SANTA INC.

BY

C.J. LIVINGSTONE

Cover illustration by Timothy Banks

Story and copy editing by Meg Mardian

Ebook ISBN: 978-0-9978070-4-2

Paperback ISBN: 978-0-9978070-5-9

For more information please visit cjlivingstone.com

Facebook: @CJLivingstoneAuthor

Instagram: @c.j.livingstone

Other books available by C.J.Livingstone:

Hogtown Book One

Hogtown Book Two

For my family

Our Lady of Mercy

This is a story set in the great city of New York. A city where buildings rise from the ground into forests of iron and stone. Where dreams linger on every intersection and evaporate into thin air like the endlessly billowing steam from the subway grates. From Afghans to Zambians, all colors and creeds have carved their paths from the corners of the seven continents.

For four hundred years it has stood as a beacon of prosperity, freedom, and the chance for a better life. A place of endless opportunity where the captains of industry walk the corridors of influence and power. Where fortunes are made and lost in a day. Where the fabulously rich live far above the crowds in the most expensive buildings in the world. But lurking below the glamor and opulence, there is also a cruel and unforgiving side. A side that shows no mercy to those who have fallen on harder times. Those for whom the great city is a manacle that is welded shut. Those who have suffered at the hard end of life's twists and its proclivity for unhappy endings.

On the corner of Gansevoort and Washington Street, in the old Meatpacking District of Manhattan, was a building that stood four stories high in brown brick, the year 1903 proclaimed in the mossy brick above its main entrance. It had four rows of large, slowly rotting wooden windows and a rusty staircase that clung to its exterior and was infrequently used as a fire exit.

From the street, a grandiose stone staircase made its way up to a front entrance of two large wooden doors. The building looked very much like any other of its type, undistinguished in most every way, and slowly falling into an old age of disrepair. Perhaps one small distinction was the three gargoyles that perched high on each corner. They were odd-looking creatures with contorted faces, bulbous noses, and wild eyes. Nobody took much notice of them, and they too had grown green with the moss of neglect.

It was perhaps the buildings that abutted to the left and right that condemned those four stories in brown into the realm of the ordinary and unimpressive, for it was dwarfed by two far bigger edifices that pushed their way skyward. In fact, most every building in the city was more spectacular, more eye-catching, and boasting significantly more height. As a result, no one ever paid much attention to that place, with its rotting windows, ancient door, and mossy gargoyles. It was forgotten and ignored just like those who lived within its walls, for it was the site of Our Lady of Mercy Orphanage——home to boys who had no home.

In the winter, the wind howled through the cracks in the window frames and sent shivers through those poor boys lying in their beds. The rain would often drip down from the leaking roof, through each floor, making its way slowly and inevitably to the ground, but not without first soaking something that very much needed to stay dry. Sometimes the electricity would go out for no reason, only to miraculously return hours later. But the building itself, with its drafts and its creaking floors was not the worst part of Our Lady of Mercy. No. That distinction was reserved for those that were charged with its management.

Sister Prudence, whose frame resembled a bag of dead branches, was thin and crooked, with pallid skin that had long given up attempting to attach itself to her bones. She moved about the old floors like a ghost. Sister Christine with her hair tied in a bun and metal-rimmed glasses was timid and conscientious.

Between them they ran the orphanage, Sister Prudence the matron and Sister Christine her deputy.

Sister Prudence dispensed punishments freely, the most common being a firm whack to the backs of the legs with a yard stick or a wooden chalk board eraser sent flying through the air toward some unsuspecting boy's head. Praise was fleeting, if at all, and she had little time for mercy.

And then there were the boys. The youngest only four or five years old, the oldest nearly full grown. Just about fifty of them in total. A motley bunch dressed in charity clothes that had already been handed down several times. Just like the city itself, their origins lay in the far-flung corners of the world, not that they would know it. They too were unified by one common theme——very few had ever known their own family. Most had simply arrived, usually before they could remember, deposited on the steps late at night or weaving through the circuitous route of temporary city accommodations. Eventually, for better or worse, Our Lady of Mercy became all they ever knew.

The building took care of almost everything to do with the boys' lives. On the top floor was the older boys' dorm, on the third floor the younger boys' dorm, on the second floor were the classrooms, and on the first floor were the kitchen, canteen, office, laundry, and recreation room. All were sparsely furnished with threadbare carpets or floorboards that jutted up at odd angles causing even the most diligent among them to occasionally trip.

There was a small outside yard, no more than half the size of a basketball court. It was all concrete and brick but nevertheless provided fresh air and a place to run, albeit in small circles. Underneath the building was the basement——cold, damp, and unexplored. Our Lady of Mercy Orphanage was no place to get a good start in life.

And then there was Eric. Lying awake in his bed on the third floor, among the rows, in the midst of twenty-five sleeping boys, the sound of air being inhaled and exhaled. All of eight years old, he had been at Our Lady since the passage of time had started for him.

It was a particularly cold night, sometime in a dark mid-November, and Eric listened to the winter storm as it battered rain against the windows. He wasn't afraid, but the blast of North Atlantic air that howled through the cracks had chilled the room. He curled up in a ball and held his feet in an effort to restore some warmth to them.

Eric imagined he was in the bowels of a ship——a freighter, in the middle of the ocean. The rain against the windows was the salty spray from the giant waves that lashed across the decks. He was headed to the Ivory Coast of Africa, and the boat rocked from one side to the other as the giant swell pushed the old hulk around like a cork. Eric peered out from his covers and looked across the large cabin. All of the other sailors slumbered in their beds, old sea dogs used to life on the ocean waves who could sleep through anything. He thought of the night watch above, clinging to the ship's wheel and attempting to blindly navigate through such treacherous conditions. Maybe they would hit a rock and sink before daybreak. Maybe a great sea creature like a giant squid or a kraken would rise up and swallow them whole. He hoped they would make it to the port of Abidjan for he had important business to conduct there. Eric's eyes fluttered a little, and the fog of sleep came rolling in from the west pushing the ship toward calmer weather and a small, sheltered bay where dreams danced across the water.

Routine

Every morning, at precisely six o'clock, the Sisters would walk through the dorms banging a large pot with a metal spoon. Clang! Clang! Clang! The boys, still half asleep, groggily rose from their beds and dressed. There was a strict uniform of black pants, a black vest, a white shirt, and a dark blue tie. There were no exceptions. Although the clothes were often well-worn and old, they were always clean and always immaculately pressed. Each boy was responsible for the presentation of his clothes and anyone who did not meet the exacting standards of Sister Prudence was punished. Eric sat on his bed, pulled up his socks, and laced up his old but highly polished black shoes. He made his bed, combed his hair, then joined the procession of trudging feet down the staircase into the main hallway and the canteen.

The canteen was a large, basic room, with rows of old benches and long metal tables, flickering strip lights, and a serving hatch at one end. Paint peeled off the walls after years of neglect, and the ever-present draft of damp, cold air whispered its way through the floorboards. Each boy stood upright and silent at the long benches. If they were not in position by ten minutes past six, there was a punishment. Eric stood next to Santiago and Lucius, just like always. Santiago with his jet-black hair and olive skin, and Lucius, with hair too short to be as curly as it wanted to be and a scrawny body underneath it. Eric rubbed his eyes awake as Sister Christine glanced at the old clock that hung on the wall. 6:09 a.m. Sister Prudence marched down each line.

"Straighten that collar," she ordered. "Re-tie that tie. Those shoes need a polish. Comb your hair."

Once inspection was complete, at the stroke of 6:15 a.m., the entire room began to recite the Lord's Prayer:

> "Our Father, who art in heaven,
> Hallowed be thy name..."

During this most sacred of rituals, the Sisters walked once more up and down the lines, their ears primed for mispronunciation. This was very important to the Sisters, and each boy knew very well the importance of keeping his voice clear and keen.

"Amen."

The metal shutters of the kitchen rolled up, clanking one after the next, and the old cook, Mister Miller, with his stained whites and his metal ladle, stood ready.

Breakfast was always the same——oatmeal——dished out from an industrial sized vat, slopped imprecisely into tin bowls like wet concrete. There was an order to everything. The older boys always went to the front of the line. They were always first, followed roughly in descending order of age but sometimes by strength or social status. Everybody knew their place.

No matter the age or size, every boy ate his full fill knowing very well that rejecting it meant not eating anything at all. They spooned the tepid gloop into their mouths joylessly. Talking was not allowed during breakfast, or any other meal for that matter. Sister Prudence said that it made boys unruly and spread bad ideas about the place. The room was silent, save for the sound of slow mastication and the odd ding of spoon against tin.

Occasionally the Sisters would leave the room, and for a few moments conversations would bloom like wildflowers, whispers blowing against the drafts. This particular morning when both Sisters stepped away, Eric leaned in closer to his friends.

"Did I tell you about the time that I sailed to the Ivory Coast of Africa?" he asked quietly.

Lucius' eyes darted about the room, wary of engaging in any conversation. He shook his head furtively.

"I know what you are thinking," Eric continued. "Why did I go to the Ivory Coast of Africa?"

Santiago curiously raised his eyebrows.

"To bring two elephants to the New York Zoo," Eric answered. "We nearly didn't make it. There was a terrible storm, and at one point a giant squid——"

"Quiet down!"

A voice cut across the room. But it was not one of the Sisters. It was Kevin O'Malley. He was the oldest boy at Our Lady of Mercy and the Head Prefect. He sat with the other older boys on the far table. At seventeen years old, he had the frame of a fully-grown man with well-developed arms, broad shoulders, and an uncommon bulkiness for his years.

There were a number of features that distinguished Kevin O'Malley. He had been sent to Our Lady of Mercy when he was seven, and he had known his parents, unlike many of the boys. His possession of a last name conveyed upon him something special in the eyes of the others, as most of the boys only had first names. He had a head of fiery red hair that, combined with his physique, enhanced his status as a leader. He was always referred to by his full name, Kevin O'Malley, an important acknowledgement in Our Lady of Mercy. Only the Sisters were more powerful than him.

"No talking," he called out.

Sister Prudence arrived back into the canteen, suspicious that something was awry. She looked about the room as each boy kept focus on the contents of his own bowl. Those who had had theirs taken in a moment's opportunity would go hungry. Breakfast was finished in silence.

Routine was everything at Our Lady of Mercy. It governed every aspect of the boys' lives from sunup to sundown. Every day was the same and started with an early breakfast, followed by a morning of schooling, and an afternoon of chores. Sunday, the day of rest, was spent at church or in Bible study. The younger boys went to bed at eight and the older boys at nine.

Sister Prudence was a firm believer that hard work and a commitment to learning were the foundations of a young man's life. So enthusiastic was she about those two things that she enforced them at almost every waking moment of every day. Lessons were in the basics: English, mathematics, history, and Bible study. They were formal and involved the Sisters lecturing before the class for an hour or more.

Eric and his friends yearned to play, but the opportunities to do so were few and far between and punctuated by long periods of intense boredom that usually required sitting very still and listening. Classes were uninspiring and dull, and lasted forever. Recess, on the other hand, passed within the blink of an eye, over before it had even started. But the chores were the worse part of all.

There were lots of chores. Endless chores. Hours of chores. There was laundry. There was cleaning the showers and toilets. There was polishing shoes. There was ironing and pressing. There was sweeping the floors. There was mopping the floors. The list went on and on. Then there were the chores that Sister Prudence held back for punishments. They were even worse that the regular chores. And so it was, life at Our Lady of Mercy Orphanage.

Class

After breakfast, the boys filed out of the canteen into the hallway and up the stairs to the second floor for the first lesson of the day. The classrooms were old, almost as old as the building itself. The single desks had little inkwell holders where in years gone by children would fill their pens with ink. Many desks had the names of those who had passed through Our Lady of Mercy scratched into them, such that their surfaces were so rough that it made writing almost impossible. The chairs were no better, hard wooden things that invariably had one leg shorter than the other and would rock from side to side with the slightest movement.

"Stop rocking!" Sister Prudence would often call out.

This resulted in the offending boy performing a precarious balancing act that invariably required more concentration than the lesson itself. Sister Prudence taught many of the lessons, everything from mathematics to English. Nothing ever changed. It was always the same. She entered the classroom with her sour face. Many of the boys were too afraid to look her directly in the eye as if doing so might turn them to stone.

"Settle down," she ordered. "Sit up straight."

She surveyed the room, always on the hunt for an infraction, some evidence that the rules had been broken. Full attention was mandatory. Any slouching or wandering eyes were punished with a swift thwack with the yard stick. But of course, even the most diligent boys sometimes found it difficult to maintain a full hour of solid math delivered in the dry monotone of Sister Prudence. The yard stick would often make an appearance.

Despite this, Eric enjoyed lessons. Learning wasn't work to him at all. His curiosity knew no bounds, and he was continuously amazed at the secrets that the world revealed to him, even inside those four stark walls. But his mind did have a tendency to drift off to more exciting places when the subject fell short of inspiring.

Sister Prudence stood up from behind a big old desk, picked up a piece of chalk, and turned to the blackboard. The blackboard itself was more white than black, owing to a thick layer of chalk residue, and made an unpleasant scraping sound as she scrawled out the letters.

"Multiplication," she announced.

5 x 3 Sister Prudence wrote on the board.

While other boys struggled by counting with their fingers or nodding along to each number with a look of puzzlement, the answer simply popped into Eric's head instantly.

"Write the answers down," ordered Sister Prudence.

After first paying close attention, Eric's thoughts, without any conscious direction, began to meander away in a completely different direction from math. There was nothing that Sister Prudence was saying that he did not already know, and so naturally his gaze took him to the window where there was a view down to the street.

He looked at the people out there. They were busily getting on with their day, carrying groceries or chatting on their cell phones. Some were drinking coffee, and some were walking hand in hand. Maybe they were trying to get to work or were late for an appointment. They never looked up at him, never even took a moment to pay any attention to that old building. It was almost as though it didn't exist.

"Eric?" boomed the voice of Sister Prudence.

She was staring directly at him from the blackboard, her face grizzled with annoyance. His head swiveled back in her direction.

"What are you doing?"

"Nothing," he replied innocently.

"Then answer the question."

"What question?" asked Eric.

A murmur of chuckling rippled through the class.

"Quiet!" demanded the Sister.

Her eyes narrowed as she trained her stare on Eric and moved toward his desk like a python.

Eric could almost see her bones through that wafer-thin skin as her claw-like fingers clenched the yardstick.

"Do you think," she asked, "that I am going to waste my time furnishing you with an education when you have no interest in learning anything at all?"

"No, Sister," replied Eric. "It's just that I already know all my multiplications."

Eric's words had a way of creating in Sister Prudence some kind of chemical reaction, such that he could see bubbles rising up through her wrinkly face and popping across her forehead.

"You already know your multiplications?" she repeated flatly. "Well, let's put you to the test."

Eric knew exactly what the order meant. Slowly he pulled his hands out and reluctantly lay them on the desk. They were pinkish white and small, quite the opposite of the Sister's. He stared at the yardstick and for a moment imagined it with an angry face, egging on Sister Prudence to thwack him down across the table. The boys watched intently for there was nothing quite so entertaining as the spectacle of a punishment.

"Seven sevens," began Sister Prudence.

"Forty-nine," replied Eric.

"Eight sevens."

"Fifty-six."

"Nine eights."

"Seventy-two."

Each correct answer inspired Sister Prudence to deliver a more complex formula.

"Eleven twelves," she continued.

Eric thought for a second. The others were amazed. Lucius gave Santiago a concerned glance, but he was too consumed in the unfolding drama to notice.

"One hundred and thirty-two," said Eric calmly.

"Fifteen fourteens."

Sister Prudence was determined to catch Eric out. She would have her vindication, of that she was certain. But Eric had a system. He knew that $10 \times 15 = 150$ and $4 \times 15 = 60$, so all he had to do was add them together.

"Two hundred and ten," he replied quickly.

An expression of determined grievance came over Sister Prudence. She pierced her lips tightly.

"Nineteen eighteens," she spat out.

This continued for more than five minutes with the increasingly irate Sister firing out larger and larger numbers. Every answer that Eric provided inflamed her annoyance until finally she stopped. She stared at Eric for a moment, eerily silent and as still as a statue. Eric was pleased. He had passed her test. He raised a little smile at her and hoped for a moment that she might be impressed with his display of mental agility.

Thwack!

She brought the yardstick down hard across his knuckles. Eric recoiled in pain. The other boys who had eagerly watched winced.

"That's for disrupting class," she said.

Eric shook the stinging out of his fingers.

"Get out," ordered Sister Prudence.

Eric's hands hurt so much that he could barely lift his writing pad and pencil. The class was so quiet as he walked out that he could hear the twenty sets of eyeballs turning in their heads as they followed his every footstep. Sister Prudence slammed the door behind him.

For a few moments Eric stood silently in the hallway listening as she admonished the rest of the boys through the closed door.

"That kind of devilment will not be tolerated in this building," she warned. "Do we have any more mathematicians present?"

There was no answer.

Eric shook out the pain from his hands one more time and made his way down the old wooden stairs to the main hallway and into the recreation room, or the *Rec* as it was commonly known. There was a ping pong table, a television that no longer worked, assorted board games, and lots of tattered books stuffed onto the shelves. There were a couple of easy chairs and deflated-looking bean bags placed upon the threadbare carpet that had been donated over the years.

There was a large fireplace with a grand stone hearth that was never used, a relic of a past time. Eric noticed that a current of icy air was funneling out of the fireplace and chilling the room. He looked up into the chimney and found that there was a sheet of metal attached to a large hinge that could be used to seal the flue. He slid the metal sheet across and the frigid current abated.

Then he went straight to the corner cupboard and opened both doors. There, in front of him resided the things that he loved most in the world——two shelves of National Geographic magazines. He smiled as he saw their familiar yellow finish, like meeting an old friend again. Eric had read all of them. Many times over. In those magazines he found solace, adventure, and an open door to the wide world that lay outside the miserable four walls of Our Lady of Mercy Orphanage.

He ran his slowly recovering finger down the spines of each one, perusing the well-worn titles. He pulled out a favorite cover featuring the ship breakers of Bangladesh, ready to read, but as he did so, he noticed that somebody had stuffed another book onto the shelf. It wasn't supposed to be there. He pulled it out and looked at it. It was an old tattered thing entitled *A Visit from St. Nicholas*. He flopped down onto a large bean bag in the corner of the room and began to read that instead.

Chores

It seemed like no time had passed at all when Eric heard the familiar sound of the boys charging down the grand staircase that wrapped around the hall. A river of screams and shouts descended from the floors above. No matter how many times the boys were ordered to be quiet or threatened with some corporal punishment, it went straight out of their minds every time class ended and a few moments of freedom beckoned. Eric placed the book carefully back onto its rightful place on the shelf as the boys flooded out into the yard for their short morning recess. Lucius and Santiago turned into the Rec where they were sure that they would find their friend.

"Sister was so mad," said Lucius breathlessly. "She made us all do multiplication for the whole lesson. And she whacked anyone who got it wrong."

"Which was everybody," added Santiago.

They both revealed a line of redness across their knuckles.

"How did you get all the numbers right, anyway?" asked Lucius.

Eric sat back on the bean bag and spread his arms out as though easing into a large armchair.

"One time, many moons ago, I traveled the length of the Yangtze River in China, far into the interior from Wuhan to Chongqing. I saw alligators, paddlefish, and even a rare Yangtze dolphin who swam up to the side of the boat and followed us for a couple of miles upstream. I was working for a trader who sold his wares to villages along the river, and during visits with his customers, he would barter the price of his goods. Once a deal

15

was struck, he had to quickly multiply the number of products that he sold by the price that he had just negotiated. He taught me his tricks for quickly and accurately multiplying numbers."

"You went to China?" asked Lucius.

"Was this before or after the Ivory Coast of Africa?" followed Santiago, somewhat unconvinced.

"Long before," said Eric.

Santiago often didn't believe the things that Eric said. He had come to Our Lady of Mercy after a few years of going in and out of other city facilities. He had experienced the hard side of life firsthand. Although he was rarely convinced, he always listened once Eric started telling his stories.

Eric could paint pictures with his words so that in their minds they felt like they were right there with him. Together they scaled the peaks of mountains, traversed great rivers, crossed deserts on the backs of camels, and camped under the stars in moonlit forests. And in doing so, just for a few moments, they too escaped the cold drudgery of their own lives.

After recess, the younger boys started their first chore of the day. Eric and Lucius were on laundry duty as usual. The laundry room was opposite the kitchen. It had a faded tile floor and strip lights that blinked on and off occasionally. There were four large washers on one side and four dryers on the other side with a large wooden table in the middle that was used to fold clothes. It was always hot and steamy in the laundry room, no matter how cold it got outside, and there was the ever-present sweet scent of washing detergent. It wafted out and danced down the hallway hooking Eric in as he got closer like a fish on a line.

Every week, each boy was required to strip down his bed, gather his clothes together, and place them into the laundry sack. The sacks were then taken downstairs to be washed. The younger boys collected all of the laundry, including those of the older boys, and hauled it downstairs for laundering. This process took place every day. When Eric and Lucius arrived, they found four large sacks waiting for them.

The most important part of the whole system was the pressing. Sister Prudence insisted that every item be pressed properly, and she had very exact specifications for what was considered acceptable. Firstly, there were absolutely no crinkles allowed anywhere, at any time. Secondly, the crease in the pants had to run from the hem to the ankle in one, perfectly straight line. She had been known to force boys to press, re-press, and press again until they got those seams just right. Eric knew all too well how the process worked. He had done it every week for as long as he could remember. Lucius and Eric began the process of loading the washer. Then they sat and watched the clothes and sheets going round and round until it was done.

After that, the damp clothes and sheets were hauled across the room to the dryers. This was always a tough job because the weight of the material increased significantly with the un-expelled water. Together, Eric and Lucius forced the mass of sheets into the drum and pushed the door closed. When each dryer was loaded, Eric went down the line and switched each one on. The electric motors whirred into action and began their hypnotic spin. Once again Eric and Lucius sat on the table and watched them go round and round.

"What do you know about Christmas?" asked Eric.

Lucius scratched his head.

"Only what the Sisters told us about Jesus, like it was his birthday."

"Some kids get presents," said Eric.

"I never got no present."

Lucius was more timid than Eric and Santiago. He was not so well prepared for the challenges that life had forced upon him. He had come to Our Lady of Mercy when he was only weeks old——too young for the place but with nowhere else to go. Sister Christine had named him after a particularly bright star that was shining that night. He had a natural desire to help people, but he often found that his efforts were confronted by hostility in that cruel and unforgiving place. He had no memory of first meeting Eric, but at some point they had formed a friendship over stories of sea monsters and tea plantations.

The dryers kicked into high speed whizzing the contents around faster and faster.

"What about Santa?" Eric asked.

Lucius shrugged.

"Do you think he is real?" asked Eric.

Lucius stared into the dryer. They always took forever, and the incessant circulation got boring very quickly. Occasionally, one of the prefects stuck his head inside to make sure that nothing had gone awry, but other than that, Lucius and Eric were left to their own devices.

"I guess it would be fun to have Christmas," said Lucius.

They sat quietly for a moment absorbed in their own imagination of a perfect Christmas Day. Lucius dreamed his usual dream——a big house full of people that he called family. He didn't know too much about Christmas Day, but in his opinion anything with a big family in it would be all that he could ask for. Eric noticed the glum expression on his friend's face. He scanned the room for something to do to take his mind off it and noticed a box of coat-hangers in the corner of the room. They were a mix of wood, plastic, and metal and were used to hang up the pressed shirts and suits. Eric jumped up and grabbed one, pushing his fingers between the hook and holding the longer flat side against his arm.

"You are my prisoner!" he called out to Lucius, pointing at him with his newfound bow and arrow.

Lucius jumped up and dashed for the box, he grabbed a metal hanger and held it like a sword.

"Never!" he cried.

"I am the greatest pirate that ever sailed the seven seas, and I demand your treasure."

The two friends inched around the room, staring intently at each other. Lucius flashed his sword at Eric, searching for a spot to land the blade. But Eric was too fast. He jumped backward and pulled an arrow from his quiver. He launched it mercilessly at Lucius. But Lucius flicked his arm at the last moment and sent the arrow whipping past him causing little more than a graze.

"If you don't relinquish your bounty," called Eric, "I'll throw you in the brig and you'll never get out."

He pointed the bow at Lucius with a look of determination on his face. Now Eric also drew his sword from its sheath——the coat-hanger held at its corner. He held it aloft and brought it down slowly onto Lucius's weapon. The blades touched momentarily, the signal for the dual to commence. The two adversaries parried this way and that, pushing each other backward, forcing their way forward. The steel clanged as the noisy battle raged around them.

Lucius was small but he was quick, and he skillfully parried one way and darted the other as he searched for a spot to land a blow. But they were well matched adversaries, and every attack was greeted with an equal defense.

Finally, Lucius pushed forward, pinning Eric into the corner of the room. But as he moved to press his advantage, he felt himself being pulled backwards by a pair of hands wrapped around his shoulders. It was Carl, flanked by Ryan.

"Hey!" he called. "Get off me."

But those boys had no intention of letting go. They had mischief in mind. It was written all over their faces. Both of them were much bigger than both Eric and Lucius. Lucius wriggled and squirmed in an attempt to get away, but they were too strong. Ryan opened up one of the washing machines.

"Sister Prudence says you don't smell good," he said with a smirk.

"You need a wash," laughed Carl.

They hoisted Lucius into the air and pushed him inside the washer. Lucius kicked his legs in an attempt to stop his body from being forced inside.

"Stop!" called Eric, marching forward to help.

But Ryan held out his hand and refused to let him come closer. Eric was no match for the larger boys. Ryan and Carl giggled with glee as their plan was executed. Lucius looked terrified as his entire body was pushed into the drum of the washer.

"Please," he begged them.

"Leave him alone," demanded Eric.

He jumped forward again and tried to grab hold of Lucius' arms but there was no stopping the other boys. Like the hyenas of the Serengeti, they were delirious with the scent of fear. With one push Carl forced Lucius inside the washer and closed the door. They howled with glee as poor Lucius peered through the small glass window.

"Spin cycle?" suggested Ryan.

He clicked the dial around. Eric could hardly believe that he was actually going to go through with it.

"Enjoy your bath," laughed Ryan.

He pushed the button. The water pump clanked into action. Lucius banged on the window, fear spreading over his face. Ryan and Carl danced around and banged on the window as their cruel plan took hold. Eric continued to try to push his way through, but the bigger boys held him back.

Then, everything stopped. The dryers ground to a halt. The strip lights flickered off. The water pump ceased. Power cut. With no exterior windows, the room fell into darkness. Ryan and Carl scuttled off, their entertainment cut short. Eric unlocked the washer and opened the door. Lucius's entire body was shaking.

"Are you alright?" asked Eric.

They stood in the blackness together. For a few moments his friend could not speak. Then the lights flickered back to life and the dryers resumed their noisy cycle. The power had returned.

"That was a close one," said Eric with a comforting smile.

He held out his hands to help Lucius out. Something much more ominous had just entered the room.

"Stop!" cried a voice.

That voice. The boys froze, Lucius still half in the washer.

"You," said Sister Prudence, pointing at Eric. "Into my office."

Magic Dust

Inside the office were two identical wooden desks, a big black filing cabinet and a wooden carving of Jesus Christ on the cross that was hung on the wall. What struck Eric the most, however, was the large pile of papers sitting on one of the desks. They looked like letters and many of them had a red coloring along the top.

Sister Prudence took a seat at the tidier of the two desks, clasped her hands together, and for what felt like a long time, stared directly at Eric. She seemed to enjoy the silence and the discomfort that it brought to those who had to endure it. Eric had stood on that spot many times. The carpet was particularly well worn where generations of misbehaved boys had done the same.

"How long have you been at Our Lady of Mercy?" she asked finally.

"I don't know, Sister."

It was true that Eric didn't really remember when he had arrived at the orphanage, neither did Sister Prudence. She just knew that he had been around long enough to know better. There was something indefinable about Eric that irritated her.

"Don't come stupid with me, boy. You're smart enough when you want to be. First you disrupt my class. Now you can't even do your chores without getting into mischief."

"It wasn't..."

Sister Prudence's stone white face momentarily flushed a shade of red. Eric stopped. He knew better than to attempt to propose an alternative opinion. He looked at her wrinkly white skin and the traces of purple veins underneath it. He wondered if she had purple blood. Or maybe it wasn't blood at all but some kind of toxic fluid like a poison dart frog from South America.

"I've had just about enough of you today," said Sister Prudence, "You can make yourself more useful by spending the rest of the day scrubbing the stairs. Top to bottom."

Eric did not attend any further classes that day. Instead he took a bucket and a hard-bristled brush from the storeroom and scrubbed the three flights of stairs in their entirety. It was a hard job. The steps were filthy from the endless march of boys up and down them. The other boys were not kind to him either. They called out to him as they passed in the corridor and deliberately made the steps dirty again when they went to recess. But Eric scrubbed every single step with care and attention to detail, and he did not cut corners or miss sections, even if the dirt was so ingrained that it was almost impossible to move.

Eric took his time, slowly and methodically, focusing on the task at hand. There was something quite satisfying about the process of cleaning. He was still working when the boys went to dinner and when they went up to their dorms to get ready for bed. His stomach rumbled from hunger but there was nothing to eat. Just after lights out, Sister Christine appeared at the foot of the stairs. She handed him a slice of bread.

"Go to bed," she said.

She watched him slowly walk all the way up the stairs then she returned to her own small room. Sister Christine had come to Our Lady of Mercy when she was little more than a child herself. She had always dreamed of helping those who were less fortunate, and sometimes the ways that the boys were treated pained her. She believed in compassion over discipline. But over the years she had no choice but to fall in line with the methods of the place. At night she would take comfort in reading her Bible, then she would pray for each and every boy's soul.

Sometime in the middle of the night Eric awoke. He didn't know what time it was, but he sensed that the night was at its darkest. Over the snores and the quiet muttering of boys deep in dreams, Eric made out another sound. It was the sound of a gentle sobbing. If it was any quieter it would not have been audible at all.

Eric sat up in his bed and looked about. Over in the other corner of the room was a boy called Roger, a prefect who was in charge of the younger boys' dorm at night. He was snoring loudly. Eric swiveled around and slowly let his bare feet touch the floor. The wooden planks were cold and instantly Eric could feel the draft begin to chill his toes. He stood and tip toed across the room being careful to avoid the stray nails that jutted upwards.

"Lucius," he whispered.

He put his hand on his friend's shoulder.

"Go back to bed," Lucius replied. "We'll get in big trouble."

"Everyone's asleep," replied Eric. "What's the matter?"

Lucius sat up furtively. Experience had taught him that waking up in the middle of the night was a sure way to a punishment. But soon he could see for himself that everyone was indeed asleep. Eric sat down next to him.

"What's up?" asked Eric again.

Lucius paused for a moment and wiped his eyes. He looked at Eric with a certain expression in the moonlit night.

"Sometimes," he started, "I have this dream. It's a wonderful dream. It's Christmas Day. I'm with my family. I'm eating pie with my mother and father. Apple pie. And I have a bunch of brothers and sisters. I can't really see them too well, but I know it's my family. And we're all eating pie. With ice cream. And we're all laughing. Everybody just keeps on laughing because they are so happy."

"That sounds like a good dream," said Eric.

"It is," said Lucius. "It's the best."

He hung his head low.

"But one by one," he continued, "my family start to leave. Until there's just me left. That's when I wake up and realize that I am still here."

Lucius started to sob again. Eric put his hand around his friend's shoulder. He could feel his body gently rocking as the tears made their way out. At that moment something very special happened. Through a crack in the curtains, a beam of moonlight shone into the dorm.

"Look," pointed Eric.

The moonlight illuminated the dust that hung in the air, giving it a magical translucent quality.

"What's that?" asked Lucius.

"That's Magic Dust," replied Eric knowingly. "When you see that, you know that good things are going to happen."

"Really?"

Eric nodded.

"Magic Dust does not appear very often. It only comes at certain times."

Lucius's eyes lit up, and in that moment, he found some small semblance of hope.

"Magic Dust," he said under his breath.

For a few moments the two boys sat on the bed and stared at it as it shimmered and glinted in the pure white light. Their concentration was broken by a rustling in one of the nearby beds. Lucius and Eric sat perfectly still until the boy rolled over and began to snore, quietly jibber-jabbering to himself.

"It's time to go to sleep," said Eric, feeling that his feet had already become extraordinarily cold.

Lucius lay back down as Eric tiptoed back to his own bed. He lay awake looking at the Magic Dust until the beam of moonlight shifted and it gradually disappeared. Eric wished that he could do something to give his friend the Christmas that he wanted. Not just Lucius but every boy. Even the terrible ones.

Bad Egg

The next day, Eric was permitted to rejoin class. When there was a break in the rain, the boys were allowed to play outside for recess. The courtyard was small, half the size of a basketball court with one flimsy, old hoop hanging off the wall at one end. The younger boys played hopscotch and tag. The older boys bounced the ball around or sat on the concrete steps talking. The courtyard was surrounded by very tall buildings on each side. If Eric looked directly upwards, he could create the illusion that they were falling over. He wondered what it would be like to look out from the top floor of one of those buildings. He wondered what kind of people were up there looking out.

"People say you're skating on thin ice," warned Santiago as he bounced a ball towards Eric.

Eric pointed upwards.

"From the top of that building I bet that you could see to the edge of all five boroughs on a clear day."

"Eric, I'm serious. Don't make trouble for no reason. Be careful."

Eric didn't know how to be careful. All he knew how to be was himself.

"I'm thinking of building some kind of flying machine," he said purposefully.

Santiago watched Eric. Sometimes he did not understand the things that his friend said.

"Let's play?" he suggested.

He pushed the ball into Eric's chest, but Eric did not take it. From out of the corner of his eye, Eric saw someone approaching. It was Kevin O'Malley.

"Sister Prudence told me to keep an extra special eye on you," he said in his deep voice.

"Why?" asked Eric.

"Because you're a bad egg," replied Kevin. "If you mess up again then we all get punished. And if I get punished, you're getting triple punished."

Eric lowered his gaze and stared at Kevin for a moment. Compared to the other kids, he was a giant. He had thick tree trunk arms and his ginger hair was parted in the middle and hung down like curtains across his forehead. He had a tough-looking face. The kind of face that you would be scared of even if there was no particular reason to be scared of it. There were some deep red hairs sprouting at odd angles from his chin.

"Do you know that you would make a good wrestler?" he said.

Santiago nudged Eric. Lucius appeared behind them, curious to see what the discussion was all about, but Santiago held him back, knowing that the outcome was not likely to be good.

"What?" said Kevin.

Eric nodded encouragingly.

"When I travelled through Mexico, I came upon a professional wrestling exhibition. They call themselves Luchadores. It just occurred to me that these guys are very similar in size and shape to you. They're big and bulky, and they like a good fight. Maybe one day, when you leave this place, you should consider going down there for a tryout."

"What are you talking about?" asked Kevin, looking confused.

"You might have to learn Spanish, but it is not a hard language to pick up. Santiago could help you. It's in his blood."

Kevin was not sure if Eric was making fun of him or not. Either way, he didn't like it.

"Watch yourself," he said.

He jabbed his index finger into Eric's chest and walked off. Santiago looked at Eric. Suddenly he burst out laughing. Lucius smiled but then Santiago's laughter was so infectious that he joined in.

"What is it?" asked Eric.

"You're crazy," said Santiago.

Soon they were all laughing, although Eric was not really sure why, but the joy of his friends made him happy. The bell rang and the three friends returned inside for the next lesson.

In the classroom, some of the boys sat down and some stood around talking. Sister Christine arrived at the door and made her way to the solid oak desk at the front. The boys took little notice of her. She turned to the blackboard to write the lesson title, but the chalk was gone. While she searched for it, the volume of chatter in the room slowly increased. Finally, she turned back to the front.

"Has anybody seen the chalk?" she asked.

No one answered. Some didn't even acknowledge her question. For some reason, she could not produce the same level of fear in the boys as her colleague. She did not like shouting, instead she preferred reason, but that rarely yielded the same results as her counterpart. Sister Christine continued to hunt for a few moments until eventually she gave up and left the room to get more supplies. At that point, one of the other boys, an eleven-year-old named David, jumped up and placed the chalk back on the desk. The boys around him chuckled in delight at their ruse.

Eric watched. Meanwhile the volume in the room grew as the boys continued to be left unattended. Eric looked down at his desk and ran his finger over the lines that had been etched into it over the years. He wondered what life was like in the year 1903 when the building was constructed. Sister Christine reappeared with the new chalk and saw the old chalk sitting on her desk. She didn't say anything. She too had been at the orphanage for a long time, and despite the fact that she had been immersed in Sister Prudence's methods, she could never bring herself to implement them in the same way. She believed that the boys could act responsibly in the right circumstances. But she also knew that Sister Prudence would never agree to those ideas. So instead she simply wrote the lesson on the board: *Bible Study*.

"Settle down," she called out.

But as was often the case when the boys had been permitted to go too far, they were unable to settle. Their minds had become too excited by the brief moment of freedom that they had been afforded.

"Quiet please," Sister Christine called out again, louder this time.

Sister Christine watched the melee continue for a few moments. Eric watched too. He was not one for being riled up.

"Settle down," she called again.

It was no use. She turned back to the black board and began writing up the lesson plan.

"Quiet!"

A different voice cut through the room like a bolt of lightning, muting every other sound in an instant. Sister Prudence stood at the door. The boys who were standing up took their seats and buried their eyes into their desks in terror. Sister Prudence stared into the room in the way that only she could. The temperature seemed to drop, and a fear was sent deep into the core of their souls, as though they were looking death itself in the face.

"Sister Christine," asked Sister Prudence. "Can you not control your class?"

"I needed to get more chalk," replied Sister Christine.

"More chalk?" inquired Sister Prudence with a puzzled tone. "I left the chalk by the board after the last lesson."

"Yes," replied Sister Christine.

"So where was the chalk?" asked Sister Prudence.

Sister Christine breathed deeply. She looked at the boys.

"I didn't see it," she answered. "I went to get more only to find that it was right there on the desk."

Eric perceived something quite interesting in that moment. Sister Christine had saved those boys. If Sister Prudence had known that someone had taken the chalk, she would have sniffed the perpetrator out like a hound dog and punished them severely.

"If you didn't see the chalk in plain sight, you may need new spectacles," suggested Sister Prudence.

Sister Christine nodded.

"And if you cannot control your class then I will do it for you."

"Thank you, Sister Prudence," said Sister Christine.

Sister Prudence glowered over the room one more time as though charging the boys with enough fear to get them through to the end of the lesson. She pulled the door slowly shut, peering through the crack until it was totally closed.

"Now then," said Sister Christine, with a forced smile. "Bible study."

Choir

E very year, in the weeks preceding Christmas, the orphans of Our Lady of Mercy performed in a carol service. The boys began practicing their songs early in November. Sister Prudence led the choir while Sister Christine provided accompaniment on the piano. They practiced for an hour every Tuesday and Thursday in the canteen, which was the only room that could comfortably hold everyone.

The boys stood in rows, tallest at the back to the smallest at the front. Their song sheets were old and tattered, having been passed down through many generations. Like all things in Our Lady of Mercy, the Sisters took the preparation of the carols very seriously. Sister Christine attacked the keyboard with gusto, her fingers banging away at the chords. Sister Prudence marched up and down the line, turning her yard stick and listening intently to every word.

"Pronunciation!" she would call out at regular intervals.

The boys cycled through the four songs to be performed: *God Rest Ye Merry Gentlemen, We Three Kings of Orient Are, Away in a Manger,* and *Oh Come, All Ye Faithful.*

Eric very much enjoyed singing. He knew all the words to the carols. There was something about a chorus of voices that gave him a feeling of great warmth down to his bones, as though it connected him to something deep within the vein of life. He liked to hear Sister Christine on the piano too. It was the only music that was permitted in the orphanage, and the sound coming from the piano gave him a sense of intense pleasure. The music filled the room and the voices rang out clear and true:

"God rest you merry, Gentlemen,
Let nothing you dismay,
For Jesus Christ our Savior
Was born upon this Day."

Halfway through the song, some of the boys began to look around, as though something was wrong. Eric didn't notice it at first, being too consumed with the music, but a loud banging, not quite loud enough to overcome the sound of fifty voices and a piano, became audible. Then, quite out of nowhere, Sister Christine stopped playing, and soon after the boys stopped too.

Bang! Bang! Bang!

Sister Prudence drove her yardstick into the wooden floorboards over and over. After some twenty seconds, she stopped. She sternly walked back down the line, taking in every single face, looking like she had sucked on a particularly bitter lemon and was struggling to hold the juice in her mouth.

"Somebody is intent on sabotaging this song," she declared. "Who is it?"

The boys were quiet and still. No one dared raise their hand.

"May I remind you," said Sister Prudence, "that this orphanage, where you all live for free, receives a generous donation from the congregation of the Church of Our Lady of Mercy each and every Christmas. And if I cannot convince them that you are deserving of their alms, they may not give us any money at all. And you will all be cast out onto the streets to starve."

Sister Christine did not like it when Sister Prudence used such terrible words against the boys. She did not think it was necessary, and she always felt bad that they had to be subjected to such unkindness. But all the same, she couldn't bring herself to speak out against her superior.

Sister Prudence surveyed the room once more, lingering on certain choice individuals——Ryan, Paul, and Umberto. Just one look from her could send a chill deep into the heart of any child.

"Sister Christine," she said eventually. "If you please."

Without a second's pause, Sister Christine struck back up on the piano from the point where she had left off. The boys began to sing. Sister Prudence marched back down the line, her ears pricked up like a meercat. When she finally arrived at the end where Eric was standing, she slowed. Each boy's heart raced a little faster as she trained her focus onto them. She stood as still as a statue with one ear pointed toward the sound.

"Stop!" she cried after a few moments.

Once more, the music ground to a halt. Sister Prudence analyzed the line, her eyes eventually resting on a boy called Clive. He was visibly shaking.

"Do you want this orphanage to receive its annual donation?" she asked.

"Yes," said Clive.

"Do you want to have every boy cast out to the streets to starve?"

"No."

"Then let us hear you sing," ordered Sister Prudence.

"Just me?" he asked nervously.

"Just you," she said.

Clive took the hymn sheet. He began to sing the words of the song. His high voice carried the tune well. But this did not make Sister Prudence happy.

"You," she said, cutting Clive off and pointing to Arthur, who was standing behind him.

Eric glanced at Arthur. He noticed that his face was very similar to the Bangladeshi ship breakers, with his jet-black hair, a dark brown coloring to his skin and brown eyes. He looked just as petrified as Clive. Arthur began to sing. His tone wasn't quite as good, but he carried the song nevertheless. Sister Prudence moved on.

"You," she said, pointing at Eric.

Eric took a deep breath, puffed out his chest and began to sing:

> "God rest you merry, Gentlemen,
> Let nothing you dismay,
> For Jesus Christ our Savior
> Was born upon this Day."

Before the first verse ended, Sister Prudence began furiously banging her yardstick. Eric persevered for a few moments but then stopped. It was clear to almost everybody where the problem lay. Eric was unable to order any of the notes correctly in the song. In fact, the melody was almost undetectable under the words that were coming from his mouth.

"You will not sing in my choir," Sister Prudence declared. "From this point forward, you will mime the words. No sound will come from your mouth. See me in my office after."

"Yes, Sister," said Eric.

Eric did not understand. To him, his singing had sounded perfectly pleasant. Sister Prudence nodded and Sister Christine began to play once more. Eric mouthed the words as he had been told to do, but it wasn't the same.

Eric stood in the Sisters' office. He was quite puzzled. He stared at the two desks and the wooden carving of Jesus. He looked at the overflowing filing cabinet and the letters with red on them. He edged forward and noticed that one of them, from the Gas Company, had OVERDUE printed in large red letters along the top.

Eventually, Sister Prudence arrived. Eric wondered if she ever smiled. She must have smiled at one time in her life. Maybe she had never smiled. Maybe she had just looked at the gas bill. It was true that the orphanage was not much fun and that the Sisters worked from morning until night. He wondered if it would be possible to get her to smile. But not today. Sister Prudence took her seat and drove her icy stare directly into Eric.

"Just what do you think you are doing?" she asked.

The Sisters had a habit of asking questions wherein the answers were not immediately obvious. Eric didn't answer straight away because he was trying to figure out exactly what Sister Prudence was asking for.

"Well then?" she prodded.

"I was just trying to sing," said Eric

"You think that you are so smart, don't you? You think that you could outwit the good Lord himself."

"If I could just practice some more, I think that we could figure it out."

"You won't sing in my choir ever again, young man. You are an instigator. You're not a bad egg, you're a rotten egg."

Eric was often puzzled by the reactions of the Sisters and this occasion was no different.

"A man who does not know himself is no man at all," said Sister Prudence. "We don't need thinkers here. We need obedient boys who know when to keep their mouths shut."

"Yes, Sister," replied Eric. "But seeing as I'm already here, I thought I would raise to you some of the problems we younger kids face day to day."

"Problems?" repeated Sister Prudence.

"Yes, like the bigger boys picking on us, and the food is not so great and it's cold at night. I don't mind it so much but——"

"Just who do you think you are?" demanded Sister Prudence, cutting Eric off.

Eric was not sure how to answer that question, figuring that the answer was quite obvious. Luckily the Sister had no intention of soliciting a response.

"You step into my office," she continued, clearly affronted, "and dare to question my methods. You boys don't know the meaning of hard work. All you do is eat and make a mess."

Sister Prudence went on for quite sometime. Eric couldn't understand why she reacted so terribly to the things that he said. Why do they get so upset? He thought to himself. Why did asking questions create so much ire? Why did boys like Ryan and Carl get away with all of their cruel pranks? They didn't receive so much as a clip around the head, but a simple question could somehow invite an uncontrollable wrath. It didn't make sense.

"Well then?" said Sister Prudence after some unknown period of time had passed.

Eric looked up at her and realized that he had not been listening to anything that she had said. She stared at him expectantly, but he had no idea how to respond.

"Can you repeat the question?" he asked.

Sister Prudence arose from her desk. She opened the door to her office and stepped out.

"Come on," she said.

Eric sensed that he would be handed the mop and bucket. Again. He foresaw a long day in front of him. But Sister Prudence's hand did not open the storeroom, instead she reached out for the door opposite the office. Her crooked twig-like fingers grasped the knob and turned it in one swift motion. The large cavernous blackness opened up before him. The basement. There was a small light bulb hanging from a single wire above the staircase. Sister Prudence reached out, unscrewed it and held it in her hand.

"In," she said, matter-of-factly.

The Basement

E ric tentatively stepped toward the doorway and peered into the expanse of darkness that lay before him.

"Sister Prudence," he said. "I am not sure that I want to go in there."

"Your problem, young man," said the Sister, "is that you don't know when to shut up."

She nudged him forward and Eric reluctantly stepped down onto the first step. He stood on the small landing and stared down a staircase that descended into sheer black nothingness.

"Now you can talk for as long as you wish," said Sister Prudence.

She shut the door and locked it with the definitive clunk of a metal bolt.

Everything was black. Eric could not make out a single shape. He lowered himself on to the step and sat down. It was musty and still. Everyone had heard stories of the kids who had been sent to the basement. That some kind of creature lived down there, a dark and foreboding beast that the Sisters fed only the unruliest of boys to. The darkness didn't scare Eric, but he did wish that had something to read. So for quite a while, he sat and did precisely nothing. Eric decided not to think at all. Instead he felt the air on his face.

He remained on the small landing for an unknown period of time until he noticed something odd. A glint of light appeared behind the door, almost as though it was trying to find its way in. Eric turned and watched it as it moved slowly and precisely. It became more concentrated until suddenly there was a solid beam cutting through the little crack between the door and the frame.

In the shard of bright yellow light that it created, Eric could see quite clearly. Magic dust. It twinkled and sparkled as the light danced off it. It hung motionless in the air, unaffected by gravity, like a lighthouse pointing the way. He followed it down the stairs and onto the floor of the basement. There were all types of boxes and other assorted miscellany stacked up down there. There were old cans of paint and tools, pieces of scrap wood, and an old sewing machine.

Eric searched for a light switch and eventually located one on the far wall hoping that maybe there was another light further down inside the basement. He flipped it on. Nothing happened. No light. He flipped it a couple more times, up and down. Nothing. Then, just as quickly as it had appeared, the Magic Dust disappeared. The shard of light was gone, and Eric was plunged into blackness once more.

For a moment he stood as still as a statue and tried to remember the footsteps that he had taken to reach where he was presently standing. The air was even cooler and more still deep in the basement. It was quite a different sensation to the drafty corridors above. He reached his hands out and felt around at the cardboard boxes. In the silence, his ears twitched. A sound. Not from above but from below. A voice, a strange voice.

Eric stayed completely motionless and waited. It came again. He couldn't make out the words as they were muffled, but he was certain that it was something. Somebody. He listened carefully. Yes! It was definitely a voice. It was a kind of sing-songy type of voice. He tried hard to make out the words, but they sounded as though they had been put into a washing machine and spun around. Maybe there was a ghost after all. It was quite plausible that this rotten place was occupied by the specters of children past.

Eric slowly moved toward the sound, one foot edging past the other, his hands moving over the boxes, feet treading carefully among the debris. He could feel all sorts of strange things. Odd textures and shapes that bristled against his hands. Maybe there were giant slugs down there. Maybe there were cockroaches with fur on their backs that were kept as pets by mutated sewer rats. He had to find the voice. He was too curious. So he kept shuffling blindly forward.

"Hello?" he called.

Eric's head bumped into the wall, and he concluded that he must have reached the far corner of the room. He rubbed his skull a little, then spread out his fingers and felt his way across the wall. Wherever the voice was coming from, it had not yet been alerted to Eric's presence, of that he was sure. In fact, if anything it was getting louder. Eric's hand rippled over something. He stopped and ran his fingers around the edges of what felt like a large grate. The grate had a metal mesh cover, and Eric touched its hard corners. He bent down and put his ear to the mesh. Sure enough, the voice was now quite audible.

"Hello," Eric called out again.

Eric wondered if someone was trapped down there. He became full of the spirit of adventure with no care for the consequences of his actions. He had to figure out where the voice was coming from and who it might be. He tugged at the grate, but it would not budge. He wrapped both sets of fingers around each of its sides and gave it a solid pull. Nothing. It was fixed tight to the wall. Meanwhile the sing-songy voice continued unabated.

"Hello," he repeated.

Whoever the voice belonged to did not hear him. Eric considered calling out louder, but he was wary of alerting the Sisters. He gave the grate another hard push, but it didn't move an inch. He ran his fingers over it again and in doing so came across what seemed like a small piece of protruding metal. Eric pulled it in every direction until eventually——click——something opened outwards toward him.

He put his hand inside. It was some kind of tunnel, made of metal, smooth and cold to the touch. He ran his hand around the outside of it and determined that it was circular. But what was it for? It was big enough for him to fit inside.

He hesitated for a moment. What if it led directly to the sewers and the voice was that of a ten-foot rat who loved nothing more than dining on orphans with his pet mutant cockroach? Or what if it led straight into the pit of hell and the voice belonged to one of those demons that the Sisters were always talking about who were out to get small boys' souls? Or worse, what if the tunnel somehow led directly to the Sisters themselves? Then he would really be in trouble.

Huxley

Eric took a breath and made his way forward on all fours. He could hear the voice getting louder. He felt a rush of excitement as the tunnel snaked around, turning this way and that. Then suddenly, Eric tumbled forwards, moving faster and faster. Without him realizing, it had dipped forward vertically, and Eric was now sliding, carried by gravity, into the unknown. Now he really did believe that he was headed for the sewer.

A light appeared in the tunnel before him, beaming up into the shaft from below. He tried to grip on to the sides to slow his acceleration, but it was no use, he couldn't stop. Instead he curled up into a ball to protect himself. He peered from behind his hands and saw the crisscross of another grate below him. He hurtled towards it at an unstoppably fast rate clutching his feet and bracing for impact.

Bang! He hit. The grate came flying off, ejecting Eric from the tunnel. Now he was in free fall. That second felt like a lifetime. Falling. Falling. He shut his eyes tight.

Gedumpf! He landed on something soft. The wind was knocked out of him a little, and he gathered himself without observing his surroundings. He spluttered and coughed but soon realized that he was not hurt at all. He had landed on a bed. He lifted his head up slowly and found that he was in a large room with high ceilings and no windows.

An old man stood in front of him, with his hands on his hips, quite shocked. For a moment, Eric sat on the bed looking at the old man and the old man stood looking directly back at him. He was dressed in a grey suit that included a neat waistcoat. His tie was a deep red and underneath it, a crisp blue shirt. He wore a pair of immaculate brown leather shoes that were intricately patterned.

"Goodness gracious," exclaimed the old man after a moment, adjusting his gold rimmed spectacles.

Eric's eyes darted around as he tried to work out where he was.

"It's rather fortunate that you landed where you did," he continued, glancing up at the grate that was swinging above them. "One foot to the left and you would have broken every bone in your body."

Eric took a moment to look around the large room and saw that it was actually the entire floor of a building that was filled with all manner of objects impossible to characterize at first glance. And all over the place, stacked on shelves that went all the way up to the ceiling were boxes and boxes of toys. All kinds of toys from wooden airplanes to jack-in-the-boxes, dollhouses to dinosaurs, soldiers to wooden bricks.

"Where am I?" he asked.

"This is my workshop," answered the old man.

Eric looked around once more and began to recognize the menagerie of objects that were in front of him——machines and tools everywhere, and in between the stacks of toys, drawings and designs pinned erratically to the walls.

"Who are you?" asked Eric.

"I might very well ask you the same question," replied the old man. "My name is Professor Owen Huxley."

He had a distinct way of talking, different from anything Eric had ever heard before. His accent, the phrasing of his words and even some of the words themselves, were all just a little bit odd.

Professor Huxley looked Eric up and down.

"You're a well-dressed fellow," he noted.

Eric wore his usual black suit, not so well fitted but neatly pressed, a crisp white shirt, blue tie, and shiny black shoes.

"What's your name?"

"Eric."

"Eric. What a splendid name. Norse in origin I believe. From what part of Scandinavia do you hail?"

"I'm not from Scandinavia," said Eric. "I'm from Our Lady of Mercy Orphanage. I was locked in the basement. Sister Prudence put me in there because she said I'm an instigator. And I ask too many questions."

"Too many questions?" said the old professor with a disbelieving huff. "How can you ask too many questions? There are more questions than we can possibly ever hope to answer so how could you ever ask too many of them?"

"I don't know," said Eric. "I don't think the Sisters like questions."

Professor Huxley pondered for a moment, then was seized by an important thought.

"Where are my manners! Would you like a cup of tea?"

"No, thanks," said Eric.

"No tea?" said Huxley, looking baffled. "How incomprehensible."

"I did once work on a tea plantation," said Eric. "In Darjeeling. But I never got a taste for it."

The professor walked over to a small kitchenette that was located among the jumble of assorted machinery.

"That is strange," he noted.

He picked up a kettle, filled it with water, and then placed it on a small electric stove top. Eric took a moment to take another good look around the place.

"You're a professor?" asked Eric.

"Aeronautical engineering," said Huxley, taking a tea bag and pushing it into a small, china tea pot. "Not that that matters much these days. I'm a toy maker."

"Did you make these toys?" Eric asked.

"Of course. I design them. I build prototypes. I test them. And then if they're good enough they go into production."

"What do you mean by production?"

"They get made. Upstairs in the factory."

Eric's eyes followed Huxley's finger upward but all he could see was the high ceiling. He looked about the place in wide-eyed amazement. Every nook and cranny was filled with some interesting object. Every color and shape danced delightfully into his bulging eyes. The kettle began to whistle, and the professor poured the boiling water into the pot. He put the tea pot onto a tray, along with a small cup and saucer, then poured a glass of water. Finally, he opened a large jar and placed two cookies on a plate. He carried the entire tray over to a small table and set it down. Eric walked over to the table and sat down.

"I must say," said Huxley, inviting Eric to sit, "you did rather give me a fright when you came rumbling down that pipe. I thought it was an earthquake."

"How come you speak funny?" asked Eric.

"Me?" questioned Huxley with surprise. "I speak the Queen's English. It is you that possesses the peculiar inflection of the mother tongue. Biscuit?"

"That's not a biscuit, that's a cookie," said Eric affirmatively.

"Let us be clear on one thing," said Huxley, holding the article aloft. "This most certainly is a biscuit. A Custard Cream. All the way from England. Air freight."

"Do you come all the way from England?" asked Eric.

"Of course I do. And we certainly don't have cookies there. Especially with our tea."

Huxley poured the steaming brown liquid into his small china cup, then added a splash of milk. Eric took a biscuit. It did look tasty, with two hard crunchy pieces sandwiching a soft white center.

"If you like, I will permit you to dip it into my cup of tea. But just the once and not too far in."

"Why would I want to do that?" asked Eric.

"Because a tea-soaked biscuit is one of life's great joys," exclaimed Huxley.

Eric placed the biscuit about a quarter of the way into the tea, then pulled it out. It was all soggy. He took a bite out of it. Immediately his taste buds reveled in the warm, sugary flavor. Huxley repeated the action with his own biscuit.

"Simple pleasures," he said with a smile as he took a bite.

Eric couldn't help but continue to stare about the room. The more he looked, the more he saw, as though the place constantly revealed new things to him. There were tubes and lights and buttons, mechanical contraptions, and designs——from great blueprints to scraps of notepaper pinned to nearly every wall.

"What do you do with all your toys?" Eric asked.

"They go to the boys and girls around the world, of course."

Huxley pulled a handkerchief from the top pocket of his jacket and wiped the crumbs from his mouth. He watched Eric for a moment.

"Do you have the slightest inclination as to where you have landed?" asked Huxley with a chuckle.

"No."

"You are at the headquarters of Santa Incorporated. Where Christmas is our business."

Toy Lab

"Christmas?" asked Eric.

Huxley nodded. "That's right." He took another sip of his tea. "I call this my toy laboratory," he said. "Would you like to take a look around?"

Huxley slowly rose to his feet, pushing himself up with one hand on the back of the chair. He walked over to the large drafting board.

"Many a great toy has begun its life right here," said Huxley, with a familiar tap.

"How do you invent a new toy?" asked Eric.

"I don't really know," said Huxley. "I suppose it's just persistence. I sit here until it comes to me."

The great room looked as though it was from some other time long passed. The machines, the table, even the kitchenette was made of cast iron and solid wood. There was a heaviness to it all, as though it would last for a hundred years. They moved on to an area that contained lots of tools——there were chisels, drills, screws of every length, hammers set around a work bench. It wasn't exactly orderly. In fact, it was quite a mess.

"This is where I build the prototypes," said Huxley.

He ran his hand over a large saw that lay idle.

"In the good old days, the elves would help me. This place was a hotbed of innovation," he continued as he regarded the silent machines arranged about the workshop. "We would rattle out prototypes by the hour."

"Elves?" asked Eric somewhat suspiciously.

"Elves," repeated Huxley.

"They're not real. Are they?"

"I should hope they are," Huxley chuckled.

The next part of the room was full of paints. Every color imaginable was arranged on shelves from the floor to the ceiling. They were all organized according to hue.

"So what happens when you finish your prototype?" asked Eric.

"Good question," said Huxley. "It goes to Santa for approval."

"Santa?" asked Eric. He couldn't quite fathom the words that he was hearing.

"Who else is going to make the decision?" asked Huxley.

"Where is Santa?"

"Up there," said Huxley. "Everybody is up there. The elves. The Factory. Santa. The Executives. The Accountants. Everyone."

Eric looked up again, but he could still only see the ceiling. Huxley sensed Eric's confusion.

"There's a whole building above us. Filled with people whose business is to make Christmas the most fantastical day of the year."

"Can I go up and see?" asked Eric.

"No," said Huxley, shaking his head vehemently. "It's busy season. Nearly the big day, young man. And there is no time to entertain guests."

Eric came to a realization. If he had made his way through the tunnel to the next building, he must be at the bottom of one of those skyscrapers. He wondered just what was up there in that building above, and for a moment his imagination ran wild thinking of Santa and Elves and all of those things that were Christmas.

"We need to get you back to where you came from," said Huxley, striding back toward the kitchenette.

"Why?" asked Eric.

In a short time, Eric had taken quite a liking to the toy laboratory. It was warm and there were interesting things to look at, and those cookies that Professor Huxley called biscuits were very tasty.

"I'm quite sure that they'll be sending out a search party if you are gone much longer," said the Professor.

Huxley began to rummage around in a large cupboard next to his small kitchen. All types of knick-knacks came tumbling out.

"I have something that may help you. I know it's in here somewhere," he mumbled with his head inside. "Aha!"

He appeared holding something that looked like an oblong piece of wood. He gave it a shake. Nothing happened. Huxley turned the device over.

"Wrong way around," he noted to himself.

He flipped a switch and a spring-loaded ladder came shooting out, narrowly missing his head.

"I knew this thing would find a use one day. Every adventurer needs a ladder, and this one can fit snuggly into your backpack."

He pushed the ladder up so that it came to rest inside the air duct. Eric climbed the ladder until he got to the top, then he peered into the black hole.

"Here!" shouted Huxley.

He threw a small flashlight upwards. Eric caught it, switched it on and illuminated his way. At first climbing up the tube was difficult. It was very nearly vertical and hard to get any purchase on the smooth interior, but slowly he made his way upwards and back towards the basement.

"Cheerio," said Huxley with a little wave.

"Can I come back and visit again?" Eric asked.

Huxley contemplated the question for a moment.

"I'm not sure that's such a good idea," he said.

"I won't make any trouble," said Eric.

"We are very busy. You know, Christmas."

Eric made his way up the pipe and back into the basement. The flashlight made it much easier to navigate his way and he was able to easily replace the grate back to its original position without any difficulty. He made his way back to the stairs but not before concealing the light by one of the old boxes where it would not be found. Then he sat on the top step and waited. And waited.

He thought about what he had seen, Professor Huxley, and the things that he had been told. He was intrigued. There was something magical about that building. There was so much more to know than his short visit had allowed. He resolved that he would visit again. He would have to, of course.

After some indiscernible amount of time had passed, the sound of feet treading hastily upon floorboards began to ripple through the cavities of the old building. Eric guessed that it was the end of the day's lessons. The footsteps rushed this way and that, accompanied by the sound of excited chattering. The door to the basement swung open and Sister Prudence stood in the doorway.

"Have you had enough time to think about what you have done?" she asked.

"Yes, Sister."

Sister Prudence moved to the side and let Eric pass.

"Go on and do your chores," she ordered.

Eric was desperate to tell his friends all about his incredible adventure. He sensed there was more to that place than he had seen. He found Santiago and Lucius collecting laundry on the third floor.

"Hey," he called out, beckoning them toward him.

"What happened to you?" asked Lucius.

"Sister Prudence locked me in the basement," said Eric.

"The basement!" his friends responded together with a look of horror on their faces.

But Eric didn't look scared, in fact he was positively brimming with excitement.

"Promise you won't tell anyone if I tell you something," he said.

"Promise," said Lucius.

"Promise," said Santiago.

Eric waited for a moment then began to speak.

"I found a grate down there, and a tunnel to the building next door."

"What?" said Santiago, suddenly feeling like he was in the middle of one of Eric's wild stories.

"It's true, and I met an old professor who makes toys."

Eric decided to leave out the Santa part, figuring that maybe they would not believe him about that.

"Did you know that the English call their cookies biscuits?" he added.

"What are you talking about?" asked Santiago.

"And they dip them in their tea," added Eric.

"Just be careful, Eric," warned Lucius. "I've heard bad things about the basement."

"I'm going to go back again as soon as I can to explore," said Eric.

Lucius and Santiago shot each other skeptical glances even though Eric appeared quite adamant about it.

Foraging

That night Eric lay in bed, unable to sleep. His mind was full of the thoughts of the world that he had discovered beyond the basement. He quietly sat up, placed his feet on the floor, and pulled his pants, shirt, and vest on. He even tied his tie. Then he tiptoed as quietly as he possibly could across the floorboards. Every other floorboard that he stepped on made an awful creaking sound, but he slowly navigated his way out of the dorm without disturbing anyone.

When he was at the top of the stairs, he put his socks and shoes on and leaped two steps at a time all the way down to the bottom. Moonlight streamed in through the windows of the large hallway, and the building itself seemed to be taking giant intakes of breath, expelling them out in one gentle movement.

Eric didn't know where the Sisters slept, but he figured that they could be lurking around anywhere, so he made sure to be extra quiet. Once he reached the basement, he placed his hand on the old metal knob and pushed the door open.

Eric felt a rush of excitement as he stepped down the stairs and located the little flashlight that he had hidden previously. With a click, the beam illuminated the basement and he made his way down the steps, across the room filled with boxes, and back to the tunnel. He carefully lifted the grate and crawled inside. Then he moved forward, feet first, and felt the bend of the pipe. He cupped his hands to his mouth and shouted.

"Professor Huxley, it's Eric."

There was no reply. He began to shuffle forward.

"Here I come!" he called out, launching himself into the tube.

In moments, he was moving fast, the still air rippling over his cheeks. It was only when he was moving too fast to stop that he realized something startling——maybe Professor Huxley was asleep in the bed that he was about to crash land onto.

"Professor!" he shouted at the top of his lungs. "Get out of my way!"

Eric hurtled out of the pipe and braced for impact. Before he knew it, he was on the bed——the soft, unoccupied bed. He wafted the dust from his face and straightened himself out. The old professor sat at his drafting board illuminated by a single light, pencil in one hand, eraser in the other. He turned around with a casual interest.

"Hello, young man," he said without a hint of surprise. "You're back."

"I couldn't wait," said Eric.

Huxley placed the pencil down.

"Actually, I am rather glad you returned," he said.

"Really?" asked Eric.

"My supplies are running quite low."

"Supplies?"

"All this designing and building and testing takes a lot of resources——paper, pencils, wood, paint——just to name a few. It's been some time since I have replenished any of them, and now they're almost all gone."

Huxley pointed around the room at the various cabinets, shelves, and drawers.

"Those paint cans are mostly empty. The only wood left is offcuts of offcuts. My pencils have been sharpened to extinction."

"You want to go to the hardware store?" Eric asked.

"Oh no," said Huxley with a chuckle. "Young man, do I have to remind you that you are at Santa Incorporated? This is where we make toys. It's all here. We just need to fetch it."

Eric was a little confused. He didn't know exactly what the old Professor was asking. But Huxley was already making his way across the lab floor to an unknown set of doors.

"Come on then," he called out.

Huxley opened up the doors, revealing a small area with a strange-looking contraption that included a harness and a pair of ropes.

"What's this?" asked Eric.

"This is how we get around. Well, one of the ways," said Huxley. "Step inside."

"What does it do?"

"It's the quickest way to get anywhere. Far superior to the staircase. Which is exhausting. The service elevator is too slow. And the main elevators are too risky."

"Too risky for what?"

Huxley ignored the question and instead placed the harness over Eric's body and secured it firmly.

"Where are we going?" asked Eric.

"Up, of course," said Huxley.

Eric looked up. Extending above them was a shaft that went as far as he could see until the remaining light dissipated into blackness.

"Where does it go?"

"It goes anywhere we want it to go. In this building, that is."

Huxley then placed the other harness over his own body, adjusted and secured the clips, then punched some buttons on an ancient-looking control module that stood next to them.

"I do sometimes worry if this old thing still works properly. Otherwise we may end up as sausage meat. The flat kind, not the cylindrical kind."

He muttered to himself as he tapped a couple more buttons on the module then pulled a lever at the side. There was a cranking sound and the long ropes started to move upwards into the cavernous space above.

"Don't be afraid, young man," said Huxley with a smile. "You're an adventurer after all. I am sure that you have been in far more perilous situations than this one."

The ropes above continued to make a terrible twisting, creaking sound, as if any moment they would snap under the pressure.

"Will the ropes break?" asked Eric.

"They're not ropes. They're elastic bungee cords. Made to stretch. Although admittedly I should do something about that awful sound. Maybe the elastic needs some kind of lubricant. I'll have to look into that."

Eric could feel the growing energy contained within the cords as they continued to screech and squirm up into the never-ending darkness. Then with a clunk, the sound stopped and there was silence.

"Ready?" asked Huxley with a smile.

Eric did not feel ready at all, but he nodded all the same. Huxley reached for a button to his left and pushed it.

"Hold on to your hat," he said.

Eric didn't have a hat, so he closed his eyes instead. Nothing happened. Huxley pushed the button again. Nothing.

"What the devil," he mused.

He tapped it a few more times. Eric felt a modicum of relief.

"Well this is quite embarrassing," Huxley said. "It should have——"

ZOOOOOOOOM!

Suddenly they were hurtling upwards so fast that Eric could hardly let the air out of his lungs to scream. They were traveling at such velocity that Eric felt as though he had left his stomach far behind.

When it finally caught him up, he was filled with a very strange sensation. As they whooshed further upwards, specks of light flickered past as though they were traveling at a thousand miles per hour. Both he and Huxley let out one long scream.

Eric had no concept of how long he had been moving for or how far he had gone, but after a few seconds they began to slow, then the slowing came very quickly. Then, for an infinitesimally brief moment, they hung completely weightless in the air, moving neither up nor down. The air that had moved so rapidly past their faces only moments before was now completely still.

"Gravity," whispered Huxley.

Now Eric became worried about something completely different, falling uncontrollably back to earth. But that did not happen. Instead, a wooden board, with a padded surface, slid out from the side of the wall, and they landed with no more than a light bump.

"It does work!" exclaimed Huxley. "I was wondering about that."

Eric breathed deep. His arms and legs felt wobbly, as though they didn't have enough blood in them to work properly. He ran his hand thankfully over the board that supported them. Huxley set about removing his harness.

"Let's go!"

They crawled to a doorway built into the shaft, then Huxley opened a door and stepped inside a narrow corridor, no more than two feet wide. He placed his index finger to his lips and signaled for Eric to remain quiet. He padded carefully down the corridor. Eric followed. They came to a small peephole that was positioned just about at eye level. Huxley peered through it, contorting his face in the process.

"Your turn," he said, moving out of the way.

Eric stood on his tiptoes, squinted, and looked through the peephole. In front of them was a large open plan office, the lights were partially dimmed.

"I was hoping, because of the hour," said Huxley, "that we would find this place unoccupied."

"What is this place?" whispered Eric.

"This is where the accountants work," said Huxley.

He tried to restrain himself but found that it was impossible.

"Look at it," Huxley continued. "They like order. They like everything to be neat and tidy. Can you imagine working in a place like that? Day in. Day out. How can anybody get anything done in such a sterile environment?"

"Why are we here?" asked Eric.

"Because there's one thing that accountants love. Paper-work. Reports. With lots of numbers. And dollar signs. They use the dollar signs so much that they have to replace them on their keyboards every second month."

There was nobody at the office, so Eric could only imagine what these accountants must be like.

"And what do you need for paperwork?" asked Huxley.

"Paper?" Eric guessed.

"Exactly. So they can print more and more reports, and look at more and more numbers."

"We're going rescue some of that paper and put it to better use. Across that hall is a storage cupboard. Inside are boxes of paper. Get the biggest box that you can find."

"What if somebody sees me?" asked Eric.

"There's nobody here," said Huxley. "They're all clocked off."

Huxley gave a little push against the wall where they were standing. Somehow, the outline of a door appeared. Eric had not noticed it before and now found himself standing in the main corridor.

"Go ahead," replied Huxley.

Eric breathed deeply, then sprang from the door like a greyhound out of a trap. He dashed across the hall and into the little storeroom. There he found all manner of supplies, stacked rows upon rows of shelves. He quickly located a large box with *Paper* written on the side. It looked like the biggest box of paper in the room. He wrapped his hands around it to lift, but it was heavy. Very heavy. He heaved it up at one end, managing to just about drag it along.

"All clear!" Huxley called from the door.

Eric half dragged, half carried it back to Huxley, who reopened the door and helped to pull it into the small corridor, then Eric scurried in behind it. Huxley shut the door quickly.

"You did it!"

Eric felt great. He was exhilarated. He could barely stop moving he felt so good. They dragged the box a little further down the interior corridor where Huxley opened another door. Inside the next room was an elevator, a great sturdy contraption with a metal sliding door and a concrete floor.

"We'll send the paper up on the service elevator and continue on our way," said Huxley, pushing the box into it and closing the metal gate with a clunk.

He pressed a button and the elevator began to ascend above them.

"Where is it going?" asked Eric.

"No time to explain," said Huxley. "Follow me."

The Luge

N ow Huxley opened another door on the opposite side to the elevator. Inside was a small circular staircase.

"How do you know about all this stuff?" asked Eric.

"Young man," he said. "I am the architect of this building."

Huxley stepped into the staircase.

"Every nut and bolt, plank of wood, girder of iron, pour of concrete. I was right here, watching. I filled it with things to make life easier, and a little more fun for everyone that worked here. But when the accountants arrived, everything changed," Huxley continued. "They don't like to have fun while they work. They just like to work. But I ask you, what is the point of work if it is not fun?"

"We work a lot at the orphanage," said Eric. "It's not much fun."

"I imagine that an orphanage is a rather terrible place to grow up," said Huxley.

Huxley began to climb the stairs. They were steep and he moved slowly, placing his hand on the bannister and pulling the rest of his body up.

"I used to run up these things three at a time," he chuckled. "But as old as I get, I always make sure to get my steps in every day. Exercise is the key to mental fortitude."

After quite a few flights, they came to another door. Huxley turned the handle and opened it. This time, he stepped out into the large open space without hesitation. Instantly, Eric's senses were alive with a very distinct smell. Huxley tapped the light switch and the strip lights flickered to life, illuminating rows and rows of industrial sized steel racks.

On those racks was wood of all shapes and sizes——from great planks as thick as tree trunks to tiny, thin pieces no bigger than a pencil. A sawdusty substance hung in the still air, and as Huxley walked across the bare concrete floor, his footsteps echoed into the distance. He tenderly touched the planks of wood one by one.

"This place used to be the busiest floor in the whole building," he said. "Three deliveries a week. Wood from all over the world. We would hoist them up the outside of the building on a giant crane and load them in through those large doors."

Huxley pointed toward a towering set of double doors in front of him. A large antiquated piece of machinery sat dormant in front of it.

"Of course, it's all plastic now," mused Huxley.

"What is?" asked Eric.

"Toys!" exclaimed Huxley. "They're all plastic. Foul stuff. A characterless, obnoxious material. But it's cheap and malleable."

Huxley picked up a four-foot plank of Douglas Fir. He ran his hand along its rough, untreated edge.

"Wood is alive. From a living organism. It has a soul. And it gives the toy a soul."

He smelled the wood, allowing its earthy scent to fill his senses. He walked over to the end of the row where a flatbed cart sat waiting to be used. Its paint had been long scratched off leaving just the exposed brownish coloring of the iron beneath. Huxley placed the wood onto the flatbed.

"We shall endeavor to give it the second life that it deserves," he declared.

Eric and Huxley wandered around the large storeroom. Eric pushed the cart as Huxley inspected the different cuts, lengths, and widths of timber and placed those he wanted onto the flat-bed. By the time they were done, the old cart, with its creaky wheels, was very heavy and hard to maneuver.

"They won't even notice it's gone," said Huxley.

Together, they pushed it slowly back to the service elevator and with all their strength, heaved it into the cage, next to the paper. Huxley pulled the large metal door closed again, hit a button, and somewhere above them a motor whirred into action. The cart, the wood, and the box of paper began to descend through the floors.

"Now," said Huxley, holding his index finger aloft, "on to our final stop."

They crossed back across the floor of the wood store, but instead of returning to the staircase, Huxley opened a different door.

"If you work here," asked Eric, "how come you're sneaking around?"

Huxley busied himself and did not hear, or at least he pretended not to hear, choosing instead to march forth leaving Eric somewhat puzzled.

He pushed open another door that revealed a small room, this time with some type of semi-circular metal track in it.

"Do you like to go fast?" asked the old Professor with a smile. "I certainly do."

The track wound its way down from the floor above and then descended to the floor below although it was not possible to see beyond that.

"When I was a young man, I was quite taken with winter sports. So much so that I dreamed of competing."

Huxley pulled a lever by the side of the track. There was a rolling sound, wheels gliding over metal, that came from somewhere above. Eric looked up to where the track was coming from but could not see anything. Huxley opened a large storage box by the side of the track and began rummaging around inside.

"Growing up, I had the privilege of wintering in Switzerland where I was introduced to the idea of shooting down a mountain as fast as humanly possible on nothing more than a glorified ice skate. It became a lifelong passion, and I resolved, when I designed this building, to incorporate some kind of similar contraption into the frame of it to allow me to indulge whenever possible."

He didn't find what he was searching for in the box, so he turned his attention to two adjacent shelves.

"I would venture that this is the only building in the entire world that contains such a thing."

The sound grew louder. Eric could tell that something, whatever it was, was on its way.

"There they are," exclaimed Huxley.

He reached back into the cupboard and pulled out two helmets as a contraption made of wood and metal shot down the track from the floor above and stopped quickly in front of them. There were two basic-looking seats mounted onto a small chassis with four small wheels underneath. A brake lever was placed just in front of the forward seat.

"This," announced Huxley, "is *The Luge*."

Huxley handed Eric a crash helmet and invited him to sit down.

"The beauty of this thing is that it runs on nothing more than gravity. Going down anyway."

Huxley clambered in and adjusted himself in the seat, being careful to straighten his bow tie in the process. Then he pulled on his crash helmet. Eric followed. It didn't fit very well at all, and there was no chin strap to secure it into place. It wobbled precariously on top of Eric's head.

"I would suggest that you use the seat belt," Huxley said, pointing to a piece of worn rope attached to the seat at one side.

Eric drew the rope over his body and fastened it at the side with the aid of a small hook. Huxley grasped the lever with glee.

Without a moment of hesitation, the old professor released the brake and the luge began to move. It was slow at first but soon the speed increased as the track dipped downwards toward the lower levels. Eric felt the air of the interior of the building rushing past his face. It felt a lot like the basement, still and cool. The wheels below him whirred around, faster and faster, louder and louder as they screeched along the track.

"We will be encountering some reasonably persuasive G-forces along the way," Huxley called out.

Some parts of the track were entirely dark, and it was impossible to know which way they were traveling, then the luge would jerk left or right and they would run along the next floor. Now Eric could see just how fast they were moving. This repeated many times as the descent continued. Huxley's grey hair fanned out from the sides of his helmet as they gathered speed. He had no intention of applying the brakes.

"Here we go," he shouted as they hit a tight corner.

Eric's body was forced into its seat. He felt as though his arms were made of lead.

"There's that G-force!" called Huxley.

Eric's stomach hurtled away from him. They circled round and down passing through the floors on a seemingly quickening journey through the insides of the building. Eric had no idea where he was and became quite disoriented from all of the spinning around, but it was so much fun that he hardly noticed the blood sloshing from one end of his body to the other. Eventually, Huxley yanked hard on the lever and the luge came to a screeching halt. They sat for a moment in silence as Huxley pushed his hair back down.

"You just travelled from the fortieth floor to the third floor in less than two minutes," he declared.

Both Eric and Huxley pulled themselves out of the luge and for a few moments they held onto the wall for balance.

"I do believe that I have quite lost my senses," said Huxley with a chuckle.

Eric thought that he might throw up.

Elves

When his head had finally stopped spinning, Eric removed his helmet and looked around the luge station. He began to get an inkling of how the Santa building worked. At least he had a theory. There was the main building with its large corridors and offices that the accountants used, and there were also other floors, some used and some abandoned. But hidden inside the building's walls was a secret world of unknown passageways, stairs, elevators, catapults, and luges that Huxley used to navigate his way around the place. It was as though there were two buildings in one. Eric wondered if perhaps Huxley was the only person to occupy this vast building.

"Does anyone else know about these things?" he asked.

"Only the elves."

"Elves," Eric whispered to himself.

The word didn't make sense. Huxley walked over to a set of double doors and placed his hand on both handles.

"Now," he said, "you are in for a real treat."

After his adventures, Eric could not imagine something that could be more amazing than what he had already experienced. He had already seen more things in one day than he had ever seen before. At least since his travels to the Ivory Coast of Africa.

"Be prepared for something spectacular," Huxley announced.

He flung open the doors and Eric's eyes bulged in disbelief.

Stretching out before them was a huge factory. There was activity everywhere, noise and movement. Machines, production lines, and all manner of contraptions whirred and buzzed incessantly. But this was no ordinary factory, with cold, grey machines, and unforgiving strip lights. The whole place was full of color. Every machine was painted in a bright red, blue, or yellow, and they sparkled and shined as though they were not more than a day old.

Eric's eyes had never beheld such a sight. It made him feel as though he were more alive than he had ever been. Along snaking conveyor belts came toys of all shapes and sizes, pumped out at a rapid rate and packed into boxes. The boxes were loaded onto pallets and whizzed away on forklift trucks. Everywhere was movement, everywhere was color. But what was most incredible of all was that everywhere Eric looked, hard at work, were tiny little men, no more than two feet high.

Eric could not believe what he was seeing. He strained to see them, thinking that somehow the perspective was off in his eyeballs. He even rubbed his eyes. But those figures in front of him remained the same size, busily occupied with their own tasks. Some had full beards, some had no beards, some had mutton chop sideburns, and a few had great mustaches that were carefully coiffured into elaborate circles. They all wore green overalls and red hard hats. Eric found that the old professor was regarding him with a smile.

"Are those...?" asked Eric.

"Elves," nodded Huxley.

Eric watched in awe. He could barely believe it.

"Are they real?"

Huxley laughed.

"Of course they are."

There was an almost incessant procession of raw materials that fed into the production lines, molding all manner of products into recognizable shapes through the process.

"Rather stunning, isn't it?" asked Huxley. "Despite the plastic."

Upon closer inspection, Eric could see that what first appeared as chaos was actually perfectly timed and coordinated. Each elf had a job and would appear at exactly the right time to perform it. The forklifts weaved around feeding the machines and taking away finished products.

"In the old days, this was all done by hand, with nothing more than hand tools. But over time, automation and machinery have been introduced. It's a year-round operation, you see."

Suddenly Eric became more aware of himself.

"What if they see us?" he asked.

"Goodness gracious," exclaimed Huxley. "I have known the elves for as long as I can remember. And they have known me for as long as they can remember. They are the life force of this whole endeavor. We built this place together. Brick by brick."

Eric watched in fascination as the miniature army proceeded with its task. Even though they were obviously working hard, something about their demeanor made it appear as though there was no effort at all. Every so often, one elf would start singing and the others would immediately join in:

> "We are the elves.
> Santa's worker elves.
> We make the toys
> For all the girls and boys"

"They all look so happy," said Eric.

"They are happy," replied Huxley. "They are doing the thing they love. This is their life's purpose."

Huxley walked toward a giant storage area dodging the vehicles that shuttled in and out carrying supplies. The elves crisscrossed in front of them, busy with their tasks, but each one greeted Huxley as they passed.

"Hello, Professor!"

"Morning!"

"Bonjour, Professor Huxley."

Professor Huxley greeted each one in turn. He knew all of their names.

"Hello, Stanley!"

"Morning, Oswaldo!"

"Bonjour to you, Jean-Pierre."

Finally, they arrived at a small corner of the factory floor where one elf sat, carefully working on what looked like a wooden train. He had meticulously assembled the pieces of delicately cut wood using tiny nails and glue to hold it together.

"Good morning, Stephen," said Huxley.

The elf looked up from his work.

"Good morning, Professor," he replied. "Haven't seen you for a while."

"Busy?"

Stephen the elf shrugged.

"You know what it's like," he said, rolling his eyes.

"I was wondering if I could trouble you for some paint?" asked Huxley.

Stephen carefully placed the wooden train on his work bench.

"I can give you a little bit, but the accountants record every ounce of what we use these days," he said, inspecting his creation. "If we use too much, we get a talking to. I'll only be able to put a couple of coats on this."

"Oh dear," remarked Huxley.

"Lofty!" called Stephen.

A younger-looking elf who was almost two and one quarter feet appeared from the storeroom.

"Yes, boss?"

"Help the professor with some paint."

"Yes, boss."

"Just the primary colors," said Huxley. "I can do the rest."

Lofty opened a storage cabinet. Every color of paint imaginable was neatly arranged, just like in Huxley's laboratory. Stephen scanned them for a moment and carefully picked out his targets, then used a sliding ladder to access that part of the cabinet, carefully selecting green, blue, red and white. He brought them down and placed them into a hessian sack.

"Thank you, Stephen," said Huxley.

"No worries, Professor. How are the new designs coming along?" the elf asked.

"Marvelously," replied Huxley.

"Fantastic," said Stephen.

Huxley and Eric walked back across the floor to the sound of song.

"It's Christmas time,
On the production line.
We'll load up Santa's sleigh,
Then we'll dance and play."

Eric tried to capture everything in his mind so that he might preserve the memory of what he had seen. They returned to the luge and loaded the cans of paint into a small space on the back of it.

"They really are real, aren't they?" Eric asked.

"Oh yes," said Huxley.

They climbed into their seats and buckled up.

"I'll go a little slower this time," said Huxley.

He let the brake off and the luge pulled away. They glided all the way down to the basement at a leisurely speed and came to a stop back in Huxley's workshop. Eric jumped out and unloaded the paint.

"What did Stephen mean?" he asked.

"About what?" asked Huxley.

"When he rolled his eyes like this."

Eric mimicked Stephen to the best of his ability.

"I don't think I saw that," said Huxley. "But I am quite parched and in desperate need of some tea. And probably a biscuit."

Mister Miller

Eric returned to Our Lady of Mercy just before dawn, back up through the tunnel and the grate and into the basement, sneaking through the hall and up the stairs, quiet as a mouse. He climbed back into his bed. He couldn't sleep for a long time as his mind raced with the excitement of Santa Inc. Finally, his eyes fluttered a little and he fell into a deep slumber.

It seemed like only minutes had passed before the Sisters were banging the pot to wake everybody up. Eric was groggy and lay motionless, dead asleep. When Sister Prudence saw that he was still in bed, she began to clang the pot at double volume just above his head.

"Get up," she yelled. "Get up!" Over and over.

Finally, Eric dragged his eyes open. He stretched and wearily pulled his clothes back on. He was late walking down the stairs, and by the time he arrived, all the other boys were already seated. It was 6:12 a.m., and the Lord's Prayer was in full flow. Sister Prudence glowered at Eric as he stood, looking slightly disheveled by the door. Lucius was very worried. Santiago shook his head. Eric went to take his place, but as he walked forward, Sister Prudence called out.

"No."

Eric stopped dead. The boys stopped dead.

"Continue," she barked.

The boys resumed. Eric joined in.

"Not you," Sister Prudence shouted.

Eric stopped. Some of the other boys stopped. Then started. Then everybody lost their place. It was quite the debacle.

"Everybody, start again, except Eric," ordered Sister Prudence.

When they were finally done, there was silence. Sister Prudence scanned over the boys. Their heads were down for they knew that something bad was imminent.

"Eric was late this morning," she said. "Therefore, you will all receive a half ration of oatmeal."

A low mumbling of discontent rippled through the boys.

"Silence," called Sister Prudence. "Eric, will hand everyone a bowl this morning and apologize to each of you for his tardiness."

Eric walked over to the serving hatch. Then the oldest boys followed, Kevin O'Malley being first. Mister Miller served up a half-measure and gave it to Eric, who handed it over.

"Sorry," he said.

Kevin O'Malley snatched the bowl with a scowl. Terrence did the same. Then Ping. It went on and on. Every boy's stomach, already empty was now consigned to a half serving of gloopy oatmeal.

"Eric will enjoy two servings today," announced Sister Prudence.

"But Sister..." protested Eric.

But he was met with a stare that could melt rock. He stopped and accepted the fact that today he would eat double, in fact quadruple, what the others had eaten.

Mister Miller served him his two bowls, and he carried them to the table and sat down. There were stares up and down the row. Forty-nine pairs of aggrieved eyes watched every bite. When breakfast was over, and his table was dismissed, he took his bowl and placed it into a large plastic tub for washing. Sister Prudence appeared next to him.

"Wait here," she said.

Eric waited until every boy had cleared his bowl and left the canteen. There were more stares, more mouthing threats. Finally, the last boy dropped the last bowl in the tub.

"Sister Christine and I both agree that you are a persistent disruption in class and that you must be removed," said Sister Prudence.

The truth was that Sister Christine had not been consulted on the matter. Sister Prudence did not believe that there was any value in discussing such matters with her subordinate.

"What do you mean?" asked Eric.

"You know exactly what I mean, young man," she replied. "And thankfully we have found a solution."

Eric did not know what she meant, but he could tell by her tone that it would most likely be unpleasant.

"If you think that you are too clever for math, for Bible study, or to sing in the choir, then so be it. We will put you straight to work."

"What type of work?" asked Eric.

"Useful work," said Sister Prudence.

She pushed open the door to the kitchen. Mister Miller was busy scraping the remnants of the burned-on oatmeal from the large pot into the trash.

"Mister Miller," said Sister Prudence. "This is the trouble-maker boy. He will work for you until further notice. See that he is put to good use and do not give him an inch. Otherwise he will take a mile."

Sister Prudence pushed Eric further into the kitchen and shut the door behind him. Eric had never spoken to Mister Miller before, despite being served every single meal he had ever eaten by him for as long as he could remember. Mister Miller wiped his hands on a dirty, old rag and walked over to Eric. He had quite a pronounced limp in his left leg, something that Eric had not noticed before. His weather-beaten face and sturdy forearms were joined to hands as big as bear claws.

"Well then," he said. "You must've done something terrible to wind up here with me."

Mister Miller grinned. His brownish-yellow teeth poked through underneath an overgrown mustache.

"So come on," he continued. "Out with it."

"What do you mean?" asked Eric.

Mister Miller leaned against the large old table that stood in the middle of the kitchen.

"Fighting?" he asked. "Have you been fighting?"

He clenched his fists and extended each arm in turn as though sparring with some invisible opponent.

"No," said Eric.

"What about carousing all night?" he asked with a wink. "Up at all hours having a grand old time?"

Eric shook his head. Mister Miller looked puzzled, as though searching for an answer.

"Then you must have been robbing," he concluded. "Got some light fingers, have ya?"

He pushed his thumb and forefinger together and delicately lifted an invisible object.

"No," said Eric, "I have never stolen anything."

Mister Miller's mustache twitched under his nose.

"Then what is it?"

"Sister Prudence says I ask too many questions."

"Questions?" said Mister Miller with a pronounced disappointment. "That's not troublemaking."

Eric shrugged.

"And sometimes she says I have too many answers. She says that's disruptive."

Mister Miller's shoulders dropped.

"Questions and answers," he mumbled to himself in disbelief. He returned to his stove and peered into the pot. "I was hoping for some good stories."

"What type of stories?" asked Eric.

"Exciting ones," said Mister Miller, "With plenty of carousing. And fighting. And a bit of robbing."

"I once sailed to the Ivory Coast of Africa," said Eric.

"You did?"

"I can tell you all about that."

"What's your name?" asked Mister Miller.

"Eric."

Mister Miller pointed to a giant sink full of hot soapy water and all of the dirty bowls sitting in the tub.

"Alright, Eric," he said with a nod. "You can wash while you go."

Eric told Mister Miller his story of the ship, the great storm, and transporting elephants all the way from the west coast of Africa to the New York Zoo. And it just so happened that Mister Miller had been a ship's cook for many years, and he had travelled the world on the high seas aboard all manner of merchant ships plying their wares from one far flung place to the other. He too had a story to tell about every country and city that he had visited.

Eric listened intently while he ran the sponge over every bowl and placed it on the side to dry. Over the course of that morning as they took care of all of the kitchen duties together, cleaning up breakfast and then preparing lunch, Eric and Mister Miller shared a great many yarns about the Yangtze River, the ports of Manaus and Belo Horizonte, and the Malay Peninsula. Eric told of his journeys to Borneo and Darjeeling and his expedition to see the Inuit Tribes of northern Alaska. He did not mention his most recent adventure to Santa Inc., however.

"There's nothing like a life on the high seas," Mister Miller mused.

The hands of the clock in the canteen ticked to midday. Almost immediately there followed the familiar sound of feet, down the staircase then down the hall, like a herd of charging buffalo through a canyon.

"Here," said Mister Miller.

He handed Eric a spare apron.

"Otherwise they're all going to think you're a waiter."

Mister Miller laughed at his own joke as Eric put the apron over his suit and tied it behind his back. The doors burst open and the canteen was again awash with sound. Mister Miller rolled up the shutters and picked up his ladle, ready for action.

"What exactly is in that?" asked Eric, peering into the giant pot.

"Bits of this and bits of that."

It was the same stew as always, bland and watery with the odd scrap of gristle or carrot added for texture. The pot bubbled and steamed but it didn't look much like something that anyone would wish to eat. It didn't even have much of a smell. The boys lined up, and as usual Mister Miller ladled out the watery brownish liquid into their bowls one by one. Eric stood to the side and observed.

So many times he had seen the process from the opposite angle, and it was quite interesting to see how things worked from a completely different perspective. As each boy reached the front of the line and saw Eric standing in the kitchen, they looked at him with the same expression of surprise. Kevin O'Malley was first.

"What are you doing in there?" he asked.

"Sister Prudence has given me a special job," said Eric proudly.

Kevin O'Malley looked suspicious but took his meal and moved on. The reaction from each boy was the same: total surprise that Eric had emerged in a position of some privilege. When Lucius and Santiago got to the front of the line their mouths dropped open simultaneously.

"What are you doin' back there?" Santiago whispered.

"I have a new job working with Mister Miller," Eric replied.

"What about classes?" followed Lucius.

"More important things to do," said Eric.

The same question was quietly posed to Eric at least ten more times over lunch. Nobody could quite believe how Eric had come to assume a role in the kitchen. Lucius snuck a look at his friend in the serving hatch. Eric met his eyes, then he pointed to himself and then motioned with his hand a downward movement, indicating that he was returning to the basement. Then he drew his finger to his lips. Lucius nodded.

When lunch was done, the boys brought their bowls and spoons back to the kitchen. Eric took them in turn and each boy gave him the same disbelieving look. As they left the canteen, chattering quietly among themselves, they concluded that far from being a punishment, Eric had somehow landed himself in a position of great importance.

Eric once more ran a sink of hot soapy water and washed the spoons and tin bowls. He pulled his hands out and looked at them. His skin was crinkly and bright pink from the water. At the other end, each bowl had to be dried in turn. As did the cutlery. By the time lunch was over and the boys began their afternoon chores, Eric was tired and his fingers were soft and tender. Mister Miller took a seat.

"A cook's life is a hard life," he said as he eased himself down onto a wooden chair.

He closed his eyes, and within moments he was asleep, his belly moving up and down slowly in a contented sort of a way. Eric folded the dish cloth and placed it onto the large kitchen table. As he removed his apron, a marvelous thought came to him. With the Sisters occupied and Mister Miller snoozing, an opportunity to return to Santa Inc. had unknowingly presented itself.

Lunch

Eric made the now-increasingly-familiar journey into the basement, down the stairs, weaving through the boxes, into the grate, down the pipe, and the final exhilarating whoosh into Professor Huxley's laboratory.

"Here I come!" he shouted as he was launched from the duct.

The old professor was sitting at his drafting board with a large sheet of the recently plundered paper in front of him.

"Hello, Professor Huxley," he called out.

There was no reply. Eric picked himself up off the bed and wandered over.

"Professor Huxley?" he asked.

Huxley was concentrating so hard that it wasn't until he heard Eric's voice right next to him that he snapped out of it.

"Ah," he called out. "Wherever did you appear from?"

"What are you doing?" asked Eric.

For a moment Huxley appeared hesitant, and a forlorn expression briefly crossed his face. It was only then that Eric realized that the sheet of paper was blank.

"I'm working on something that is proving to be a considerable vexation to me."

Huxley spun around on his chair to face Eric. He placed his hand on his head, consumed with this particularly challenging problem.

"I need a new toy," he said matter-of-factly.

"To play with?" asked Eric.

"I need to design a new toy," replied Huxley. "A brilliant toy. Possibly the best toy that the world has ever seen. Something so incredibly fantastic that every child, young or old, girl or boy will demand that they simply must have one."

"Why?" asked Eric.

"Because that is what is needed," said Huxley without a moment's thought.

He swung back to the desk and busied himself by sharpening a pencil that already looked sharp.

"Christmas is nearly upon us," he continued. "If I can finish something soon, it's still possible. Maybe the elves will work a little later into the evenings. The machines can run over time."

Huxley stared at the blank page as if willing for something to appear on it by magic.

"But I am blocked!" he cried, raising both hands in the air and shaking them.

He turned to Eric.

"Do you have any ideas?"

Eric thought for a while.

"How about a ship? Like a pirate ship? Or an old freighter that crosses the sea and delivers cargo from the Ivory Coast of Africa, or the Port of Manaus, or makes its way up the Yangtze River to where the river dolphins swim?"

Huxley screwed up his face.

"That's just a toy boat. That's not new."

"How about a backpack that contains enough food for a four-day trek across the Andes on a Llama?"

Huxley shook his head back and forth.

"Think back to your best Christmas ever, remember how you felt when you unwrapped that present, the surprise, the excitement, the sheer joy of the moment."

"I don't think I have one of those memories," said Eric.

"What do you mean? All your Christmases must be fresher than fallen snow in your mind."

Eric shrugged.

"You mean they don't give you a Christmas in that orphanage?"

"No," said Eric.

"What a wretched place it must be. Every child should get at least one present."

"Christmas is no different to any other day of the year. Except that we go to church and sing. But this year... Who knows?"

Huxley sat back in his seat to take in the news.

"I don't understand. How can any child not experience the joy of Christmas? It doesn't make any sense."

"Maybe you're just thinking about it too much," said Eric, turning the conversation back to the blank paper.

"You could be right," said Huxley.

Eric tapped the drafting board.

"Sometimes if I sit in one place too long, I get bored. If I get up and walk around, I get new ideas."

"That's it. We need an injection of inspiration," said Huxley, standing up.

Huxley and Eric made their way back to the factory, this time by way of the service elevator. When they arrived at the factory floor, everything was quiet.

"They must be at dinner," said Huxley.

"But it's only just been lunch," noted Eric.

"The elves stick to a very strict schedule," said Huxley. "They believe that they get more done in the morning and therefore the earlier they start, the more productive they are. They get up at 3AM every day. They have breakfast three hours before the sun comes up so by 10AM they're ready for lunch. Then they eat dinner at 2PM. They go to bed at 7PM for a full eight hours of sleep."

They walked across the dormant factory floor to another doorway. Huxley pushed it open, leading the way through a small courtyard. In front of them was a small building in the style of a Swiss chalet with a door no more than four feet high.

"They're in the Elf Lodge," said Huxley.

Eric repeated the words *Elf Lodge* to himself. A great noise reverberated from the building, the sound of cutlery banging against tin and a thousand voices all chitter-chattering. Huxley pushed the door open to reveal rows and rows of long wooden tables crammed with elves enjoying a hearty meal. They were talking, eating, and laughing. It reminded Eric of the orphanage except that everyone was happy and the food looked good. Huxley bent down and made his way inside. Eric followed.

"Where could they be?" Huxley asked over the din, peering over the room. "Aha!"

He started off walking down the lines of tables, greeting many of the elves as he went. Eric recognized two of the elves, Lofty and Stephen, from the previous day. They were sitting at the end of a far table. Stephen raised his hand and beckoned them over. Eric felt like a giant as he made his way through the raucous canteen.

"Sit down!" called Stephen, clearing space for them.

They sat down on the small wooden bench. A large bowl was dropped in front of Eric. Steam curled upwards into his nose. The aroma was absolutely delightful.

"Is this for us?" he asked.

"Of course," said Stephen.

"What is it?" asked Eric.

Huxley and the surrounding elves looked at Eric in disbelief.

"You don't know?" asked Stephen.

"No," said Eric.

"This," announced Lofty, "is Spaghetti Bolognese."

"And this," declared Stephen, "is Parmesan Cheese."

He sprinkled a dusting of the grated white cheese over the meal. Eric's stomach rumbled in anticipation as he took his fork and pushed it into the spaghetti. He spun it around and wrapped the pasta, meat sauce, and a good amount of cheese into one large bite, then placed it into his mouth. Even before tasting it, he knew that this would be the most scrumptious mouthful of food that he would ever taste. And he was right. Its flavor was so intense, so fantastically wonderful that it almost made him want to get up and do a little jig.

"Good?" asked Huxley with a knowing smile.

Eric shoveled another mouthful in. And another.

"We elves make the best food," said Stephen proudly. "If we didn't like making toys so much, we would have opened a restaurant."

As Eric ate, he listened to the conversations that Huxley had with Stephen, Lofty, and the other elves sitting around them. They talked about materials, how things could be made, what was working, and what needed to be improved. Eric was fascinated. He had never heard such interesting subjects being spoken about over a meal. It was as though a whole new world of possibility had opened up to him.

"What I am really looking for," said Huxley, "are ideas. What kinds of toys are you making this year?"

"We're making everything," said Stephen. "I mean everything. You name it. We're making it."

Eric noticed that Huxley looked a little forlorn.

"What's the big-ticket item?" he asked.

"Boys still love to smash things up, and fight, and shoot things," said Lofty.

"And girls tend to be more creative, they like to make things," said Stephen.

"But some girls like to smash things."

"And some boys like to build things."

"So we've made something for everyone, because all children are different," added Jean-Pierre, who was sitting across the way.

Huxley was not satisfied with the answer.

"What else?" he asked.

"Cars, trains, ponies..."

"Rocking horses, crayons, paints, teddy bears..."

"Giraffes, doll houses, building blocks, chemistry sets."

The list went on and Huxley listened intently. Eventually the plates were cleared away and Eric found that his stomach protruded out from his body. That had never happened before. Then the elves picked up their knives and forks and began to bang them in unison on the tables until eventually there was one consistent beat——BOOM-BOOM-BOOM-BOOM-BOOM. Then, in one perfect chorus, the elves began to sing:

> "We are the elves.
> The Santa Inc. elves.
> We make the toys
> For all the girls and boys."

> "We need our meat and pasta
> To keep us working faster.
> We'll build and work all day.
> And then we'll dance and play."

In one movement, the elves stood up and continued the beat by stomping their feet. Then they filed out of the canteen and into the courtyard. It was very orderly, but because Eric and Huxley were sitting on one of the far tables, they had to wait some time before it was their turn to leave.

As they streamed out and the singing slowly dissipated into laughter and conversation, they heartily patted each other on the back. But after a few moments, there came a bumping and jostling at the door which soon spread. Something was happening at the head of the line that nobody could quite see, a commotion. Huxley sensed that something was wrong as the elves drew back and their happy demeanor was replaced by an anxiousness. A tension fell over the room and the happy chatter stopped.

Trouble

"Let's wait here," suggested Huxley.

The elves had gathered in the courtyard as whispers and questions rippled through the crowd.

"What's happening?" asked Eric.

"I don't know," said Huxley, though in truth he did have an inkling of an idea.

Together, they peered furtively out of the window as the great factory door opened slowly. Out stepped a man. He was as thin and boney as Sister Prudence. He wore a black suit with white pinstripes that ran lengthways from his shoulders to his ankles. His jet-black hair was neat and short and matched his well-polished shoes. He wore a crisp white shirt and a red tie. Huxley took a sharp intake of breath.

"Who's that?" asked Eric.

"Wormwood Grubbs," said Lofty. "One of Santa's suits."

Just the mention of his name sent a chill through those within earshot. Eric looked at the man's angular face as he silently stared out over the elves. It was clear that he did not carry a natural affection for them. In fact, his expression was a mixture between sneering and menacing.

"Well then?" he asked finally.

There was a ripple of chatter among the elves, then one elf began to make his way forward from the middle of the crowd. The group opened up and let him through.

"There he is," said Huxley.

"Who?" asked Eric.

"That's Robbo. All elves are equal, but he is their designated spokesman."

Robbo stepped forward to where Wormwood Grubbs was standing. His greying mustache curled around in two perfectly symmetrical circles at the sides of his face. He did not look anxious like the other elves. In fact, he was positively bristling for a showdown. Two elves hoisted him up onto their shoulders, raising him by two feet, then four elves hoisted them up raising Robbo by another two feet so that now he stood just over six feet tall. It was all performed in an effortlessly acrobatic way so Robbo could look directly into Grubbs' eyes.

"Now see here," he called, addressing his fellow elves as much as Grubbs. "You asked us to work double time. You asked us to split our shifts. You asked us to increase our productivity. Well I'll tell you this, Mr. Grubbs. We know how to work. We already do good work in good time. In fact, we were doing it long before you arrived. So here's my answer: We won't do it!"

There was a cheer from the elves, but Grubbs was not about to back down either.

"I told you that we needed to make more toys and cut more costs. It's as simple as that," stated Grubbs.

"How can we make more toys? We're already making more toys," argued Robbo.

Mumbled agreement pulsed through the crowd.

"Then you leave me no choice. I will be forced to consider other options," stated Grubbs.

"Then you go ahead and consider your options. We elves work hard every day, from morning until night," said Robbo firmly. "But we also need to have fun!"

There was a huge cheer. And with that, the elves broke out into a chorus of dancing and singing.

"Elves just wanna have fun!
Elves! Elves! Wanna have fun. Fun!"

"Silence!" Grubbs called in his most dastardly voice. "This is a business. It's not about having fun. It's about making money."

"Where is Santa?" asked Robbo. "How come he sends you down here, but he won't come and talk to us himself?"

"He's busy," said Grubbs dismissively. "He's got a multinational business to run. Do you think he's going to jump at your every groan and gripe? You're wasting his time."

Quiet returned for a moment, save for a few murmurs of discontent. Eric watched, intrigued to see what would happen next. The two parties had come to an impasse.

"We need a work-life balance," a voice called out.

Grubbs' face contorted with annoyance.

"Who said that? Who said it?" he demanded. "Who said those vile words?"

Lofty slowly raised his hand.

"You," cried Grubbs pointing at the young elf. "You're suspended for forty-eight hours."

Lofty immediately burst into tears as Stephen put a conciliatory arm around him.

"You can't do that!" said Robbo.

But Grubbs was in no mood for apologies.

"You've all gotten a little too big for your small boots," he said. "We will increase productivity. And we will make more toys. We'll outsource it if we have to."

Grubbs waited for the response, but it did not come. Instead the elves just waited and stared at him. Realizing that his hard line may have worked, he took on a somewhat surprised and overly satisfied look as the elves stood passively in front of him.

But he had declared his own victory too soon. In one coordinated motion, a giant roar swelled up from the crowd and with it a wall formed. Three elves high, they marched toward Grubbs howling their battle cry. Grubbs' smug expression quickly turned to panic as he hastily backtracked all the way to the factory door. But the wall would not stop. The roar got louder as the elves marched on, letting their discontent ring out for all to hear.

"You have not heard the end of this!" Grubbs cried as they forced him back.

He tried to make one last defiant stand, but the strength of the mob was too much for him, and he realized that there was no option but to retreat. He opened the door and shut it quickly behind him, scampering off to the elevator. The biggest cheer of all went up in the factory, and the elves began to sing once more as they returned to work:

> "We are the elves.
> The Santa Inc. elves.
> We make the toys
> For all the girls and boys."

> "We like to work!
> We like to play!
> And Wormwood Grubbs
> Can go away!"

The Bottom Line

Whatever the commotion died down and it was safe to leave, Huxley and Eric returned to the laboratory.

"What's a work-life balance?" asked Eric.

Huxley mumbled a few words, but they did not become a satisfactory answer.

"So the elves are mad at Santa?" Eric surmised.

Huxley placed one hand on his forehead. Eric noticed that that was a habit.

"I think we had better have a cup of tea," he said.

Huxley brewed a pot of tea and placed four biscuits on the plate. They sat down at the table in the small kitchen.

"You have correctly observed that things are not all rosy at Santa Incorporated at the present time," said Huxley.

"Because of Wormwood Grubbs?" asked Eric.

"That's not the whole story..."

Huxley sipped his tea and thought carefully. He did not particularly care for this subject of conversation but concluded that Eric deserved a proper answer.

"This all started when we were still at the North Pole," he said eventually.

"You were at the North Pole?" asked Eric.

"Oh yes," said Huxley. "Everything was perfect. Life was simple. January was always vacation. Somewhere hot, with a beach, like Timbuktu or Rarotonga. In February we came up with ideas for new toys, and in March we would finalize the designs. Then in April we would go into production all the way up to Christmas Eve. One coordinated effort, all working in harmony."

"So what went wrong?" asked Eric.

"Santa read a book. It was all about men and women who had built great business empires and amassed great fortunes and became fabulously famous. *Great Industrialists*. He started to believe that his small-time operation was going nowhere. So he bought more books. Books about marketing and sales and production and finance and all the things that are required to run a business. He wanted to be one of those people."

"A great industrialist?" asked Eric.

"Correct."

"And what happened?"

"We made more toys. We made them a little quicker, we made them a little better, and we made them a little cheaper. Everyone was happy. Except for Santa. He had found something that fired his imagination. It was as though a whole new world had revealed itself to him."

Huxley dipped his biscuit into his tea and took a bite.

"Business," said Huxley as pieces of half-chewed biscuit were launched from his mouth like a volley of miniature mortars. "From then on, everything changed. Santa was suddenly driven to expand. He decided that the north pole was too far away from anything to succeed. He wanted to come to the center of the business world."

"New York," Eric added.

Huxley nodded.

"So we built this place. A factory, an office, a dispatch center, all under one roof. We made more toys for more children and became more famous than ever before. We had tie-ins and endorsements, movie deals, and commercials. We had more money than we could ever imagine. Everything was wonderful."

"You don't mean that, do you?" said Eric.

"No," said Huxley.

"Santa took the company public. We were registered on the venerable New York Stock Exchange."

"What's that?" asked Eric.

"It's where people buy and sell companies."

Huxley was animated but then almost immediately became dejected.

"Somewhere along that road we lost our way. Gone were the January vacations. The time to be creative was no longer important. The hours went up. The fun went down. And everybody focused on the bottom line."

"The bottom line?" asked Eric.

"Money," said Huxley, as though the very utterance of those words produced a foul taste in his mouth.

"And he hired people like Wormwood Grubbs and his army of accountants to make sure that not a single penny was misplaced. Those shareholders must be satisfied. And Christmas became business."

Huxley chewed his biscuit with a look of melancholy.

"In my opinion we have wandered too far from the true spirit of the season. That is why I must invent a new toy," Huxley continued. "Something real. Not some nasty piece of injection-molded plastic. Something that has been crafted by a real person. Or a real elf. With care and attention to detail."

Eric didn't say anything. He was too busy percolating all of the information that his visit had provided.

"I'm sorry," said Huxley as he finished the last of his tea. "I would dearly love to have offered you a better story."

Eric made his way back up the ladder, through the pipe, and into the basement. As he opened the door, he could hear the boys playing at recess. He desperately wanted to find Santiago and Lucius, just to tell them something. Just another little hint of what he had seen.

"You!" came a voice.

Eric stood as still as a statue. He turned and found Mister Miller staring at him. Eric began quickly assembling his excuses in his mind, but the old cook had no interest in where he had been.

"Time to get the dinner going," he said, pushing his way back through the swinging kitchen door. Eric followed.

"What do you call the stuff that we have to eat?" asked Eric.

Mister Miller thought about it for a while.

"I guess it's just stew," he said eventually.

"Can you make Spaghetti Bolognese?" asked Eric.

"Of course!" shouted Mister Miller. "I can make anything."

Eric thought about the Spaghetti Bolognese——deliciously tasty, meaty, and cheesy.

Mister Miller took the large pot that was used for every meal and filled it with water. Then he limped over to the stove and dropped it down with a clang.

"Stew," said Eric.

Mister Miller turned up the heat, then he took some yellowish powder and dropped it into the water. Then he opened up a large can of carrots and tinned celery and dropped them in. Finally, he opened a can with the word *Meat* printed on the side. It made a sucking sound as Mister Miller forced it out of the container and let it drop into the pot where it floated, perfectly cylindrical, in the warming liquid.

"All done," he said. "Give it a stir every five minutes or so."

Eric gave the pot a stir with a large wooden spoon. It slowly turned into the same unappetizing mixture of murky-looking liquid with the occasional carrot making an appearance on the surface. Its contents were not too different from the used sink water after the washing up was done.

"So how do you make it?" asked Eric. "Spaghetti Bolognese."

"Meat," said Mister Miller. "Olive Oil. Garlic. Tomatoes. Oregano. Salt and pepper. And spaghetti. Lots of spaghetti."

"And cheese?" added Eric.

"Parmesan cheese. No imitations. When I was on the ships, the Italians on the crew would have thrown me overboard if I didn't give them the real thing."

Eric imagined a mob of angry Italian sailors waving fake Parmesan cheese while hauling Mister Miller over the side into the dark ocean.

"So, who decides on the food that you cook?" asked Eric.

"I do," said Mister Miller, as though the thought of someone interfering in his kitchen was ridiculous.

"Are we allowed to make Spaghetti Bolognese here?" Eric asked.

"Allowed?" asked Mister Miller.

"Do you think we could try one time?"

Mister Miller mumbled something unintelligible, not unlike Huxley. Eric peered into the stew again.

He couldn't figure out why Mister Miller was so into stew when other far tastier foods were available. He decided not to pursue it any further. Dinner was rapidly approaching, and the boys would soon appear. He set up the spoons and bowls ready for serving. When everything was prepared, Eric looked at the old canteen clock and realized that there were five minutes to spare.

He pushed the door of the kitchen open, walked down the hallway, past the office and the basement and into the main hall. There he opened the door to the courtyard and stepped out into the cold, early evening air. The winter sun was already sinking low in the sky where it projected an orange hue onto the great buildings of the city.

Eric's eyes started at the bottom and gradually made their way to the top of the mighty edifice that stood before him. He wanted to see what the Santa Inc. building looked like from the outside. He had looked up at it many times before, but this time was different. This time he knew what was inside. He had been given an inkling of its secrets. From the outside, the building gave nothing away. How would anyone have ever known that it held so many stories?

"What are you doing?" came a voice.

Eric spun around. It was Sister Christine. She stood with her hand on the door looking suspiciously at him.

"Get inside before you get in more trouble," she ordered.

Eric turned and walked through the open door.

"You set yourself up for strife, young man," she said as she escorted him back to the kitchen.

"I don't mean to," said Eric.

Sister Christine did not respond. Eric noticed that she was carrying a stack of letters, very similar to the ones that were permanently parked on her desk.

"What do you have there?" asked Eric.

"Bills."

They reached the office and stopped.

"Bills for what?" asked Eric.

"Everything," said Sister Christine.

"What are you going to do with them?

An odd look came over Sister Christine's face.

"On you go to the kitchen," she said.

Catapult

The next morning, during breakfast Eric noticed something different. Santiago and Lucius did not arrive together. Instead Santiago sat with Arvin and Paul. Lucius was on his own. Eric smiled at him, but Lucius did not look happy. He once again motioned downwards but Lucius just shrugged. Eric felt bad for his friend.

When breakfast was over and the last of the bowls were washed, Mister Miller sat down on his wooden chair. He started reading his newspaper, but within moments he was asleep, snoring loudly. So loudly in fact that it sounded like someone was sawing logs with a chainsaw.

Eric watched him for a moment as the old cook's chest expanded and contracted with every booming breath. He realized that Mister Miller's predilection for daytime slumber revealed itself with some regularity, and he estimated that he would have an hour or more of freedom. He pushed the kitchen door ajar and looked directly down the hall. Sister Christine had closed the door to the office. Santa Inc. was calling.

Eric shot out of the air duct and landed on the bed. He had become quite accustomed to the process now. He shook himself down, stood up, and scanned the room for Huxley, but there was no sign of him.

"Professor?" Eric called.

Eric wandered around the laboratory. All was quiet. The prototype toys sat motionless on the shelves observing his every move. Eric stood over the drafting table where a partially drunk cup of tea and a saucer containing only crumbs had been left. He wandered over to the tools and took a good look at each one.

"Professor Huxley?" he called out again, a little louder this time.

Eric concluded that the old professor must be visiting with the elves again. Or maybe he had gone for more supplies? Maybe he was visiting with Santa? Maybe he was meeting with Wormwood Grubbs to work things out? Eric decided to make his way to the factory. After all, Huxley would likely need his help.

He walked over to the catapult and inspected it for a moment, trying to remember exactly what the professor had done to get the thing working. He cranked the wooden wheel around and slowly the harness descended from above. He inspected the console. Eric pulled the harness over himself and secured it into place with three clicks, just like he remembered. Easy. Next he looked at a conversion table, written out carefully in neat handwriting.

"Distance multiplied by weight" Eric read aloud.

Eric didn't know how much he weighed, and he wasn't sure how far he was trying to go. He punched some numbers into the ancient control module and hoped for the best. Nothing happened. He hit a few more buttons until high above him the cranks began to turn. By the time that Eric was done, the bungee cords were as tight as steel. That looks about right, Eric thought to himself. He double checked the calculations. The bungees creaked a little more. He sat back in the harness, took a deep breath, and pressed the release button.

The mechanism worked perfectly, and he was launched upwards so fast that he could hardly see. The acceleration wouldn't stop. Further and higher into the building he hurtled. He cranked his head around to see just how far he had travelled. One thing was sure, he was going a lot further than the elf level. Up and up he went. It was only then that Eric realized he must have pulled the bungee far too tight.

He covered his eyes, though that had no effect on slowing him down. The air rushed in through the tiny cracks between his fingers, whistling with glee. He opened them a little and realized that a new problem was rapidly approaching——the top of the shaft. He could just about make out a flat square of solid concrete in the black. He was traveling so fast toward it that he was sure he would crash. Maybe he would smash through it and be launched into space.

Eric recoiled against the inevitable impact as his face came within an inch of the ceiling. He was so close that he could smell the dry, cool concrete. Then suddenly he stopped, and for half of an instant, just like when he was with Huxley, he hung motionless in the air, completely unconstrained by gravity. He waited. He waited for a millisecond that felt like forever, hoping for that board to slide out and for him to drop softly onto it. But that didn't happen. Instead he began to fall, faster and faster, accelerating back toward the ground.

Now the endless abyss was below him, screaming ever closer as gravity dragged him uncontrollably toward earth. Now he could hear the creaking of the bungee cords tightening once more. He felt himself slowing down as the cords tightened and brought his fall to a momentary stop. Then he was on his way back upwards.

This continued for quite a long time. Up and down. Up and down. Each time the distance from the top and the bottom getting smaller, the rate of acceleration slightly less. Finally, the bungee, the harness, and Eric came to a complete stop leaving him dangling precariously somewhere in the middle of the shaft. Eric felt as though he had been put on the spin cycle in one of the giant drying machines. He took a breath and tried to regain his senses. For a few moments he let the harness hold him as he recovered, at which point he realized that he was stuck.

"Professor Huxley," he called.

But he knew that the professor was not likely to respond. He would have to navigate his own way out. There was an entry way to the side of him, but it was a good five feet away. He began to swing himself to and fro, slowly at first but gaining momentum as he forced his body back and forth.

Finally, he moved his body to a point where he could grab hold of a metal step that protruded from the side of the shaft. His hand latched onto it, and he pulled his body toward it with all his strength. He unbuckled the harness and pulled himself out of it. For a moment he hung over the shaft, unsecured. One wrong move and he would plummet hundreds of feet to the ground. With a burst of strength, he pulled himself onto the step, then managed to crawl into the doorway and to safety.

Once on firm ground, he stood up, gathered himself, and walked down an interior corridor. It was almost identical to the accountants' level. Eric walked up and down the corridor looking for a door that might give him access to the main floor, but he could not find one. He could not even find one of the peepholes that he and Huxley had peered out of. He wondered if there was no door. He walked back to the shaft and looked down.

"Professor Huxley," he called out again. "I'm up here."

His called bounced all the way down the shaft and then back toward him. No answer. Eric walked back down the corridor. He wondered if he would be stuck there forever. He pushed on every part of the wall as his search for an exit became more desperate. No luck. He was stuck.

He fell back against the wall, exhausted. But to his surprise, it was not a wall at all. He rolled out through a concealed entrance and onto the main floor of an office. The entrance closed behind him, disappearing instantly. Eric stood up and brushed himself off. He was standing in some kind of a waiting room.

There were people sitting on chairs. They wore suits and ties, just like him, and clung to manila folders with papers in them. They waited silently with anxious-looking faces. None of them noticed that Eric had somersaulted into the room in front of them. Eric sat down. He noticed that they all had nicely polished shoes, just like him.

"Are you an orphan, too?" Eric asked a man next to him.

All he got was a very odd expression in reply. A door opened and all the people in the room looked up. A woman appeared. She was also nicely dressed.

"Are you next?" she asked Eric.

"Yes," he replied without hesitation.

"Follow me."

Eric stepped forward. The woman held the door, allowing Eric to pass through, then closed it behind her. There was another room with a small round table and four chairs.

"Take a seat," she said.

The Interview

Eric was not sure why he was in the room with the round table and four chairs, but it all seemed to be quite interesting. He was also relieved that he was far away from the catapult shaft. Eric sat down.

"My name is Yolanda Fleming," she said.

"My name is Eric," said Eric.

"What's your last name?" she inquired.

"It's just Eric."

Yolanda looked up from her notes.

"Did you bring a copy of your resume?" she asked.

"What's a resume?" asked Eric.

"You don't have a resume?" she asked.

"I don't think so," said Eric. "What does it look like?"

Yolanda suspected that Eric was in the wrong place.

"Are you here for the Global Logistics Manager position?" she inquired.

"Sure," said Eric.

Yolanda looked Eric up and down. There was something not quite right about him, but she could not put her finger on it. After all, he did look like the other applicants with his shiny shoes, well pressed suit and tie. She decided to give him the benefit of the doubt with one last question.

"What do you know about Santa Incorporated?"

"Oh, I know a lot," said Eric confidently. "There's Santa, and Wormwood Grubbs," said Eric. "And the accountants. They want to make lots of money. They want to make things faster and cheaper. And there's shareholders. And elves. The elves work in the factory. They're not happy right now. They want to make toys the way they've always made them. But most of all they want a work-life balance. But the shareholders only care about the bottom line."

Yolanda looked surprised.

"Yes," she said. "I guess that's right. But what I really meant was, what do you know about this organization with reference to the job that you are applying for?"

Eric thought for a moment.

"I already have a job working in the kitchen with Mister Miller," said Eric.

Yolanda Fleming became more perplexed with every word that Eric spoke, but she took a deep breath, closed her eyes momentarily, and forced a smile back to her face.

"Today we are interviewing people for the position of Global Logistics Manager. This job requires you to have an intimate knowledge of cargo and freight processes. You will coordinate the distribution of toys all over the world."

Eric's face lit up.

"I know all about that," he said. "I brought elephants from the Ivory Coast of Africa to the New York Zoo."

Suddenly Yolanda felt as though she had made a breakthrough.

"That's good," she said.

"There was a great storm, and we nearly got eaten by a giant squid. Or maybe a kraken. But we made it. And the elephants were safe."

"Interesting," she said, jotting down notes. "Worked with high value cargo."

"I also worked on a tea plantation in Darjeeling, India," said Eric. "The tea gets shipped all over the world, you know. A lot of it goes to England."

"This is just the type of experience we are looking for. Please tell me more," said Yolanda, becoming more optimistic.

"I worked with a Chinese trader on the Yangtze River. We delivered all kinds of goods. That's how I got so good at math," said Eric.

"Math is very important for this job," said Yolanda.

"I'm so good at math that I got thrown out of math class," said Eric.

Yolanda laughed, although Eric didn't think it was funny. She was warming up to him.

"Have you ever seen a Yangtze River dolphin?" asked Eric.

"No," said Yolanda.

"They are very rare."

"This job could involve some travel," said Yolanda, changing the subject. "Will that fit into your lifestyle?"

"I've been almost everywhere already," said Eric. "Newfoundland. Australia. Brazil. Bangladesh. You name it."

Yolanda looked at her notes.

"Good at math. Experienced in high value cargo. Willingness to travel. You do look like you have all the skills that we are looking for. Do you have any questions for me?"

"There is one thing," said Eric. "Am I too young to have a job?"

Yolanda smiled and shook her head.

"Santa Incorporated is an equal opportunity employer," she said. "Age is not a factor for us."

"Alright then," shrugged Eric.

Yolanda looked at him.

"There's something about you that gives me a good feeling," she said. "I can't quite put my finger on it, but I'm prepared to make you an offer. How much money are you looking for?"

"I don't know," said Eric. "I hadn't thought of that."

"Very shrewd," said Yolanda. "Getting me to make the first offer. You're going to need that when you negotiate with our distributors."

Yolanda took out her pen and wrote a number on a piece of paper. She passed it over to Eric. His eyes nearly popped out of his head when he saw how big it was.

"Is that in your ballpark?" she asked.

Eric could not help but grin as he left the interview. He had gotten himself a job at Santa Inc. That was very exciting. He stepped back into the waiting room feeling very proud. As he crossed the floor, he noticed that something odd was happening. His legs were no longer propelling him forward. It was a strange feeling, as though he was floating on air, and for a moment he thought that it must be the excitement of the situation. He was walking on air. But then he looked up and realized that he was actually being hoisted into the ceiling through an open panel. It was Huxley. He had hooked Eric by his vest collar using an industrial sized fishing line to reel him in.

"Whatever are you doing?" he asked in a whispered panic.

"I got a job," said Eric proudly.

Huxley quickly replaced the panel, then marched Eric along the thin beam of the ceiling cavity, through a small doorway and back into the internal corridor where he had started.

"However did you get here?" Huxley demanded.

"I took the catapult. I was looking for you, except I don't think I got my calculations right."

Huxley thought for a moment.

"What is the job?" he asked.

"Global Logistics Manager," declared Eric proudly.

Work Day

On Eric's first day of work at Santa Inc., he was up early. He had given his shoes an extra polish and they were so shiny he could see his face in them. His shirt was a crisp white and the creases in his suit pants were as straight as a yardstick. When the morning routine in the kitchen was done, and as soon as Mister Miller had drifted off to sleep, he quickly made his way to the basement.

Huxley was pacing nervously when Eric arrived. He had been up all night worrying about the situation.

"This is not a good idea," he said, shaking his head.

"Why not?" asked Eric.

"Because too many things can go wrong."

"Professor Huxley, they need me," said Eric.

"What do you want to work in that awful office for anyway?"

Huxley was quite bothered, so much so that he found it impossible to stop moving.

"Just think of all the paper I can get," Eric said.

Huxley was not convinced.

"All of this is proving a considerable disruption to my work," he moaned.

"I have to go now," said Eric. "I don't want to be late on my first day."

"Let me escort you up there," said Huxley reluctantly. "I don't need anybody knowing how you came to be here."

"Professor," asked Eric, "I thought you worked here. So why don't you want anyone to know where you are?"

Huxley sighed. He had always felt the inevitability of this conversation, and now it had arrived.

"The truth is," he said, "I've been busy with my designs down here for so long that I'm not sure anybody up there remembers me. Only the elves. The company has changed so much. I don't even know where I fit in anymore."

"What about Santa?" asked Eric.

"The next time I see Santa will be when I present the prototype for the greatest toy the world has ever seen. Not before."

Eric thought that Huxley's position on the subject was quite odd, but he very much needed to get to work, so he did not press the matter further.

"Come on," said Huxley. "If you must go."

"I would rather not take the catapult," said Eric.

With a grumbling reticence, Huxley escorted Eric to the service elevator, which they took to an unused floor. They then crossed over to the main elevator bank. Soon its doors pinged open and Eric stepped inside. He pressed the button with the number twenty-seven on it.

"Good luck," said Huxley. "And please avoid saying anything about me."

The doors closed. When they opened again, Yolanda was waiting for him with a smile.

"Good morning, Eric."

"Good morning, Yolanda Fleming."

"Please follow me."

She held her ID card up to a scanner and the office door clicked open. They walked into an open area that was full of office cubes, square boxes each occupied by a single worker. Each was identical——a monitor, a phone, and a swiveling office chair. Some people had decorated their spaces with photos, a calendar, or a picture with a phrase that said something like *You don't have to be crazy to work here, but it helps.* Eric thought that was funny.

"How was your commute?" asked Yolanda.

"What's a commute?" asked Eric.

"You know, how did you find getting to the office?"

"Oh," said Eric. "It was fine. I only came from next door."

Yolanda gave Eric a surprised look.

"The first thing we need to do," she said, "is get you an ID card."

She ushered Eric into a small internal room where a man sat in front of a large computer screen.

"This is Shen," she said. "He does all of our IT. Shen, this is Eric. He needs an ID."

Yolanda guided Eric to a white wall.

"Stand there for a moment," she said.

Shen scooted over to a camera that was situated just in front of Eric.

"Smile," he said.

Eric smiled his biggest smile.

"A little less than that," said Shen.

"Santa Inc.," said Eric. "Where Christmas is our business."

The camera snapped a few times and Shen returned to his computer. Eric and Yolanda waited as he tapped at the keyboard.

"Here you go," he said eventually.

He handed Eric a little white card. On the front was the photograph of Eric with *Santa Inc.* printed above it.

"Wow," he exclaimed. "Is this for me?"

"That will get you in and out of the building," said Yolanda.

"This is fantastic," said Eric, clutching his newly prized possession.

"I know it's your first day," said Shen, "but there's no need to be that enthusiastic."

They left Shen and continued walking through the office. More and more people arrived, removing their overcoats, unpacking their things, placing their bags down and beginning their day of work. Finally, they reached a corner desk where Yolanda stopped.

"This is you," she said.

"Me?" asked Eric with surprise.

Yolanda nodded.

"Your computer is all set up. There's a stationary cupboard across the hall. I'll let you get situated, and I will check back with you later."

With that, she walked off. For a few moments, Eric stood at the desk. It was much nicer than those old wooden things at Our Lady of Mercy. He sat down on the seat. It was springy and comfortable. And it had wheels. He put his hands on the desk. Then he opened all of the drawers. They were empty except for a pad of sticky notes and a couple of pens. Eric spun the chair around a couple of times. When he did it a third time, a woman, who had just arrived, walked past him and gave him a very disapproving look. He stood up and surveyed the office. Despite being over half full, it was very quiet. No one was shouting. No one was pushing someone else out of their way. It was very calm.

Eric decided to draw on the pad of sticky notes. The first thing he drew was a Yangtze river dolphin. Then he sketched out a picture of a freighter carrying elephants to the New York Zoo. He soon found that one sticky note was not sufficient for this task and so he began to peel them off, sticking them together into a patchwork. It was so much fun that Eric barely noticed the time passing. Later in the morning, Yolanda returned to find an entire pad of sticky notes covering Eric's desk.

"How's it going?" she asked, rather shocked.

"Fantastic," said Eric enthusiastically.

"Are you getting through your dispatches? Hopefully it's all self-explanatory. We're very busy at this time of year, so it is very important for us to hit our daily targets."

Yolanda noticed that Eric's computer monitor was off.

"I've been trying to calculate just how big a giant squid could get."

Yolanda looked at Eric with a mixture of confusion and panic. She reached over and turned Eric's computer on.

"You need to start on your work," she said.

"Oh sure," said Eric. "But I do have to help Mister Miller out with lunch in about five minutes."

"Who's Mister Miller?" asked Yolanda.

"He's the cook."

Yolanda was even more perplexed.

"Do you have another job?" she asked.

"At Our Lady of Mercy," said Eric. "I work in the kitchen."

Yolanda had seen Our Lady of Mercy Orphanage many times on her way to work. She had looked at the decrepit building, with its rotten window frames and those hideous gargoyles perched on the roof. Sometimes she even observed the forlorn-looking boys staring out. She had two young children herself, and every time she saw those boys, a pain tugged in her heart a little.

"I see," she said. "You're a volunteer. Hence only coming from next door."

She could not in good conscience be annoyed with Eric for giving up his free time to help those poor young boys.

"Very well," she said. "I'll help you get started after lunch."

Kitchen Duties

Eric returned to the orphanage. He slowly opened the door of the basement out into the corridor. But as he pushed the door open wider, he nearly jumped with fright. Sister Prudence was standing only inches away with her back turned toward him. She was berating Terrence for his creases.

"You're one of the oldest boys here. You should know better. This is pathetic."

Terrence kept quiet and simply nodded in agreement. Eric pushed the door closed and stood very still for a moment, unsure of what to do.

"Go on, press those pants again and bring them back for inspection," she ordered.

Sister Prudence sensed something and turned, and that was the point where she nearly jumped out of her skin with fright. Sister Christine came running at the commotion.

"Sister Prudence, what is the matter?"

But Sister Prudence was fixed upon Eric with an icy glower.

"What do you think you are doing?" she demanded. "Why are you sneaking up behind me like some kind of creature?"

"I don't know," said Eric innocently.

"Out of my sight," ordered Sister Prudence, pointing to the kitchen.

The kitchen had a set of doors that opened directly on to the street, which on this occasion was open. A cold draft rattled in, along with a woman who pushed a cart loaded with boxes. Her work shirt displayed a tag that read *5 Boro Food Service*. The woman thrust two pieces of paper into Mister Miller's hand.

110

"Same as always," she said.

Eric noticed that the delivery lady had a name tag which read *Norma Jean* sewn onto her shirt. She left and then returned with a large box with *Rolled Oats* printed on the side.

Eric peered inside the other boxes. One contained large cans with *Meat* printed onto a white label. There were two boxes of canned carrots, two boxes of canned celery, and a large box that said, *Powdered Bouillon.*

"I'm not sure what y'all are cookin' up here, but I'm sure as heck glad that I'm not eatin' it," said Norma Jean.

Mister Miller signed the invoice and handed a copy back. Eric followed Norma Jean to the doors.

"Is this all you deliver?" he asked.

"If you can eat it, we can deliver it" she said. "That's our slogan."

Eric pulled the doors closed. The artic draft whistled through the cracks. He and Mister Miller dragged the boxes of rolled oats, meat, and vegetables to the pantry where they stacked them up onto the shelves.

"Why do we have to eat oatmeal and stew every day?" asked Eric.

"Ask Sister Prudence," replied Mister Miller.

Inside the pantry, Eric noticed that there were all types of jars filled with various powders and dried goods. They had interesting colors——hues of deep red, yellows, earthy browns.

"What are these?" he asked.

Mister Miller placed his hand on one of the jars containing a yellowish powder.

"Spices."

"What do they do?" asked Eric.

"They are used to flavor food."

He took the jar with the yellow-brownish powder in it and unscrewed the top. Then he offered it up to Eric's nose.

Immediately Eric got a sense of the full aroma that was contained inside. It was like nothing that he had ever smelled before. It was overwhelming and deliciously pungent.

"Cumin," said Mister Miller with a smile. "From Chandni Chowk in Old Delhi."

He returned the jar and pulled another one down. It was a deep red color. Once more he unscrewed the top and presented it to Eric. The smell was quite different, fiery and sweet.

"Smoked Paprika," said Mister Miller. "Made from dried red peppers. I bought this from an old man who cooks Paella on the beach in Nerja."

"The Southern-most tip of Spain," Eric noted.

Mister Miller was impressed.

"You know your geography," he said.

"I've been around," said Eric.

Finally, he took one more jar down. It contained a dark brown course powder.

"Now this one," he said, "I picked up in Singapore."

Eric inhaled deeply, expecting another delicious aroma, but instead the smell immediately turned his stomach.

"Dried fish," said Mister Miller, bursting into laughter.

Eric rubbed his nose and backed away from the foul stench that wafted out of the jar.

"Close it up," he called out.

Mister Miller was highly amused by Eric's stomach-turning reaction and spent a good amount of time guffawing and waving the jar about before sealing it up.

"Do you ever use them?" Eric asked as his eyes wandered over the others.

"In this place?" said Mister Miller with a sour chuckle. "It would be a terrible waste. No, these are no more than bottles of memories now. Reminders of a life once lived."

He took a long look at the dried fish. It conjured in him some lost memory of an exotic expedition. He smiled a little and shook his head, remembering a particularly wild night of carousing at the Port of Singapore. Then he placed it back onto the shelf.

"So why can't you just make Spaghetti Bolognese?" asked Eric.

Mister Miller ignored the question and instead busied himself with placing the rest of the boxes onto the shelves. Eric helped.

After lunch, it was straight back to the office. Thankfully Mister Miller's nap proved to have all the regularity of the large old clock in the canteen, and Eric calculated that he could predict almost to the minute when he would shut his eyes. Eric stepped back into the office as the minute hand ticked over to one o'clock, just as Yolanda was approaching purposefully.

"Let me show you how it all works," she said, directing his attention toward the computer monitor.

"Santa Inc. sends packages all over the world. Mostly by container. Once they leave the factory, they go by truck, rail, air, and sea to every single country. It's very important that the right container goes to the right place and gets there at the right time."

Eric nodded in agreement.

"That's your job."

"It is?" said Eric with some surprise.

Yolanda took a deep breath.

"You will call our cargo distributors and schedule the container pickup. Then you will track it all the way to its final destination. You log it all in the system."

Yolanda pointed to the screen.

"This one is going to Nairobi. This one is going to Edinburgh. This one to Ulan Bator."

"Wow," said Eric. "This stuff is going all over the world? From right here."

Yolanda nodded.

"Does this make sense?" she asked very clearly.

"Oh yes," said Eric. "I get it now."

Global Logistics Manager

Once Yolanda had explained the job, Eric immediately set about working as hard and as fast as he could at it. First, he sat in front of his computer for about an hour, tapping the keys and seeing how the mouse moved the curser. Eric had never used a computer before, let alone used one to facilitate the transportation of cargo around the globe, but he found it to be quite straight forward once he had mastered the controls.

When Eric's phone rang for the first time, he stared at it. He had never spoken on a phone before. Nobody had a reason to call him.

BRIIING! BRIIING!

Finally, he picked it up.

"Hello?" he said tentatively.

"Hello," came a voice on the other end. "This is Francisco from Peru."

"Oh. Hi," replied Eric.

"Where is my order?" asked Francisco.

"What order?" asked Eric.

"I made an order three months ago, and it has still not arrived."

Eric searched his computer, but the truth was he had no idea what he was looking for. Then a call came in on another line.

"This is Barry from Alice Springs. I'm expecting a delivery but it's not here."

Then another call came in.

"This is Mayumi from Tokyo."

At that point Eric became completely overwhelmed. The man in the next cube appeared above the partition. For a moment he watched Eric zig-zagging his cursor across the screen and making very little progress. Eric's phone was flashing.

"You need the container number," he said.

Eric looked up at him.

"Ask for it and enter it into that box," the man continued pointing at the screen.

"What's your container number?" Eric asked.

Francisco gave him a long number.

"Sorry," said Eric. "It's my first day."

Once Eric had the number, he tapped it into the computer.

"Hit *ENTER*," said the man over the partition.

Eric followed the instruction and sure enough the information popped up on the screen.

"There," said Eric, "the container has been unloaded at the port of Lima."

"Excellent," said Francisco.

Eric repeated the process with Barry and then Mayumi. Once he hung the phone up, having successfully provided both of them with the right information, he breathed a sigh of relief. He felt very good that he had managed to figure it out. Eric turned to thank the man in the neighboring cube, but he had already disappeared from view.

Eric finally began to understand how the system worked, and when a customer would call him, he could give them all the information about their delivery. From his computer, Eric could track the products moving through the factory, see when they were transported to the warehouse, and when the container was filled. When the container was full of toys, it was marked as complete and sealed. Finally, it was assigned a very long number so that it could not be mixed up with any other container. At that point, it was ready to be shipped on to its destination.

After a few days, Eric found himself a routine that started in the kitchen of Our Lady of Mercy for breakfast, then got him to Santa Inc. by eight o'clock to begin his working day, back to orphanage for lunch and cleanup, then back to the office for the afternoon, then finally returning home for dinner.

Each night as Eric climbed into bed, his eyes were shut before his head even touched the pillow. Lucius desperately wanted to talk with him, to ask him how life was in the kitchen and what he was doing, but they barely had the opportunity. He was lonely without his friend, which was made even worse because Santiago had left him too for a new set of friends. To all the other boys, it appeared as though Sister Prudence was working Eric to the bone. When the morning came, he was gone again, up before the rest of the boys had so much as stirred.

But Eric loved the idea that the containers being loaded in the factory that he was working in would soon find their way to the most far flung and exotic places. He got to know the people in those places——Mayumi was learning origami, Barry liked to practice meditation, and Francisco was expecting his first daughter. They all liked Eric a lot because he would not stop until he had solved their problems. When it came to negotiating with them, Eric found it easy to strike a deal.

The truth was that Eric didn't really feel like he was working at all, he enjoyed every moment so much that it felt like fun all day long. He had a window out into the big wide world.

During that time something quite curious occurred. As Eric became more familiar with his job, it took him less and less time to complete his duties. What first required an hour, took him a half hour, and then just ten minutes. Eric got so good at what he was doing that eventually he was able to complete his tasks for the day in less than one hour. It was at this point that he started to take more notice of the other people in the office.

One afternoon, when he had completed all of his own tasks in record time, he decided to take a walk around the place. He found his colleagues at their desks all working quietly or talking on the phone. When he saw the man who had helped him on his first day filling a large bottle at the water cooler, Eric decided that he would introduce himself. He walked over to the cooler, found a mug on a nearby shelf that said *Santa Inc.* on the side.

"Hello," said Eric.

"Hi," said the man in a somewhat serious tone.

"I'm new here,"

The man nodded.

"What do you do?" asked Eric.

"Processing," he said as the container reached half full.

"Processing what?" asked Eric.

"Invoices," said the man.

"What are invoices?" asked Eric.

The man looked a little surprised.

"Invoices, like bills for payment. You know, invoices."

"Like the Gas Company bill?" asked Eric.

"Kind of," said the man. "When the invoices come in from our suppliers, I check that they are correct, then I schedule them for payment."

"I see," said Eric. "I think that's what Sister Christine has to do. Can you show me how it works?"

"I guess so," said the man.

"My name is Eric," said Eric.

"I'm Gopal," said the man.

They walked back to Gopal's desk. There were lots and lots of books stacked up on his desk.

"What are all of these books for?" asked Eric.

"I'm studying for my Master's in Business Administration."

"What's that?"

"I'm learning how to run a business."

Then Gopal explained how the invoices were received, matched to orders, verified, and then sent for payment. He pointed to a lady across the room.

"She's the one that cuts the checks."

Then Gopal pointed to another lady.

"She's the one that records all entries in the system. She's the bookkeeper."

Eric was surprised that Gopal was not just familiar with his own job but everyone else's too.

"Wow," said Eric. "You must love working here."

Over the course of that afternoon, Eric came to realize that all the people who worked on his floor, including him, were interconnected. Every person had a different job, but they all somehow depended on each other to do it successfully. Eric was intrigued and spent a good amount of time introducing himself to each person in turn, going cube to cube.

At first, he was greeted with some suspicion, especially when he started asking questions about what people did and how they did it, but when they realized that he possessed a genuine interest, they opened up and told him everything that they knew. He felt like he had learned more in a few hours than an entire year spent in the classrooms of Our Lady of Mercy. He could not believe that it was not just the people that worked on his floor who were connected but every floor in the whole building and in the entire company that was spread across the world.

"This is amazing," he told a lady called Linda.

She gave him the same look that Yolanda, Gopal, and many others had given him. Eric wondered how they all came to possess it. He called it the *Santa Inc. Look*.

Undeterred, he followed the trail of connections up and down the floors, talking to each person in turn, and introducing himself. There were a lot of people, and he tried his best to remember all of their names. Linda was particularly memorable. She was in charge of a department called *Document Control*. That sounded like a very important place to Eric, and Linda agreed.

"This company produces hundreds of documents a day. Without filing them in the right place, we would tie ourselves up in knots," she said. "I make sure that everything is filed correctly."

Linda showed Eric how she organized the documents alphabetically, in rows and rows of filing cabinets that could be moved up and down in a large storage room.

"Have you ever seen Santa?" asked Eric casually.

"Once or twice" said Linda. "He's up on seventy-seven. He doesn't come down here."

The people of Santa Inc. were very different to the people at Our Lady of Mercy. They listened to each other when they spoke. They talked to each other with polite words, and the smaller ones didn't get punched if they did something the big ones didn't like. One of Eric's favorite places was the staff canteen. There was an almost unending stream of people to talk to who all provided Eric with new and interesting information.

The canteen was quite different from that of Our Lady of Mercy too. It was bright and clean with plastic chairs, a machine that dispensed free coffee, and a snack vending machine. Eric made a point to introduce himself to every person who arrived.

"My name is Eric. What do you do?"

He found that people were usually very willing to tell him all about themselves and what they did, and they were always surprised by how genuinely interested he was in their jobs. Eric soaked up the information like a sponge. His co-workers delighted in his stories of the Ivory Coast of Africa, the Yangtze River, and his time picking tea in Darjeeling.

Once Eric figured out that he could get all of his work done in the morning, he would use the afternoon to wander the offices, continuing his conversations with as many people as possible. He chatted with the accountants about Generally Accepted Accounting Principles. He listened to the designers as they debated materials and the compromises needed for production. He sat with the warehouse workers as they took a coffee break from loading the containers with pallets of toys.

After not so much time at all, Eric came to know very well how Santa Incorporated worked. It was as though he could see the entire organization in his mind. To him, the way that the company worked was almost as magical as the elves that were in the factory below them making the toys. He understood how each person fit into the process of building a toy. Figuring this out was like a game, and Eric began to spend whole days thinking about it.

During this time, one thing struck Eric as odd. It didn't matter which department the people worked in, it didn't matter whether they were working at a desk, heaving boxes, or cleaning the floors, once Eric got to know them, he discovered that they all had a lot of ideas about how the company could be better.

"If I was the boss of this place, I would do it all differently," said Linda one afternoon over a cup of coffee. "For a start, I would change this awful brew."

"I wish that they would give us a little bit of time off to study," said Gopal. "That would be very nice."

"The computers that they use here are super old," said Shen. "They need to change them, but the management doesn't listen to us. Plus, the coffee is bogus. It pretty much sums up what the suits on the seventy-seventh floor think about us."

Every employee that Eric chatted with had the capacity to go on for hours about how there was too much to do and not enough time to do it.

"If I was the boss..." was a regular theme.

One of the most common topics was the coffee. Nobody liked the coffee. It was bitter and had a bad aftertaste. When people drank it, they thought bad things about Santa Inc.

"It's the cheapest coffee around."

"It tastes like tar."

That didn't stop them from drinking it. Though some people went all the way out of the building, down the street, and to a coffee shop on the corner to buy a cup, a process that often took more than twenty minutes. This process fascinated Eric even though he had never tasted coffee in his life.

Yolanda found Eric at his desk one Friday afternoon.

"I had my doubts about you at the start," she said. "But I wanted to let you know that I've been very impressed with your work."

Eric felt so proud in that moment that he thought he might burst. He puffed his chest out and spun around on his chair a couple of times in sheer delight. Yolanda gave him the *Santa Inc. Look.*

Administration

Huxley was waiting for Eric when he returned from the office.

"What exactly is going on up there?" he asked inquisitively.

"It's such a fantastic place to work," said Eric. "Everyone is so nice. Especially the accountants. I think you have it wrong about them."

"The accountants?" replied Huxley looking perplexed.

"They all drink coffee and do their jobs, and some of them have started talking to me."

"I hope you have not mentioned this place," said Huxley.

"No. I didn't," said Eric. "But..."

"But what?" said Huxley.

"But you might like them," said Eric. "Maybe I could introduce you?"

"Never," said Huxley.

Eric could see that the old professor was still laboring over a blank sheet of paper that had not changed since the morning. He simply shrugged and climbed the ladder back to the orphanage.

Later that day, when the lunch service was done and the boys had returned to their classes, Eric pushed the swinging door of the kitchen open and walked quietly down the corridor toward the basement. But as he got closer, he realized that he was about to find himself with an unexpected problem. The door of the office was wide open.

He moved forward slowly and found Sister Christine at her desk. She held her head in her hands and was staring very intently at something. There was no way that he could open the door to the basement without being seen. He stood perfectly still as he contemplated his options. Maybe she too was sneaking a quick after-lunch nap? Maybe he could furtively open the door? But it was not to be. Sister Christine suddenly looked up, her face flushed red. Eric assumed that she was angry about something.

"What are you doing?" she asked.

"I just finished with the washing up," said Eric innocently.

He walked forward tentatively and saw that her desk was full of papers, stacked high on both sides. One in particular, which was full of red markings, was the focus of her attention.

"Sister Christine?"

"What?" she answered curtly.

"Do you need some help?" Eric asked with a nod toward the stack.

"There's nothing that you can help me with," she said.

"There might be."

"Go back to the kitchen," she ordered.

But Eric would not give up. Even though he knew that it could very well get him into more trouble, he was certain that he could apply some of his newly acquired knowledge to Sister Christine's task.

"I can see that you have a lot of papers on your desk," he said. "I can help you to file them if you like."

Sister Christine was suspicious. She wondered why he would offer his help, but at the same time she was also in a predicament of her own. She had been given the role of Orphanage Administrator some time ago by Sister Prudence. Her duties included paying the bills, monitoring the bank account, organizing the files, and generally making sure that all of the tasks necessary to keep the orphanage running were taken care of.

It was a job that she neither wanted nor had any aptitude for, and as a consequence, many of these tasks had not been attended to for a good amount of time. The late bills were piling up. There were important letters strewn about the office in no particular order, and nobody had checked how much money was in the bank account for months. Now Our Lady of Mercy was being threatened with the complete cutoff of water, electricity, and sanitation.

Eric had just happened to walk in on Sister Christine when she had come to the realization that she would need to make Sister Prudence aware of this unfortunate situation. Her red face was not anger but panic. And as Eric appeared at the door, she was not working but instead saying a prayer to the good Lord to send her help in whatever form it might take. She did not expect that help to come in the form of Eric. But Eric was what she had received, and being quite aware that the divine often works in mysterious ways, she decided to accept.

"Alright," she said. "Show me."

Eric sorted through the bills on Sister Christine's desk. They were very much like the invoices that Gopal worked with every day. They reviewed each invoice in turn and wrote a check out for each one. Then Eric wrote *Paid* on each one with the day's date.

Eric spotted a bookkeeper's logbook behind some other old files. He pulled it out and looked at it. It looked like it had not been used for a long time, but he opened it on a fresh page and wrote the date, then together they recorded each bill that had been paid, what it was for, and how much it was. Eric had learned this from Ngolo in Accounts. Finally, Eric opened up the large black filing cabinet that was behind Sister Christine. He peered inside and pulled out some of the papers.

"These are very old," he noted, looking them over. "I don't think we need them anymore."

Eric remembered Linda from document control. She had some wise advice about old files:

"If it's more than three years old, get rid of it."

They removed all of the old files and replaced them with the new ones. Eric found a special place for the bookkeeper's logbook. The whole process took no more than an hour. When they finished, Sister Christine knew exactly how much money she had at the start of the month and how much money she had at the end, after paying all of the bills.

"All done," said Eric.

There was a visible expression of relief on Sister Christine's face. For the first time in a long time, her desk was clean and tidy.

"Back to the kitchen," she ordered.

Eric left the office and shut the door. As it clicked closed, he caught sight of Lucius. He was in the Rec sitting on the beanbag with a copy of National Geographic. Lucius felt more alone than at any other time during his life. He felt abandoned. Lucius looked up with a sad expression. As if life could not become any harder, his two friends had been taken away from him. Eric could see Lucius wanted him to go and sit with him, but he was already late. He waved and smiled. It felt like they were so far apart from each other, like a great chasm had opened up that prevented them from seeing each other. At least that's how Lucius felt. Eric resolved to talk to his friend as soon as possible.

Corporate

When Eric finally returned to his desk, it did not take him long to complete his tasks for the afternoon. He sat at his desk thinking about Lucius and how sad and lonely he looked. After some time, he decided to take a walk. He wandered around his floor for a while, but everybody else was hard at work. He went to Gopal's desk.

"Can I borrow one of your books?" Eric asked.

Gopal pulled out a book from his collection called *An Introduction to Business Administration* and handed it to him but couldn't talk because he was busy. Eric went to the canteen, but for some reason it was empty, so he decided to explore the other floors of Santa Inc. He concluded that he should at least try to find Santa, just to have a look at him.

He summoned the elevator and waited. When the doors opened, he stepped inside, ran his fingers down the long bank of numbers, and pressed number 77. The elevator doors closed, and it began to ascend. When the doors opened, Eric stepped out onto a floor that was quite different to any other. There was a plushness to it, the carpets felt a little thicker under his feet, there was a pleasant smell of jasmine, and all of the furnishings carried an air of luxury.

A lady sat behind a desk with a high ledge in front of it. Eric stood on his tip toes and peered over the top so that only his eyes and the top of his head could be seen from the other side.

"Hello," he said in his usual friendly way.

"Hello," said the woman in a voice that indicated that she did not particularly want to talk to him.

"My name is Eric. I'm the Global Logistics Manager. I work on the twenty-seventh floor."

"Uh huh," said the woman.

"Do you know Gopal and Linda?" asked Eric.

"No," said the woman.

"Have you been to the twenty-seventh floor?"

"Is there something I can do for you?" asked the woman in a tone that implied that she was unwilling to do anything.

"You should go one time," said Eric. "Everyone is so nice down there."

"Uh huh," the woman repeated.

Her eyes returned to her computer screen. The entire conversation was conducted with both parties unable to see each other. Eric thought it best to walk around to the side of the desk where he could see the woman better.

"What happens on this floor?" he asked.

She appeared a little shocked that he was suddenly standing next to her.

"This is corporate," she said dismissively.

"Does Santa work here?" asked Eric.

"Who are you?" the woman asked.

"Could I take a look around?"

"Do you have an appointment to meet with someone?"

"No," said Eric.

"Then I suggest that you return to the twenty-seventh floor."

The woman focused on her computer as though trying to pretend that Eric was no longer there. Eric peered behind her down a long, wide corridor that had paintings hanging on each side and big wooden doors that gave the place a look of impenetrability.

As Eric stood there taking in the new surroundings and the pleasant floral bouquet, the doors to the elevator pinged open and the sound of raised voices filled the space. A huddle of individuals in dark suits stepped out, busily talking at one another. Eric watched as each person jockeyed to insert their opinion into the conversation with little interest in what the others had to say.

"The bottom line is that we are not going to hit our revenue targets," said one man. "That's all that matters."

"That's the symptom, not the cause," said a woman.

"We've been off plan for too long," said another.

"Staff productivity is too low," another chimed in.

Eric saw Wormwood Grubbs in the thick of the group. He was wearing his black pinstriped suit and his hair was combed back against his head. He too was trying desperately to get a word in.

"We have to drive down costs," he said. "We're carrying too much overhead."

Eric observed that the cluster of people were quite worked up. So much so that they seemed unable to move more than a few feet from the elevator. It was not until one particular man, who was right in the middle of the group, started to talk that everyone else hushed down to listen.

"Wormwood is right. We have to make cuts and improve efficiency," he said. "And we need to do it fast. It's time to take action. That's the only way we'll fend this off."

Eric looked at the man. He had short white hair, and a neatly trimmed white beard. There was a healthy glow to his old face. He wore a dark blue suit and a crisp white shirt with a blue tie, not unlike Eric. There was something undeniably familiar about him.

"So where do we start?" he added.

The crowd pondered the question for a moment and then began barking loudly in unison.

"Creditor Days."

"Labor."

"Materials."

"R and D."

"Shipping."

"Enough!" shouted the grey-haired man. "What's the plan?"

"We'll form a steering committee," said one man.

"Hire consultants."

"And write a report," said another.

"I don't want a committee, consultants, or a report," said the man with grey hair. "We haven't got time for that. This company is under attack! A takeover is in our midst. We need action. Now!"

For once the group was silent. They were all thinking very hard, but Eric could tell from their faces that none of them had a satisfactory answer. The man with the white beard grew impatient.

"Come on," he called. "Give me ideas?"

"What about the coffee?" said Eric.

Everybody turned in unison to face him. They looked him up and down and soon figured that he was just a boy in a suit with a tie and very shiny shoes. They turned back to the man with the white beard.

"We'll come back to you with a plan tomorrow morning," said one man with a bald head, ignoring Eric's comment completely.

The group nodded together.

"Explain," said the man with the white beard.

"We'll assemble our thoughts and——"

"Not you. Him." The man with the white beard pointed at Eric.

"If you're looking for ideas to make your company better," said Eric, "why not start with the coffee? People don't like that coffee. They say it tastes bitter. Some of them even go all the way down the street to get their coffee. That takes a lot of time. The coffee makes people feel bad about being at work."

There was a mumbling among the group.

"I don't know who this person is," said a woman in a grey suit. "But we will..."

"Now just wait a minute," the man with the grey beard cut in. "What exactly do you mean?"

"If you gave them better coffee, maybe the people that work here would feel better and spend more of their time working."

"See!" said the man with the grey beard. "This is action."

He stepped forward toward Eric.

"What's your name?"

"Eric."

"I'm Santa," said the man, extending his hand.

He had a firm grip and looked Eric directly in the eye.

"Santa?" said Eric.

Eric was suddenly quite speechless. The man was very different to the person in his imagination. There was no red suit, no protruding belly, no joviality.

"Come to my office and we'll talk about this some more," he said.

Santa strode ahead and Eric jogged to keep up. The receptionist watched in disbelief as the gaggle of suits followed. Santa pushed open the double doors to his office and walked in.

"Why don't you leave me and Eric to discuss this?" he suggested to the others. Although by the tone of his voice, it was clearly meant as an order. The gaggle backed out and Santa closed the door, leaving them on the outside.

"All I get from them is a bunch of business school mumbo-jumbo," Santa moaned.

Eric immediately ran to the window. In front of him was a panoramic view of the entire city of New York. The Empire State

Building, the Statue of Liberty across the river, and in front of them a great forest of skyscrapers. Eric's eyes feasted upon the sight. He had always dreamed of this view and now it was right in front of him, and even more magnificent than he could have ever imagined.

"You want to know what got this view?" asked Santa.

"What?" asked Eric.

"Hard work."

Santa stood for a moment and observed Eric.

"Now come on," he continued. "There's no time to stare into space. We just got word that we're in the sights of a hostile take-over. A corporate raider!"

"Like a pirate?" asked Eric.

"Exactly," said Santa.

"Can you get onto the roof of this building?" asked Eric.

"I have no idea" said Santa.

"Have you ever flown a paper plane off it?"

"No."

"But it would fly for miles from up here."

"I'm trying to defend my company from attack!"

"If I help you, will you fly paper airplanes off the roof with me?"

Santa sat down behind a large solid oak desk. He was not used to being presented with ultimatums from his staff.

"Tell me more about this coffee idea," he said.

Eric took a seat.

"I don't know a lot about coffee" he said. "But I do know that everybody else likes it a lot, and they get really annoyed when it's no good. They say the company doesn't appreciate them. They spend a lot of their day talking about the coffee or getting coffee. If we give them coffee they like, they will spend more time working and feel better about it."

"I like that," said Santa.

Santa sat for a moment and thought about what Eric had said.

"This is my problem," said Santa. "Another company has been busily buying up our stock."

"Stock is like a part of your company, right?"

"That's right," said Santa. "They're trying to take us over. But we're going to put up one heck of a fight. We're going to drive up our stock price so they can't do it. There's only one way to do that."

"Increase the bottom line?" guessed Eric, remembering his conversation with Huxley.

"Precisely," said Santa. "Maybe this crazy coffee idea will work. Staff morale has been low lately. I'm putting you in charge of it. Can you handle it?"

"Sure," said Eric.

"Good, I want you to drop everything and do that."

"Could we fly those paper planes now?" asked Eric.

Santa's phone rang. He pressed the button and the voice of the receptionist outside came through.

"Santa, your three o'clock is here."

"Thank you, Martha," said Santa.

He clicked the button off and returned his attention back to Eric.

"Not today, kid. Go order the coffee."

Hard Knock Life

The decrepit halls of Our Lady of Mercy were a far cry from the plush interiors of Santa Inc. This became ever more obvious to Eric each time he returned. The carpets were threadbare, and the wooden floorboards had been worn down so that the nails that had been used to affix them so long ago now protruded upwards, ready to ensnare an unlucky foot. The paint was peeling off the walls and there was a damp and musty scent about the place. And of course, neither the heating, nor the electricity, nor the water worked very well at all.

It was a glum sight, a laboriously dull place to return to after the excitement of the building next door. Eric stood in the main hallway holding Gopal's book and observed the decay. He wished that he could make this tired, old orphanage better. Not just a little better, but immeasurably better. For his friends, for the other boys, for every single person who dwelled beneath its leaky roof. Then an idea came to him from out of nowhere like a little whisper in his ear. Probably the best idea that he had ever had. A quite marvelous conception, even by his standards.

He ran down the hallway to the kitchen and pushed the doors open. As usual, the pot was bubbling for dinner. Grayish-brown pieces of meat surfaced every once in a while before returning to the murky depths. Mister Miller sat at the table reading the newspaper. Eric peered into the stew. It was very similar to the orphanage itself——routine, lacking in excitement, and as gloomy as the cloudy December skies above. Eric's marvelous idea continued to fully reveal itself in his mind as he busied himself in the kitchen, glancing over at Mister Miller every so often, waiting for the right moment. Eventually, the old cook stood up, folded his paper, and stretched.

"Hitting the head," he said.

Eric watched as he hobbled out of the kitchen and the doors swung shut. Immediately, he ran into the food store and located the jars of spices. He ran his finger over each one——turmeric, ginger, garlic powder, oregano, five spice, paprika. He grabbed the paprika and the garlic powder and returned to the bubbling pot. Quickly he unscrewed the containers. Immediately, the scents intertwined and travelled deep into his senses.

He remembered reading about an old man on the beach in Southern Spain and how he had a giant shallow pot called a *paella* dish that would sit on a roaring fire made of logs. The man would throw rice, chicken, and fresh fish that the local fisherman had landed that morning into it, and the ingredients would spit and crackle as they cooked in the deep green olive oil. Then he would throw in cloves of garlic, paprika, and other spices. Finally, he would add the stock, a brown watery mixture in which the rice would cook.

Eric added each spice in turn to the stew. It bubbled for a moment as the liquid gradually enveloped it. Eric swiftly returned the spices to the pantry, being careful to make sure that they were replaced the same way as they were found. Shortly after that, the doors to the kitchen opened and Mister Miller walked back in.

"That's better," he declared with a satisfied grin. "Couple o' pounds lighter now."

He threw his paper in the garbage.

"Come on," he said. "Let's get ready of dinner."

Eric worked extra quickly to prepare the kitchen for dinner. He laid out the spoons, the bowls, and the water cups. When he was done, there was time to spare. He left the kitchen and walked back down the hallway to the office. He slowed as he approached, being careful to determine exactly who was inside before he got too close. He found that Sister Christine was at her desk in deep concentration. He stepped forward and knocked on the door quietly.

"Sister Christine, did the filing work?" he asked.

"Yes," said Sister Christine.

Eric nodded with a smile. He turned to leave, but Sister Christine added, "Now I have a new problem."

"What's that?" asked Eric, stopping himself.

"Now that Sister Prudence actually knows how little we have, she has told me the we have to save more money."

Sister Christine looked down at the bookkeeper's log in front of her and shook her head.

"I just can't see how we can spend any less. We can't turn the lights off. We can't turn the heating off. We can't stop buying food."

Eric thought for a moment. Her problem was not too different from Santa Inc., and as Eric had come to know, there was always a solution. It was just a matter of figuring it out.

"Maybe I can help you," he offered.

They looked at each bill that had to be paid every month—water, electricity, gas, sanitation. Each was quite expensive. Eric stared at the numbers and tried to think how they could be reduced.

"I have an idea" he said. "We will get every boy to use ten percent less of everything. We will turn lights off when we leave the room. We will shorten our showers. When we do our laundry, we'll make sure the washers and dryers are always full. We'll see if that can save some money."

Sister Christine looked encouraged. She smiled at Eric which was quite a surprise to him.

"That's a good idea."

"The difficulty will be getting the boys to do it," said Eric. "But I think I have a plan for that too."

"How do you know these things?" asked the Sister, quite bemused by Eric.

Eric shrugged. Then he handed Gopal's book, *An Introduction to Business Administration* to Sister Christine.

"I thought you might like to read this," he said.

Sister Christine looked at the book, front and back.

"Where did you get this?"

"In the basement."

Eric left Sister Christine. There was someone else that he needed to speak with before the dinner bell rang. He looked up at the clock in the main hallway. It was close to five. The afternoon of chores was drawing to a close and there was a ten-minute break before dinner time when the boys put their cleaning supplies away, washed their hands, and made their way to the canteen. Eric made his way to the older boys' dorm room on the fourth floor, a perilous act in itself. He stood in the empty room and waited.

He walked over to the window and inspected the frame. The wood was rotten. He easily pulled away a large splinter as a draft of icy air whistled through it. He wondered if there was a way to fix it. Then he heard the inevitable drumming of feet as the boys charged upstairs. The older boys began flooding into the dorm. Terrence and Ping came first. They saw Eric and immediately charged for him as though he were an enemy soldier caught in the heart of their camp.

"What you doin'?" they demanded with raised voices.

"Waiting for Kevin O'Malley," said Eric.

"What do you want with him?"

Other boys gathered round aghast at Eric's guile.

"He needs a punishment," said one.

"For the oatmeal," added another.

Ryan sidled up casually and tried to stomp on Eric's foot, but Eric saw it coming and moved out of the way at the last minute.

"You need teaching," grumbled Ryan.

"What are you doing up here?" a deep voice boomed across the room.

Kevin O'Malley marched forward.

"I came to talk with you," Eric replied.

"Talk to my fist," answered Kevin.

There was no way, in the middle of his peers, that the Head Boy would show any weakness.

"It's about food. Better food."

Kevin O'Malley paused, his hand raised above his head, and wondered whether to bring it smashing down on Eric without another word spoken. But the word *food* had made him think twice. When he was a young boy, he knew very well the delights of a good meal. His mother, who was Sicilian-Irish, often cooked him all manner of delicious pastas. At the weekends they would go out for cannoli. His stomach still yearned for those things, he could almost recall their flavors in his mouth, and yet he was always left wanting more. Kevin O'Malley knew better than most just what they were missing.

"I've been working in the kitchen with Mister Miller. You've seen me, right?"

"You're punished," stated Kevin O'Malley.

"I was punished," said Eric. "But I did such a good job that they asked me to stay. Now I am working on something else. I need to speak with you about it because you are Head Boy."

"Out with it then."

"Only you. It's top secret."

Kevin O'Malley looked around at the gathered faces, all eagerly awaiting the excitement of a good punishment. But something in Eric's words or maybe the rekindled memory of his mother made Kevin opt for a different course of action.

"Everybody out," he ordered.

"What about the punishment," they grumbled.

Reluctantly the other boys dispersed and made their way downstairs.

"Come on then," said Kevin O'Malley. "Out with it."

"We want to make the food better. Delicious food like Spaghetti Bolognese. Food that everybody wants to eat. But we don't have any money to do it. So we came up with a plan. If we spend less on water, electricity, and gas, we'll have more money to buy better food."

"Who's we?" asked Kevin.

"Me and Sister Christine."

"Liar!"

"I can prove it," said Eric.

He moved in closer as if to disclose some highly confidential information.

"Tonight is our first experiment. Nobody knows about it. We made the food just a little better, just to give everyone a small taste of how it could be."

Kevin O'Malley was not fully convinced, but he hated the food as much as anyone in that place. If there was an opportunity for it to be just a little better, then he would take it.

"What do you need me for?" asked Kevin.

"You're the only one that can make the boys change," said Eric. "You're the top dog. The head honcho. The big cheese."

"That's right," said Kevin, puffing his chest out a little.

Kevin O'Malley stared hard at Eric with his meanest grimace.

"I'll need you to make sure the other boys stop taking long showers and turn the lights off and do all the things that can save us money."

"Alright," he said. "But if yer makin' a fool of me, I'll bust yer head open."

Eric ran all the way down the flights of steps.

"Eric!"

The voice stopped him. It was Lucius. His friend ran toward him.

"Where have you been? I have hardly seen you. Are you alright?"

Lucius had that worried look on his face.

"I have to go," said Eric. "Let's meet tonight. After everyone goes to bed. Tell Santiago."

"Santiago has got new friends now," said Lucius.

"Just us then," said Eric.

Lucius watched as Eric ran down the rest of the stairs and back to the kitchen.

"Where've you been?" asked Mister Miller.

"Had to hit the head," said Eric.

The old cook smiled. Soon after, the sound of trampling feet began to swell, and the room was again filled with hungry young men. Mister Miller stood in front of the pot, ready with his ladle, and Eric stood next to him, so that he could pass the bowls. The older boys swarmed to the front of the line as the younger ones held back.

Sister Prudence stood sentry while Sister Christine paraded up and down. Mister Miller began to ladle the stew into the bowls. Kevin O'Malley appeared, making his way to the front, his eyes rested expectantly on Eric. He took his bowl, walked to the table and sat down.

Eric watched carefully as he spooned his first mouthful. For a moment there was nothing, but then he saw Kevin's expression change a little. There was something different, something that acknowledged that the food he was eating was somehow improved. Kevin took another spoonful. Then he looked over at Eric and with the faintest tip of his head he nodded.

That night as Lucius was sleeping, there was a tap on his shoulder. At first he did not wake, but as it persisted, he eventually roused. He opened his eyes and found a shadow standing above him——Eric. They both tiptoed to the toilets, and quietly closed the door.

"What's going on?" asked Lucius. "When are they going to let you back?"

"The thing is," said Eric, "it's more incredible than you could ever imagine. You see, the building next door belongs to Santa."

"Santa?" repeated Lucius.

"Yes!" whispered Eric excitedly.

"A huge company called Santa Inc., where they make toys." Lucius couldn't believe what he was hearing.

"I went through the grate and then I got a job there and now I send toys all over the world. They even gave me an ID card."

"What's an ID card?"

"It's a card with my photo on it that tells people who I am."

"Don't they know who you are?"

"Yes, but..." Eric paused. "But there are problems. Big problems. The elves are mad, and there's a pirate who is trying to take the company off of Santa. And Professor Huxley——"

"Wait," said Lucius as he struggled to take in all of the information.

Eric realized that he would have to start at the beginning to have it all make sense. So that is what he did, and he didn't miss a detail. When he finished, he waited expectantly for a gasp of amazement or for Lucius to ask to come along with him on his next visit. But that didn't happen.

"I miss you, Eric," said Lucius. "Can't you just stay here?"

Coffee

It was morning. In the Santa Inc. building, people were arriving for the day. They came with their lunch bags, depositing containers into the fridge, and settling in for eight hours of work. They arrived at their desks, taking their jackets or overcoats off and hanging them on the backs of their chairs or on hooks. Then they would turn their computers on and usually get up and go back to the kitchen. Each had his or her own unique routine that remained almost identical day after day.

Much like the Australian wombat, humans were creatures of habit, Eric determined. Gopal gets a coffee as soon as he walks in, and he usually drinks it very quickly while his computer is booting up. Mary sits in her overcoat for five minutes then takes it off. Linda buys a cereal bar from the vending machine, and when she's done, she goes back for a coffee with her mug that says *I'm the Boss!* on the side. Shen always shows up with a coffee, whereas Larry goes out for a coffee about half an hour after he gets in. These routines rarely changed.

Eric watched Gopal as he walked into the canteen. Gopal quickly noticed that something was different. Instead of the usual pot of joe, there were four different types of coffee set out in large stainless steel urns. The selections came from Bali, Costa Rica, Hawaii, and Ethiopia. He watched as Gopal tried to figure out the new situation.

Each type of coffee was presented in a different urn with a description of the process that it took for them to arrive at their present location. The man who had sold Eric the coffee, who had an elaborate mustache not unlike an elf, was very keen to emphasize its *provenance*. Eric had no idea and simply made the choices based on the interesting countries that they came from.

Gopal inspected each container in turn, reading the descriptions that the coffee seller had provided. This one has notes of dark chocolate and hints of raspberry, that one has a touch of cinnamon, this is smooth, that is rich. There was also a choice of milks: half and half, whole milk, two percent, almond milk, soy milk, and oat milk. Eric had learned that the milk was just as important as the coffee. As a result, he had replaced all the little packets of powdered creamer.

Gopal filled his coffee mug with the Balinese variety and added a splash of half and half. He took a sip and almost immediately his expression turned to one of pleasure. Gopal walked over to Linda. Eric could see them discussing the coffee. Linda got up and filled her *I'm the Boss!* mug. Soon the canteen was full of people filling up their mugs with the new coffee, even Shen poured his store-bought coffee away and filled his cup. There was an upbeat buzz on the office floor that morning, and everybody was just a little more peppy than usual as they went about their day with an added zing.

"Have you tried it?" asked Yolanda, who appeared to be in a particularly good mood.

Eric decided that he should probably give it a taste. He took a mug and filled it up. He pressed the mug to his lips and took a sip of the black liquid. Immediately his mouth crinkled as the bitter taste invaded his taste buds.

"That is disgusting!" he called out.

That made all of his co-workers laugh and only added to the day's light mood.

Cayenne Pepper

Later that day, Eric found himself alone in the kitchen as the dinner was being prepared. Seeing his only opportunity, he quickly dashed to the pantry and grabbed as many spices as he could. Quickly he unscrewed the lids and added oregano, garlic powder, and Cayenne Pepper into the stew. He didn't really know what he was doing, and he wasn't sure if those spices would taste good together, but he figured that some taste was better than no taste. He doubled down and poured a little more of each one in. Before he had a chance to taste it, Mister Miller appeared.

"Get the bowls and spoons out," he ordered.

Soon after the boys were called down. Eric ladled the stew into the bowls and the boys sat down at the long tables to eat. Eric watched carefully for their reactions. He was very interested to see how his concoction would be received. The boys shoveled the stew into their mouths with gusto and Eric was pleased that his skill as a chef was improving. Cooking was easy, he thought to himself. But then something happened. Paul began waving his hand in front of his mouth as though he was trying to put out a fire. Umberto followed.

"Sister Prudence, can I get some water?"

He was barely able to get the words out. Sister Prudence nodded her approval and Umberto jumped up and ran to the fountain.

"Walk!" called the Sister.

But moments later every boy was waving his mouth in the same way as if a fireball was present in their mouths, gasping for liquid.

"Water," they called through the pain.

"What is going on?" asked Sister Prudence.

Sister Christine looked bemused. She had no idea. Mister Miller looked perplexed too. Within moments the boys couldn't take it. They all jumped up and ran to the fountain.

"Walk!" called Sister Prudence.

But even she couldn't keep them from the water. They pushed and fought their way to the fountain gathering around it like a giant herd of wildebeest at a watering hole. It was total chaos. There was pushing and elbowing as each boy desperately tried to extinguish the fire in his mouth. Eric quietly dipped a finger in the stew and put it into his mouth. A hot stinging sensation invaded his taste buds.

"Oh boy," he said to himself quietly.

It took some time before Sister Prudence gained control again and allowed each of them to drink in an orderly way.

After dinner, when the burning in their mouths had finally subsided, the boys were enjoying their hour of recreation time before bed. Most were in the Rec, watching an intense game of ping-pong. The rule was that if you lost, you were off the table. But if the prefects were playing, which they were on this occasion, they had a way of bending the rules so that they never left. The rest of the boys stood and watched. Other boys were upstairs in their dorms relaxing.

Eric left the kitchen and walked down the corridor toward the main hallway and the Rec hoping for an opportunity to talk with the other boys about dinner. But suddenly he felt a hand grabbing him by the shoulder and pinning him against the wall. It was Kevin O'Malley.

"What's your game?" he asked with a sneer.

"Nothing," said Eric.

"What's with the food? You're trying to get us all punished again."

"I'm not," protested Eric. "It's just that I didn't know that Cayenne Pepper was so hot. I'm still trying to get it right."

Kevin O'Malley stared at Eric for a moment as though he was trying to see the truth.

"Don't give up," said Eric. "I'm trying to make things better. I promise."

"I don't know about you," he said.

"I promise. Tomorrow it will be better."

Slowly Kevin O'Malley released his grip. He desperately wanted Eric to be right.

"One chance," he said. "Otherwise I'm bustin' your head."

Eric nodded and continued toward the Rec. There he found Santiago and Arvin engaged in a game of checkers.

"Where's Lucius?" asked Eric.

"Don't know," replied Santiago.

"Are you guys not friends anymore?"

Santiago shrugged.

"He needs you," said Eric. "And one day you might need him."

But Santiago was never going to show any sign of weakness, especially not in front of Arvin.

"Have you guys noticed anything about the food?" Eric asked, changing the subject.

"Are you kidding me?" Santiago replied. "I thought my head was going to explode tonight."

"I think I prefer it the old way," said Arvin.

Lucius appeared, hovering around in the background, feeling out of place.

Santiago tried not to notice.

"I think it's better," said Santiago. "Maybe just a little less of the heat."

"We're going to make the food better for you guys," said Eric. "But we're still trying to get it right."

Santiago and Arvin resumed their game, moving the pieces about the board. Santiago took Arvin's last counter as Kevin O'Malley appeared in the room with more boys in tow whom he had summoned from their dorms.

"Quiet down," he ordered.

Slowly the entire Rec came to order as all fifty of them waited for their leader to speak.

"Listen up. Things are gonna change," he announced. "New rules. No more than two minutes for a shower. Turn the lights off when you leave a room. Keep the doors and windows shut. And the washers and dryers must be full before you run a load."

"What's all this for?" asked Umberto.

"We're tryin' to save money, aren't we?"

"What's in it for us?" asked Ryan.

"How about no punches in the face?" said Kevin.

The other boys laughed.

"Quiet," said Kevin.

He was in no mood for joking. This was serious business.

"We've all seen the food's gotten better."

There was a murmuring about the place and a few of the boys touched their tender tongues to their teeth.

"It's getting better," Kevin clarified. "And it's going to get a lot better."

He stared at Eric, and Eric nodded back in agreement.

"But the Sisters need more money to pay for better supplies."

Kevin O'Malley looked over the room. He had a commanding presence and an effortless way of making the other boys pay attention to him.

"So we have to help them save money. Anyone caught breaking the new rules gets double punishment. Alright?"

The boys nodded in unison. Kevin left. Eric was pleased that his plan had taken a large step forward. He wanted to get back to the kitchen, but Lucius began to set up the checkerboard again.

"Let's go," said Arvin.

He and Santiago got up and stood in line for the next turn at the ping pong table having noticed that the prefects had vacated.

"I'll play with you," said Eric.

Lucius moved his counter first. Then Eric moved his.

"Everything is going to get a whole lot better around here," he said quietly. "You watch."

Caught

The following day the first shoots of change began to appear in the orphanage. Sister Christine was satisfied that she was starting to make modest progress with the sorry state of the orphanage's financial affairs. It had taken some time, but there was now at least a little hope that order could be reinstated. She sat back in her chair for a moment to think, and in doing so, she noticed the book that Eric had given to her.

"An Introduction to Business Administration," she read aloud.

She picked it up and read the first page. Much to her surprise, she found it to be quite interesting. She had never read a book about business before. In fact, it was all quite foreign to her. But there was something in those pages that piqued her interest and she continued to read. Soon she was on page two.

In the kitchen, the pot bubbled away. Eric peered at it as steam rose up and condensed into thin whispers, and the odd gloopy bubble popped on the surface. Eric wondered what new ingredients he would add this time.

"Mister Miller?" he called out.

There was no answer.

"Mister Miller?" he called again, just to be safe.

He hopped down from the stove top and made his way swiftly to the pantry. He knelt down to look at the spices, his eyes scanning quickly across the various jars filled with different colors and textures. For some reason his attention settled on a jar of brownish powder with the name *Garam Masala* written in pen on a small label. He pulled it down and unscrewed the lid letting the aroma fill his senses.

He closed his eyes and thought of Chandni Chowk in Old Delhi, India. It took him back to the ancient building, the spice traders, the intoxicating aromas that had permeated the very walls of the that old market. He screwed the top back on and returned to the pot where he quickly poured the powder into the stew. It bubbled and slowly absorbed into the mixture.

Eric took the ladle and stirred it in so that soon its presence was undetectable by sight. Then he took a little taste. It was better, but it needed something more, some garlic salt perhaps, definitely none of the cayenne pepper. He turned to dash back to the pantry but was stopped dead in his tracks. Mister Miller stood in front of him, arms folded, watching every move.

"What's going on, boy?" he asked.

Eric was silent, frozen. Mister Miller walked forward. He simply held out his hand.

"You better have a very good explanation for this," he said.

"I do," said Eric, passing him the jar.

But Mister Miller was not in the mood for explanations.

"They told me you were a bad egg," he said, voice rising, "but I told them I'd take yer in. I said you couldn't be that bad."

"But——" said Eric.

"But nothing. You are a thief," said Mister Miller. "The worst kind."

"I thought you liked thieves?" said Eric.

"Not in my kitchen," snapped Mister Miller. "Come on, we're going to see Sister Prudence."

"Wait," said Eric. "Sister Prudence already knows about this."

The old cook was unprepared for Eric's reply.

"What do you mean?"

"She already knows that I have been adding spice to the food. It's all part of the big plan."

"What big plan?" asked Mister Miller.

"I guess it's time to tell you," said Eric.

"I guess you better had," said Mister Miller.

"Have you noticed just how bad things have gotten around here?"

"Not really," said Mister Miller.

"Well, things are very bad. You couldn't walk up the stairs without getting kicked. Boys playing nasty pranks. Calling names. My friend Lucius even got put in a washing machine. Only a power cut saved him."

"Is that so?" said Mister Miller.

"Things went from bad to worse. Fighting. Thieving. Carousing all night."

Mister Miller's eyes lit up.

"It got so bad that the Sisters decided to do something about it. They decided to try an experiment. They figured if the food got a little better, maybe the boys might behave better too."

. Eric's words ticked over in Mister Miller's head. He wasn't sure whether to believe them or not. It seemed plausible. But then it also seemed implausible.

"So why is it such a big secret?" he asked.

"Because if everybody knew about it, then it wouldn't work, would it?" replied Eric.

Mister Miller scratched his head, still not fully convinced.

"What about you? Why would they choose you to do it when you're a bad egg?"

"Do you remember why I'm a bad egg?" asked Eric.

"Because you ask too many questions," said Mister Miller.

"Is that what bad eggs do?"

"No."

"Exactly," said Eric. "I am a good egg pretending to be a bad egg. I am here to make things better."

Eric took back the garam masala.

"Now, Mister Miller, you're in on it," he continued. "The plan is working, but I need your help. We need to give these boys a little more flavor in their food."

Taking Care of Business

Another week went by and Eric found that he was busier than ever. The frantic run into Christmas saw everybody at Santa Inc. working longer and longer hours as they desperately tried to ship as many products as they could before the stores closed for the holiday. Luckily Eric's coffee gave them the extra pep they needed to see the long days through, and everybody carried with them a spirit of good cheer that was fitting for the season.

At the orphanage, the boys practiced their carols every day, sometimes for two hours at a time. They sang so much that some of them lost their voices as Sister Prudence rehearsed them like an unforgiving drill sergeant. Eric listened to them as he worked in the kitchen. He did miss singing and sometimes found himself quietly joining in as he polished the spoons. There wasn't quite the same feeling of Christmas cheer in the orphanage, but all the same, the boys did sense that a special time of the year was close, even if they did not quite know why.

It was also during this time that something else happened. After choir practice, Clive approached Lucius.

"I can hardly speak," he said. "But I like singing those songs all the same."

Lucius was wary at first. He didn't like to talk to the other boys, but Clive seemed to have a warm and honest smile.

"Me too," said Lucius.

Over the course of just a few days, Sister Christine whipped through Gopal's business book, devouring every page. It had given her more good ideas about how she could improve the orphanage, and she thought about writing them down so that she could share them with Sister Prudence. She located Eric in the kitchen one morning after breakfast.

"Eric," she called.

Eric walked over to her as Mister Miller nodded a greeting. Sister Christine handed over the book.

"Would you like another one?" asked Eric.

Sister Christine paused for a moment. She did not want to appear too enthusiastic, but the truth was that she had found the content to be quite exhilarating.

"Yes," she said quietly. "I would."

With that, she left. Mister Miller looked at Eric for a moment.

"I told you I was a good egg," Eric smiled.

Eric had gotten into the habit of bypassing Huxley on his way to and from work. It wasn't deliberate, it was just that he was usually pressed for time between leaving the kitchen and getting to his desk. Usually, he would have to run as fast as possible so that he was not in a permanent state of being late. This particular morning, Huxley was sitting at his drafting table as Eric came shooting out of the grate.

"Good morning, Professor," he called without breaking stride toward the elevator.

Huxley would often call out his own greeting without breaking his concentration, but this morning was different. An odd feeling came over him as though some equilibrium had been altered. He looked up from his desk and turned to Eric, who had almost reached the service elevator.

"Young man," he called out.

Eric stopped.

"What?"

"Do you know what day it is?"

"It's Friday," said Eric.

"It is Friday," said Huxley. "But it is also another day."

Eric stopped and thought for a moment. He had been working so hard and for so many hours for as long as he could remember that he didn't really know whether it was morning or night.

"It's Christmas Eve," said Huxley.

He smiled.

"Are you excited?" he asked.

"Sure," said Eric. "But I have a lot to do."

"I suppose that I have missed another year," said Huxley, suddenly becoming forlorn.

"The last containers leave in two hours," noted Eric.

Huxley screwed up his sketch into a ball and dropped it into the trash can.

"So much for that."

He eased himself up and walked over to the kitchen.

"Will you join me for a cup of tea?" he asked.

"It's kind of a busy day," said Eric apologetically.

"Of course it is."

Huxley remembered all those years ago when he was in the cut and thrust of things. Sometimes he, Santa, and the elves would work for forty-eight hours straight from the day before Christmas Eve to the end of Christmas Day. Those were his fondest memories. Now he had little more to do but drink his tea, and even though he was buoyed by seasonal cheer, that thought made him feel a little blue. Eric pulled shut the metal sliding door of the elevator and was soon gone.

When Eric arrived at his desk, there was already a fervor of activity. Everyone had a mug of coffee in their hands. Linda was buzzing around the office like a spinning top, and Gopal was typing furiously fast on his keyboard. Eric replaced the book and pulled two more out.

"Borrowing these," he said.

Gopal was so focused on his task that he did not break his concentration. The office was decorated with miniature Christmas trees, tinsel, and baubles, and despite their hard work, most everyone carried a smile on their faces. The holiday was close. Some people played Christmas songs at their cubes. At his desk, Eric found that there was a message for him:

Go to Santa's office.

Eric made his way to the 77th floor.

"Good morning, Martha," he said as he dashed past.

"Good morning, Eric," said Martha, raising a steaming cup toward him in greeting.

Eric knocked on Santa's door and entered. Santa was standing at his window. Wormwood Grubbs sat in a chair by his desk.

"Aha!" called Santa when he saw Eric.

Grubbs didn't give him the same warm reception.

"The situation has developed," said Grubbs. "Things have gotten worse."

"What do you mean?" asked Eric.

"This corporate raider," said Santa.

"The pirate?" asked Eric.

"His name is Max Rupee," clarified Grubbs.

"That's him, the one who wants to take over my company. He's hoovering up stock like a street sweeper."

"Is that bad?" asked Eric.

"Of course it's bad," said Santa. "Soon he'll control the company."

"Can you call him and ask him to stop?"

Grubbs started to laugh. It wasn't a friendly laugh.

"Do you understand the first thing about business?" he asked.

"No," said Eric.

Santa paced about the room.

"But that coffee idea has worked well," he said. "Productivity is already way up. People are zipping around the place like they're running on batteries. But it's too little, too late."

"Maybe you should send everyone on a vacation for the whole of January?" suggested Eric.

Santa thought about Eric's idea, and somewhere in his mind a memory was sparked, a memory from long ago.

"That's a ridiculous proposal," protested Grubbs.

"There's no time for a vacation," said Santa. "We've got to fight this interloper with everything we've got."

"Will you be sending presents to Our Lady of Mercy Orphanage this year?" asked Eric.

"If they purchased them in the store like everyone else," said Grubbs.

"I don't think they can get to a store," said Eric.

"This is not a charity," said Grubbs.

"Although we could certainly use that kind of a tax break right now," said Santa.

Grubbs nodded in agreement. Santa paced some more, intermittently looking out of the window.

"What if we cut those pesky elves loose?" suggested Grubbs. "We could get twice the amount of toys from a machine with no back talk."

Santa thought about that idea. But something held him back. He couldn't let the elves go even though he had not spoken to them in some time.

"Are you excited for Christmas, Santa?" asked Eric.

"I haven't got time to be excited," Santa replied.

"Why don't you take the day off?"

"Ridiculous," said Santa.

"Then when all of the staff return, go talk to them?" suggested Eric.

"What do you mean?" asked Santa.

"The staff have lots of ideas about how this place can be run better. In fact, it's really all they talk about."

"Talk to the staff?" said Grubbs as though a foul odor had crept into the room.

He was nearing the end of his patience with Eric.

"Explain," said Santa.

Eric sat back and thought for a moment, then ideas came to him quickly.

"Mary in Accounts has to run a report every day that is exactly the same as the one that John does. That makes her mad. Gianna has to get three signatures for her expenses, but she says no one ever checks them. Larry spends a lot of his time sitting in the lobby. That really annoys Harry who has double the amount of work to do. Linda says the company that does the shredding is no good and that they charge too much. Gopal says that we don't always pay our invoices on time, even after he sends them to Mary early and that we get charged late fees."

Eric went on and on. He described very precisely to Santa exactly how Santa Inc. worked, from the smallest details to the biggest issues that the company was facing. He set out all the things that worked well and all the areas where things could be improved. Santa sat in his seat and listened very carefully to every word that Eric said.

"What I am trying to say," Eric concluded, "is that we waste a lot of money because we don't think about doing things in a better way."

Santa pushed his hands together, rocked back in his chair, and thought deeply for a moment.

"This is quite incredible," he said finally. "You've gone deep. You really get it."

Eric smiled.

"How long have you worked here for?"

"About four weeks," said Eric.

"That's amazing," said Santa.

"Maybe if we made all these changes and saved a bunch of money, there would be enough spare to give the boys at Our Lady of Mercy Orphanage a present?"

Grubbs guffawed at that suggestion.

"Santa," said Grubbs. "There's money to be made here if we play this right. And an opportunity to cut all of the dead wood out of Santa Inc. Eric could be just the right person for this job."

Santa turned in his chair and stared out of the window.

"Let me think it over," said Santa.

He didn't seem to be looking over the city but past it. Lost in his own thoughts. For once, he didn't know what to do.

When Eric returned to his cube, he found an envelope sitting on his desk with his name written on it. He opened it up. Inside there was a note which read:

No surname in system, so we made your paycheck out to cash.

He pulled out the paycheck. He could not believe how much money it was for.

Christmas Eve

Most of the staff had left Santa Inc. by 3PM on Christmas Eve to enjoy the holiday with their families. Their work was now done. Busy season was officially over, and any remaining toys would have to wait until the next year to be sold. Eric returned to the orphanage early that day too. His first task was to deposit the new books in the office. They were called *Practical Bookkeeping* and *Getting the Most from Your Organization*. He left them in Sister Christine's inbox, under a pile of letters, so that only she would find them. Then he took his Santa Inc. paycheck and placed it in the letterbox by the front door so that it looked as though it had been received in the post.

In the kitchen, Mister Miller had only just taken out the pot and placed it on the stove in preparation for dinner.

"Remember," said Eric, "that we have started a new way of doing things."

"What's that?" asked Mister Miller as though their previous conversation had been forgotten.

"What spices could we add to this stew to give it a bit more pep?" asked Eric.

"Are you sure about this?" asked Mister Miller with an unconvinced frown.

"Very sure," said Eric.

The old cook sighed.

"Oregano, pepper, and garlic."

Eric dashed into the pantry before he had a chance to change his mind. The ingredients were not so easy to find. They were mostly stuffed in the back corners of cupboards in old-looking

161

containers, but Eric eventually located them and brought them back into the kitchen. Mister Miller scooped a good amount of each one and deposited into the pot.

"Give it a good stir then," he said.

Eric took the large wooden spoon and slowly churned the mixture.

They left the stew to cook. Mister Miller sat down with his newspaper. Eric prepared the bowls and spoons.

"Mister Miller?" asked Eric with a curious tone.

"What?" he replied, somewhat puzzled by an article about the benefits of clean coal.

"So you don't ever go into the other parts of the orphanage?"

"Why would I?"

"I guess you don't know too much about what life is like in here then?" asked Eric.

"Don't care to."

"It's not much fun most of the time."

"That's the way life is, kid," said Mister Miller. "Life's tough. The sooner you figure this out the better."

"But the boys have responded very well to the better food. That's a proven fact. If we could get some variety, something tasty, I think life would improve a little more," suggested Eric.

"Steak and caviar for all?"

Mister Miller laughed to himself at the ridiculousness of the idea.

"If we could get some bread with our dinners? Just to fill our stomachs a little more."

The words hung in air for a moment.

"No money for it," said Mister Miller flatly.

Some time later, there was a knock at the side door of the kitchen. Mister Miller got up from the table, walked slowly over, and opened it up.

"Good evening to you!" said Norma Jean, pushing her cart toward the pantry with a spring in her step.

As Eric watched her wheeling the large tins of *Meat* and *Carrots* to the pantry, a wonderful idea came to him.

"Ma'am," he said finally.

The delivery woman turned to Eric.

"Yer don't need no graces with me," she said. "Call me Norma Jean."

"Norma Jean," said Eric. "I was wondering, do you ever get any spare food?"

"Spare food," she said. "How do you mean?"

"Maybe some bread that's a little old, maybe some vegetables that are past their best?"

"Oh we got plenty of that," she said. "It's a cryin' shame what we toss in the trash sometimes."

"Do you think that maybe we could have some of it?" asked Eric.

"For what?"

"For eating," said Eric.

"Can't do that," said Norma Jean. "Company won't let us. It's against policy."

"Oh," said Eric.

As Norma Jean finished unloading the delivery, she took a good look at the pot of brownish liquid bubbling on the stove. Then she thought about the delicious food that she would be sharing with her own family over the holiday. Something about that situation didn't feel right to her.

"Let me see what I can do," she said.

Norma Jean went out to her truck, pulling the empty delivery cart behind her. Moments later she reappeared, holding a large box.

"It just so happens," she said. "That we have a box of spoiled goods. Those fancy restaurants that we deliver to, they won't take them. Normally I take them back to the warehouse and throw them out. But no one ever checks up so you may as well have them. They're good enough to eat."

She placed the box down on the kitchen table. Eric and Mister Miller peered inside.

"Can you use them?" asked Norma Jean.

There were some potatoes that were a little green and some onions that had large green shoots spouting out of them. A bunch of celery had gone limp. Finally, there was bread that had turned quite hard.

"Sure we can," said Eric.

"Alright," said Norma Jean. "It's all yours. Merry Christmas to yers."

"Merry Christmas," said Eric.

Norma Jean left and pulled the doors shut behind her.

"Look at this stuff," said Mister Miller. "It's not fit for a dog."

"But..." said Eric, "it's food."

"I'm not putting this out. I won't do it."

"Mister Miller," said Eric. "The boys will be glad of it. I'm sure you could make something with it?"

He picked up the celery as it drooped in his hand.

That night Eric found it hard to sleep. He was taken with the idea of Christmas, and his mind was too occupied thinking about all the toys that he had helped transport all over the world. He sat up and looked about the place, then he slowly stood up and walked over to Lucius.

"Lucius," he whispered, gently tapping his shoulder. "Wake up."

Slowly Lucius came around.

"I have more to tell you," said Eric.

Once more they tiptoed to the toilet block and Eric described all of the incredible adventures that he had been having. He recounted using his computer and speaking to people around the world on the telephone. But it was the part when he described actually meeting Santa that was the most incredible to Lucius. He couldn't quite make sense of it.

"You mean Santa is in the building next door?" he asked.

"Yes!" said Eric. "But not just Santa——Gopal and Linda and Shen."

"Who are they?" Lucius asked.

"My co-workers. They're so nice. They don't call each other names."

Lucius began to imagine the wonderful place next door that was full of nice people and tasty snacks.

"They taught me all about filing and bookkeeping, and then I showed it to Sister Christine."

"You did?"

Eric nodded.

"Tell me more about Santa," said Lucius.

"He's a little bit grumpy and kind of stressed out," started Eric.

He told Lucius as much as he could until he began to yawn uncontrollably. Suddenly Eric felt very drowsy and could barely hold his eyes open.

"I think I need to go back to sleep," he said, and with that he made his way quietly back to his bed.

Christmas Morning

Sister Prudence walked through the dorms clanging her pot. The boys awoke as usual and made their way to breakfast. They promptly assembled in the canteen. Inspection was completed and the Lord's Prayer recited. Then they lined up as usual for their oatmeal.

"Today is Christmas Day," Sister Prudence announced. "The Lord Jesus Christ's birthday. There will be no classes."

There was a little flutter of excitement among the boys, but it was soon quashed.

"We will complete our chores this morning. Then we will go to Our Lady of Mercy Church after lunch. We will spend the rest of the day there. You will all be on your best behavior. Any boy not on his best behavior will be punished. Is that clear?"

There was no Christmas spirit in her words, no joy or lightness.

"Yes, Sister Prudence," came the reply in chorus.

Sister Christine, however, was different. She did carry with her the spirit of Christmas. She always had. She loved the excitement of Christmas Day. She loved everything about it from the moment she awoke until the moment she laid her head on her pillow. She loved to sing and to play games and to exchange presents. But years with Sister Prudence had driven that joy deep inside so that on the outside she appeared just as stern and cold as her counterpart. She scowled at each boy in turn not daring to furnish them with a season's greeting. Nobody knew that below the surface, locked away somewhere in a discarded vault, was the ember of a happy soul.

"It's a shame," said Mister Miller, watching the boys as they trudged out glumly.

"What is?" asked Eric.

"I never had the best upbringing," said the old cook. "We never had much. Sometimes we had nothing. But we always had Christmas Day to look forward to. We always got something. Even if it was the smallest little nothing present you could imagine. I've been here for a good few years now, and I've never seen them do a thing for you boys. Not so much as a toy, or a book, or nothing. It's not right."

Eric scrubbed the bowls at the sink.

"Life's tough," said Eric. "The sooner they learn that the better. Right?"

"Not on Christmas Day," protested Mister Miller.

He walked into the pantry and picked up the box of food that Norma Jean had left.

"Christmas Day is different. There's a little bit of magic to it, and I for one will not deny it."

Over the course of that morning, Mister Miller did his best, with the limited ingredients available to him, to assemble a different kind of stew. He pulled down his chopping board and took out a knife that Eric had never seen before. It was a special knife with a razor-sharp blade and a handle made from ebony. Mister Miller used it to chop the old sticks of celery, slicing them wafer thin at a speed that Eric did not believe was possible.

Eric did not interfere with the old cook, keeping himself instead to the washing up and cleaning. He did, however, observe him most keenly, noting that there was a vigor to his work that he had not seen before.

Close to lunchtime, Mister Miller called Eric over.

"Give this a taste," he said.

Eric took a spoon and dipped it into the bubbling liquid. He blew on it and tasted it.

The stew tasted far better than Eric's concoction of surreptitiously assembled spices. It was wholesome and hearty and with a quite delicious flavor. It contained all the ingredients that Norma Jean had given them the day before.

"You made this with those ingredients?" asked Eric.

"Yup."

"How did you do it?"

"I've been cookin' a good long time," said Mister Miller with a wry smile.

When the boys arrived for lunch, Eric watched closely as they began to eat. He could see that they were quite delighted with the food that had been presented to them. They scarfed it down so fast that there wasn't even an opportunity for it to be taken away. Eric had filled the bowls with a little more than usual so that they could all get a good belly full.

In some small way, Eric felt that Mister Miller's food had charged them with enough good cheer to get them through the day. Christmas Day was not an easy day to be an orphan. Kevin O'Malley gave Eric another nod as he left the canteen, which he took as a good omen. Eric noticed that Clive had joined Lucius at the table, sitting where he used to sit.

After lunch, the boys lined up at the front door and Sister Prudence inspected them one more time. She would certainly not stand for any of her wards to be scruffy in public. When she was sufficiently satisfied, Sister Christine opened those big wooden doors, and they marched two by two, like beasts leaving the ark, down the steps and the few blocks to Our Lady of Mercy Church.

It was not until Eric had finished clearing everything up that he realized the entire building was unnaturally quiet.

"Mister Miller," he said. "I think they left without me."

"Well, there's no dinner tonight on account of them singing. So I suppose you're free to do whatever you choose. Merry Christmas."

Instead of his usual snooze, Mister Miller packed up his things, which consisted of placing his newspaper in an old plastic bag, and left.

Paper Planes

When Eric got to Huxley's lab, he found that the professor was not there. He suspected that he was spending the day with the elves, as was the tradition on this most sacred of all days. He would certainly pay him a visit later if time permitted. However, a more pressing need had overtaken him.

Eric took the elevator right to the 77th floor and walked down the long corridor to Santa's office. He knocked on the door and pushed it open without waiting for a reply. Santa was sitting in his chair, glasses perched upon his nose, drinking a coffee with a stack of papers next to him.

"What are you doing here?" he asked.

"It's Christmas," said Eric.

"I know that," said Santa.

"Have you made all your deliveries?" asked Eric.

"I don't do that anymore."

"Why?" asked Eric.

Santa was determined to concentrate and ignored Eric's question.

"What are you reading?" asked Eric after a few moments.

"Production reports."

"I thought we could fly paper airplanes."

"I haven't got time for that," said Santa.

"You did say you would do it," Eric reminded Santa. "And today there is nobody in the building. Everybody else is having fun."

"I have to figure out how to save this company," said Santa. "The buck stops here."

Santa tried to focus, but Eric stared at him. This time he was not taking no for an answer. Eventually, Santa felt the strong pull of a duty to his word.

"That coffee is very good," he said as they left his office.

Eric pushed open the door to the top of the building with excitement. A great whoosh of freezing cold air hit his face. Santa followed behind holding a box of printer paper.

"Just slow down there!" he called as Eric rushed to the railing that separated him from a sheer drop of a thousand feet. "Last thing I need is a lawsuit."

Eric peered over the railing, all the way down to the street below. He was too consumed with the rush of elements against his face to take any notice of Santa's warnings. It was a very long way down. The people below were like little dots moving about. Even the cars were like miniature models of the real thing. Eric remained there for a good minute until it became too unbearably cold to stay any longer.

"There are some really good gusts, and maybe even a couple of thermals," he said, turning his attention back to Santa. "Do you know how to make a paper airplane?"

"Of course," said Santa.

Eric took a single sheet of paper and folded it, expertly fashioning his flying machine. Santa folded the paper one way, then changed his mind and folded it another way. Then he completely unfolded it and started again.

"Do you really know how to do this?" Eric asked.

"It's been a while," said Santa.

It soon became clear to Eric that Santa did not know how to make a paper airplane at all. He took the piece of paper from Santa.

"Fold here, here, and here," he said, quickly fashioning it into the right shape.

He handed it back.

"Now," said Eric, brimming with excitement, "be sure to give it a good launch."

"I've only got ten minutes for this," said Santa.

"Try to hit an updraft to get some more lift," said Eric.

They held their planes aloft as Eric performed the all-important countdown.

"Three. Two. One."

With a gentle push, the planes were released into the air. They glided away and snaked downwards towards the ground. Santa's hit the side of the building and spiraled down uncontrollably, but Eric's managed to make it a few blocks until it disappeared from view behind a building.

"Let's try again."

They each took another sheet of paper. Reluctantly Santa made a better attempt at his own plane.

"I'm going to put some wing tips on mine. See if I can get a little more lift," said Eric.

"It's coming back to me now," said Santa.

In moments, they were ready again.

"Three. Two. One."

The planes fared better. They were more stable, and neither one plummeted toward the ground.

"Good try," said Eric.

"Thanks," said Santa. "That was fun. Now let's go back inside."

"But we just got started," protested Eric. "We have hardly had time to refine our designs."

Santa sighed again. He picked up more paper and this time made a much better airplane, carefully folding the wings and the fuselage. He also added some wing tips.

"Three," Eric started the countdown.

Santa joined Eric. "Two. One."

They let the planes fly from their hands once more. This time, both performed well. Instead of immediately descending toward the ground, the planes were carried by a sudden updraft of air from the city below. This propelled them forward, diving and rising, banking and circling.

"Look at that!" called Eric.

Santa could not help but smile, and after that, he stopped asking Eric to leave and accepted that for the foreseeable future he would be up on the roof. The process of gradual refinement continued for more than an hour. They tried folding the paper the opposite way. They tried small wings and big fuselages, they tried big wings and small fuselages. They tried wing tips, flaps, and tail planes. Some worked, some didn't work. Something quite strange happened to Santa during that time. He didn't think about Santa Inc. or any of its problems. For a few moments, he simply thought about making the best airplane that he possibly could.

"Alright then," he said when it seemed like they had reached the zenith of their designs. "The one who can get it furthest is the winner."

"What does the winner win?" asked Eric.

Santa thought for a moment, but Eric already had an idea.

"How about the winner gets to say what we do next?" suggested Eric.

"Deal," said Santa, who was not one to back down from a challenge.

Eric was inspired to be even more creative in the construction of his next airplane. He spent a good five minutes carefully folding each piece. He ran his fingernail down each fold to make it as crisp as possible. He added flaps to each wing for extra lift. Not to be outdone, Santa came up with his own unique design. He increased the wing area for maximum glide. With the heightened competition came increased secrecy. Santa turned away from Eric to protect his idea, only revealing it at the very last moment.

"Now let's see who is the best at making these things," he said.

One more time the countdown began. The airplanes soared into the air. Each one fared much better than its predecessors, gliding steadily out toward the river. Santa and Eric watched. Santa's plane took an early lead, its increased wing providing for more lift. Eric's, on the other hand, dived and circled.

"Looks like I'm going to be champion," said Santa with a satisfied smile.

The planes travelled much further than the previous attempts, moving block after block until it became quite difficult to see them. Then disaster struck as Santa's plane was hit by a downdraft of wind, and the lift that had held it so firm and steady suddenly evaporated, sending the paper craft spiraling toward the ground.

"No!" called Santa in desperation.

Eric jumped around joyfully, and they watched until his plane disappeared from view, almost reaching the river.

"I win," shouted Eric victoriously.

"Now what?" asked Santa. "Watch TV?"

"Christmas dinner with the elves," said Eric.

Christmas Dinner

"**I** can't go down there," said Santa as they walked back inside the building.

"Why?" asked Eric.

"Because," Santa stuttered, "I'm too tall, and I always bang my head on the door."

Eric called the elevator.

"Have you ever had their Spaghetti Bolognese? It's so delicious."

"Of course I have," said Santa. "I know how delicious it is."

The elevator doors opened, and Santa reluctantly stepped inside.

"This is a very bad idea," he said as the elevator descended all the way down. "It will be weird."

Eric didn't answer. He was thinking of Spaghetti Bolognese. The elevator stopped and Santa let out a deep breath.

"This is not how I planned on spending my day off," he said, lingering inside.

"It's way better than reading production reports," said Eric.

Eric marched purposefully past the silent production lines. It had been some time since Santa had been in the factory. But as he walked through those idle hunks of machinery, he felt a connection to something that had long been missing. It wasn't even possible for him to say what it was, but it was certainly there in its faintest form.

As they approached the elf lodge, a sound became louder and louder. It started as a muffled beat, but as Eric pushed the factory gate open, it became clearer——music, laughter, and fun.

"Maybe we should come back later," suggested Santa as they reached the front door.

"Later will be too late," said Eric.

He pushed the door open. Santa ducked down and stepped inside. In an instant, the entire room fell completely silent. The music stopped. The laughter stopped. Every elf turned and looked directly at the two unexpected visitors.

"Well, this is uncomfortable," Santa sighed.

There was a whispering somewhere in the room. Then Robbo stood up and walked down the rows of elves seated along the tables. When he reached the visitors, he planted his feet firmly and crossed his arms. He had a very stern expression, and his mustache twitched a little.

"Santa," he said. "What brings you here?"

"Well," said Santa, shuffling about a little, "we thought we would come and pay our season's greetings to you all."

Robbo stood for a tense moment and considered Santa's words carefully. He was not prone to making rash decisions.

"We have had our disagreements this year," he said eventually. "But it is a firm and fast rule for us elves that on this very special day we celebrate and we welcome visitors who happen to come by our home. I guess that goes for tyrannical captains of industry too."

Santa nodded. Robbo's expression started to change. His stern face softened a little, then the sides of his mouth curled upwards. Finally, a huge beaming smile planted itself on his face.

"Merry Christmas!" he called out.

"Merry Christmas!" came a chorus of elf voices.

The music and laughter resumed. Robbo led Santa and Eric down the line and showed them to a seat.

"Where's Professor Huxley?" Eric quietly asked Stephen and Lofty.

"He was just here," said Lofty, looking about the room.

"Maybe he ate too much turkey and it made him sleepy?" Stephen replied.

"Perhaps he went for a snooze," added Jean-Pierre, leaning in.

Eric was disappointed that Huxley had vanished, for the truth was that he had hoped to reunite Santa with the old professor. He thought that if they could talk, there may be a way to bring Huxley back into the company, but he soon forgot all about it as a huge plate of food was dropped in front of him. Eric inspected the contents. It was not Spaghetti Bolognese. It was turkey, cranberry sauce, stuffing, gravy, and lots of vegetables. Eric took a bite, and his initial disappointment was soon dissipated by the fact that the meal was, in its own right, quite delicious.

"Do you remember the year that the production lines stopped working three days before Christmas?" asked Robbo.

"I do," said Santa, recalling the incident. "Boy oh boy, was that a crazy seventy-two hours."

"We had to finish everything by hand," said Robbo.

"There were some raised voices that year, I'll tell you."

"And some fruity language."

The elves began to recount all of their stories from the old times——the ferocious cold of the North Pole, the difficulty getting supplies, the many trips circumnavigating the globe each Christmas Eve, the winter storms in the north, the summer storms in the south, the times they were nearly caught by children who had stayed up past their bed time. After a while, Santa relaxed and joined in, recounting his own versions of the same events.

"It was you who woke that kid up," he said to Robbo. "After you dropped his present all the way down the chimney and the dog started barking."

"That's not how I remember it," said Robbo. "As I recall, you tripped over the dog because you had your eyes on the cookies that were left out."

All the elves around them erupted in laughter. Soon the entire room joined in, listening to their fabled history of the special night.

The next event was dessert. A giant Christmas pudding was pushed out on a cart by four elves. Its dome-like shape was filled with dried fruits, brown sugar, and soft cake. The lights were dimmed, and Oswaldo poured brandy all over it. Then Lofty struck a match and held it close to the giant dessert. A blue flame consumed the pudding as all the elves clapped and cheered. Jean-Pierre stood by with a fire extinguisher, but luckily it wasn't needed. After the show, the lights came on and the giant dessert was carved up. A bowl was placed in front of Eric with a generous helping of white custard to accompany it.

"I expected to see Huxley here," said Santa as he shoveled a large serving into his mouth. "He does love a good Christmas pudding."

Eric was shocked.

"That's a secret. How do you know about him?"

Santa laughed.

"He occupies a whole floor of this building. Why wouldn't I know? I know he takes the paper from the stationary cupboard. And takes wood from the timber store. 'Liberating it,' I think he calls it."

"Why haven't you done anything about it?" asked Eric.

"Wormwood keeps telling me to make him pay rent or kick him out, but I can't bring myself to do it. He never could see the point of this company. But he's an honorable man."

By the time dessert was over, Eric was so full of food that he felt as though his stomach was going to burst. Finally, came the highlight of the entire evening: the exchange of gifts. Each elf was presented with a small present, which they unwrapped gleeful-ly. The presents were simple and usually pertained to their area of expertise. Stephen was given a new chisel, Lofty a new paint brush. Robbo got a clipboard, which he was very pleased with.

Not long after the exchange of presents, Jean-Pierre approached their table.

"Santa, there's something that you might like to see," he said.

Santa and Eric followed him out of the elf lodge.

"Wow!" exclaimed Santa. "Look at that."

In front of him was his old sleigh, in perfect condition, gleaming under the lights. And there, tethered together, were his eight reindeer. Santa went to each one in turn, greeting them by their names and letting them nuzzle against his face.

"I've missed you boys," he said quietly to them.

It was clear that the reindeer had missed him too. They pushed their noses close to him as though they didn't want him to leave. He stroked their coats and inspected their antlers. They were indeed fine creatures and were very well taken care of by the elves. They stamped their hooves upon the floor and huffed air from their noses. They were ready to fly.

"Good boys," said Santa.

Eric watched as the normally tough-talking businessman softened in the presence of his old friends. He then turned his attention to the sleigh.

"I figured this thing went to the scrap heap," he said.

"No," said Jean-Pierre. "We keep it just as it has always been kept. You never know when it might be needed."

Santa ran his hand down the metal siding. It gleamed red under the lights of the factory. He touched the old leather seat that he had used for so many years. It brought back to him so many memories that he could barely count them before the next appeared.

After the formalities were done, the music started again. The elf band set up and played all the old classics like *Highway to Elf*, *Elf Me Rhonda*, and everybody's favorite *I'm Leaving on a Jet Sleigh*. During all the singing and dancing, Santa turned to Eric.

"Thank you," he said.

"For what?" asked Eric.

"This has been the best Christmas I've had in a long time," said Santa.

"Me too," said Eric. "But there's something else that I would like to show you."

"What?"

"Can you get into the building next door?"

"Of course I can," said Santa. "I have a skeleton key to every single building in the world."

Just a few minutes later, Santa and Eric stood in the doorway of Our Lady of Mercy Orphanage. Santa pushed the door closed and placed a large key back into his pocket.

"What is this place?" he whispered.

"This is where I live."

Santa took a step forward and looked around. Then he walked forward into the great hall. Eric noticed that Santa's footsteps were as silent as an ant walking on snow.

"Follow me," said Eric.

In the dark of that Christmas night, Eric showed Santa around the old orphanage——the canteen with its rows of hard benches, the classrooms with their old chairs and desks, the dorms with their metal beds, and the Rec with its tattered books and old games. Santa felt the old floorboards beneath his feet and the icy draft of air on the back of his neck. He saw the drips of water making their way slowly through the building.

"This place is terrible," he whispered.

Eric nodded.

"That's not the worst of it," said Eric. "Not one of these boys got a present for Christmas."

"Why not?" asked Santa.

Eric shrugged.

"I guess they just can't afford it."

"That's outrageous!" said Santa, raising his voice a little.

"I guess that's just the way it is," said Eric.

Santa mumbled something quietly, but Eric couldn't tell what he said. It was clear though that the orphanage had affected him. There was a change in his demeanor. They continued to look around some more until Santa finally turned back to Eric.

"I think I have seen enough," he said.

The Pirate

Sister Christine woke early and turned on the lamp by her bedside table. She pulled one of Gopal's books from under her pillow and began to read. It was so interesting that she had read it until she had fallen asleep the night before. It gave her knowledge that she had never possessed before, and with that knowledge came a growing feeling of confidence and understanding about how other parts of the world that were far removed from her own worked.

Just like Eric before her, she began to understand how a company ran and how all of its parts were intertwined. More importantly, she began to understand how those principles could be applied to the orphanage, and many ideas began to formulate in her mind about how she could make the place better. She enjoyed that feeling very much.

Eric also awoke early and made his way out of the third-floor dorm, down the spiral staircase, across the main hallway, and along the corridor to the kitchen. He was still a little weary from the festive revelry but found that Mister Miller was already working when he arrived. Eric noticed that there were some new ingredients on the table.

"What are these?" Eric asked, rubbing his eyes and yawning.

"Sultanas and raisins," said Mister Miller.

He was stirring the large pot, a little more enthusiastically than usual.

"I had a hunt around for some ingredients to drop in."

There was a large tin which read *Evaporated Milk* next to the stove. The contents had been extracted leaving a sharp edge of metal around the cylinder.

"What's *evaporated milk*?" asked Eric, imagining that the liquid had somehow disappeared into the ether.

"It's long life milk," said Mister Miller. "Doesn't go off. We use it on the ships."

Eric then noticed that the oatmeal had a much creamier consistency than usual. Mister Miller took the sultanas and raisins and dropped a good amount into the pot, then finally scooped up a large cup of brown sugar and poured that in too.

"It was all just lying around, so it may as well get used," said Mister Miller matter-of-factly.

Eric took a spoon and sampled the contents of the pot. The gloopiness was gone, and instead there was a sweet, milky taste with the occasional burst of dried fruit.

"I think that's the best oatmeal I have ever had."

"Alright," said Mister Miller. "Let's get these back in the pantry."

As Eric heaved the bag of brown sugar off the table, he noticed Mister Miller's paper opened at the *Business* section. He let the sugar drop onto the table with a thud as he read the headline.

Santa Inc. Takeover Complete.

At his first opportunity, Eric ran all the way to Santa's office without stopping. He could hear the raised voices through the heavy wooden door of Santa's office from down the hall. He pushed it open and found Santa pacing up and down while Grubbs, the man with the bald head, and the woman in the grey suit sat quietly and listened. The look of distress was clear on Santa's face.

"He's done it," Santa called to Eric. "Max Rupee has bought Santa Inc.!"

Santa sat down. Then stood up again.

At just about the same time, out on Gansevoort Street, a man of about thirty years, stepped out of a large black car. He looked unassuming in his turtleneck sweater and khakis as he walked up the steps of Santa Inc. Inside, he took the elevator to the 77th floor.

When the doors opened, he stepped out and took a good look at the executive suite, with its plush carpets, big offices, and fancy pictures on the wall.

"Can I help you?" asked Martha, greeting him with the same surly tone that she had first used with Eric.

"My name is Max Rupee."

"I don't know any Max Rupee," she said. "Do you have an appointment?"

"I just bought this company," he said with a smile. "Please let Santa know that I would like to meet with him."

Max smiled. Martha picked up the phone.

"Someone called Max Rupee is here," she said.

She waited for a moment, listening carefully for instructions, and occasionally looking up at Max, then finally put the phone down.

"This way, Mr. Rupee, sir."

Martha showed Max to the boardroom. Max was in no hurry. He lingered in the hallway and peered into people's offices. He looked at the paintings on the wall. He even noticed the pile of the carpet beneath his feet.

"Would you like a coffee?" asked Martha.

"No thanks," said Max. "I'm cleansing."

Martha raised her eyebrows dismissively at that comment.

"Take a seat," she said. "Someone will be right in."

Max didn't take a seat. Instead he observed the magnificent vista of New York. He had always believed that he was destined for great things. It wasn't beyond the bounds of his thinking that one day he could own the entire city. Now he had just acquired his first major property in Manhattan.

"Mr. Rupee," came a voice.

Max turned around. It was Wormwood Grubbs. Santa had sent him in as an advance party. For once, he appeared to be unsettled.

"My apologies, but we were not expecting you."

Max smiled. "I know," he said.

Grubbs smiled cordially, but he too was unsure about how to proceed.

"Santa will be right in," he said.

Max's expression did not change. "That's okay," he said. "I can wait."

Max always reserved judgment until he was in full possession of the facts. There was only ever so much you could know about a business from the outside looking in. He simply turned back to the view.

When Max bought a company, and he had bought a few of them, he always showed up alone and unannounced on the first day. It was the only way to see where all the cracks were. How the place really operated before there was any time for window-dressing. If he was honest, he also enjoyed watching the panicked executives scrambling to organize themselves.

After some indeterminable period of time, the door to the boardroom opened.

A smile came across Max's face. "You must be Santa," he said, extending his hand.

"I am," said Santa, looking Max directly in the eye and shaking his hand with a firm grip.

"I'm Max," he said confidently.

"How can I help you?" asked Santa, sitting down at the head of the long table.

"I'd like to take a look around."

"Well, here it is," said Santa holding out his hands.

Max smiled.

"In my experience, the plush surroundings of the executives rarely represent the company that sits underneath them."

"It's a little difficult to do that right now. People are starting their workday," said Santa.

"I was so excited to become majority shareholder that I just couldn't wait. So I'd like to have a look around all the same," said Max with his omnipresent relaxed smile.

Max had chosen his words carefully, making it clear that Santa had little choice in the matter. Santa did not like the situation. Not one bit. But he also knew that there was little that he could do but comply with Max's request.

"Wormwood!" Santa called out.

Grubbs, who was hovering behind the door and doing his best to eavesdrop on the conversation, appeared.

"Give Max the tour."

A Plan

Max spent the rest of the day looking around Santa Inc. He started on the 77th floor and made his way down through every level. He spoke to the people that worked on the floors——Linda and Gopal, with Shen and Yolanda, Larry and Harry. Like Eric, Max also possessed the gift that enabled him to see the entire company as a whole, operated by many but ultimately as one single unit.

He was already familiar with the company, after all he had first taken an ownership interest in it some time ago. But he often found that it was not until he started talking with people that the truth of the place really came through. Santa, on the other hand, could do nothing but pace up and down all day long. He cut a somewhat forlorn figure as he stared glumly out of his office window during the periods when the pacing stopped.

"I don't know what to do," said Santa. "The barbarians have broken through the gates."

For once Eric was not sure of what to say either. The fate of Santa Inc. now lay in other hands.

In the late afternoon, Max returned to the 77th floor. He was very courteous and waited until Santa was ready to see him. He, Eric, and Grubbs had been discussing the options. Max strolled into Santa's office and sat down, like he was on vacation or a day off.

"This really is a great view," he said.

"Years of hard work got me this view," Santa said proudly.

"I don't doubt it," said Max. "You have built an impressive company here."

Santa nodded, uncomfortable with the compliment.

"But times change, and now you are faced with an organization that's out of date, inefficient, and losing money."

"Now wait just a second..."

Max's composed demeanor did not change. He had expected that reaction from Santa. He had seen it often in leaders who had stopped being able to see their companies as anything but their own darling babies. He patiently listened to Santa justify why his company was still great.

"I don't like fancy offices," stated Max after Santa was done. "You know why?"

Santa felt the hairs on the back of his neck bristle.

"Please tell me."

"Because I've found that the fancier the office, the less anyone who works in it really knows what's going on in the company below."

"I know plenty about what's going on in my company," protested Santa.

"Half of this building is empty," said Max. "It's filled with scrap wood, and old toys that no one wants. This city has the most expensive buildings in the world, and you've got space to spare. Your production lines are a hundred years old."

"We're trying to modernize them, but the elves..."

"There are antelopes on the third floor," Max cut in.

"They're reindeer," protested Santa.

"They have no place in this building," said Max, his ruthless streak suddenly slicing through his easy-going exterior. "Things are going to change around here."

He pulled his phone from his pocket and held it aloft.

"This is what kids want these days," he said. "This can give them everything they want. They want to be a pirate? This is for them. They want to race cars? Or play soccer? This is for them.

They want to dress up, be a princess or a king or even an ante-lope? This is for them."

Max looked around the room to make his point clear.

"This," he said, looking at the phone, "is the future."

"This is Santa Inc." said Santa. "We make toys."

"Made toys," corrected Max. "But I'm here to make money."

Grubbs' eyes lit up at those words.

"The factory goes," said Max. "Who has a factory in Man-hattan? That's ridiculous. We get a team of coders in to start de-veloping mobile games. The best team that money can buy. We'll keep the back office and move to a co-working space in a cheaper area. We re-launch Santa Inc. for the twenty-first century."

"And how can we afford to do that?"

"Sell the building," said Max.

"No way," said Santa.

"We'll keep the top floor. That's it," said Max.

Santa was out of ideas and out of time. In that moment, Eric knew that Santa Inc. would change forever, that the great old building that Huxley and the elves had constructed would be no more. Eric didn't want to see that happen. He had come to love that place dearly. He thought and thought and thought. He wracked his brains. And then an idea came to him and he saw that there was perhaps just one shot left to save Santa Inc. A plan quickly formulated in his mind.

"There's one thing that you don't know about," said Eric.

Max turned his attention to Eric.

"I didn't even mention the child labor," he said. "I don't even want to go there."

Eric proceeded undeterred.

"We have been working on a top-secret project," he an-nounced. "The greatest toy that the world has ever seen. A toy so amazing, so fantastic that every child, big and small, boy or girl, will demand one. A toy that will sell year-round, not just at Christmas, and by the million!"

Santa looked at Eric, and in that moment, he too saw that this was his last shot.

"Yes!" cried Santa, quickly following Eric's lead. "That's exactly it. This thing is going to blow up. It will be huge."

Max thought for a moment.

"There's no time for that," he said.

"It's already finished," said Eric with a smile. "Done. Complete. Ready for market. The feedback is through the roof. But we're going to need this factory to produce it."

"What is it?" asked Max.

Santa turned to Eric, hoping for a good answer.

"Come back tomorrow and we will show you."

Max looked at Santa and Eric. Despite the fact that he was set on his plan, he had also learned to accept that in the twists and turns of business, opportunities often presented themselves in the least obvious ways. He was planning to build a company to last a hundred years, and as a consequence, twenty-four hours was not a lot of time to lose.

"Alright then," he said. "I will see you tomorrow."

Max left.

"What's the plan?" asked Santa.

"No time for that," said Eric, already running out of the door. "I'll be back."

Eric took the luge from the 77th floor to Huxley's lab. As he rocketed through the building, he carried a sense of urgency about his task. He couldn't wait to tell the Professor about the important role he was about to play in the future of Santa Inc. Huxley was working away at his drafting table, pencil in hand, as Eric whizzed into the basement and screeched to a halt.

"Professor!" called Eric.

He tried to jump out of the luge, then realized that he was still strapped in.

"What is it?" said Huxley.

"Santa Inc. needs a new toy," said Eric, straining to unbuckle himself.

Huxley, too involved with his work, was only half listening.

"I promised Max that I would bring him a new toy. This is your chance. The fate of the company depends on it."

Eric ran over to the drafting table.

"Young man, I have no idea what you are talking about," said the old professor without looking up.

Eric started again.

"Max Rupee has taken control of Santa Inc. He's going to make games for phones. No more toys. He's going to sell the building."

"Who is Max Rupee?" questioned Huxley.

Eric took a deep breath and told Huxley the entire story from the start. A look of recognition crossed the old professor's face as he slowly pieced together what Eric was saying.

"You told Santa that you could bring him a brand new toy?" he asked when Eric was done.

"Not any toy. The best toy that the world has ever seen. One of your toys."

Now the information truly started to percolate in Huxley's brain.

"And when are you planning to deliver this marvel?"

"Tomorrow."

"Tomorrow!" Huxley leapt out of his seat. "You want me to present the best toy that the world has ever seen, tomorrow?"

Eric filled up the kettle in the kitchenette. Huxley began to pace frantically around, muttering to himself about ridiculousness and hair-brained flights of fantasy. Eric waited patiently while the water slowly came to a boil.

"This is a nightmare of gargantuan proportions," declared Huxley.

"Why?" asked Eric.

He took a tea bag from the little box and dropped it into the pot, added the boiling water, put the lid on, and placed the tea cozy over the top. Then he moved it to the table, carefully noting the time on the clock. Eventually Huxley stopped and looked directly at Eric.

"How can I possibly succeed at this insurmountable task that you have laid down before me? How can I produce the greatest toy ever made?"

"Because you already have hundreds of designs. Just pick the best one."

"They're not good enough!" Huxley replied, his voice rising higher.

"It's great," said Eric.

"How could you do this to me?" he continued.

"Professor Huxley, now is your time. Santa needs you. Otherwise, he will lose everything. You have spent your entire life working on this. Who else is better for the job? What better time than now?"

Huxley thrust his hand against his forehead. Eric found a clean cup and saucer and placed them on the table, then located the biscuits and placed four of them onto a plate——two Jammy Dodgers and two Bourbon Biscuits. He placed the plate next to the pot then sat down to wait. Huxley put a biscuit in his mouth and continued muttering about impossibilities.

"Professor," said Eric. "How long were you planning on waiting until you were ready to show them what you could do?"

Huxley stopped again.

"Forever!" he shouted.

The old professor was quite perturbed. He finally sat down and picked up the tea. As he brought the cup to his mouth, another thought crossed his mind.

"Did you tell them about me? Did you tell them about this place?"

"Max is going to sell this building if we don't come up with a toy. There will be no toy laboratory if we cannot convince him to keep making toys."

Eric did not know how he could make the severity of the situation any clearer.

"I'm sorry," said Huxley. "I cannot help you."

Laksa

Eric was passing the office on his way to the kitchen, his thoughts consumed by the unfolding drama in the neighboring building.

"Eric," came a voice from inside.

It was Sister Christine. Eric stopped and turned, hovering by the door. She sat at her desk. The office was neatly organized and there was nothing in front of her but a pen, a notepad, and a calculator, a measurable difference to the cluttered mess of old. Sister Christine appeared different too. She sat up a little straighter and there was a visible confidence about her. She looked at Eric for a moment, as though trying to figure something out.

"I wanted to say thank you," she said finally.

"For what?" asked Eric.

"For helping me. Our books are in order, the bills are paid, we even have a few dollars to spare. The boys don't know it, but you have helped them all. For that you deserve all of our thanks."

"You're welcome," said Eric casually.

"And look at this," she continued. A bright smile appeared on her face. "Some generous soul left us a check. It's a lot of money too." She held Eric's check up with delight.

"Wow," said Eric. "That's great!"

He turned to resume his walk to the kitchen, but Sister Christine wasn't done.

"How did you figure all of this out?" she asked. "The bookkeeping. The filing. The bills."

Eric paused for a moment.

"I don't think you would believe me if I told you," he said eventually.

"Try me," said Sister Christine.

"Sister, I don't really want to get in more trouble."

"You will not get in any trouble," Sister Christine assured him.

Eric waited for a moment, weighing up the situation in his mind. But looking at Sister Christine, he felt sure that she would honor her word.

"I got a job working at Santa Inc."

"Santa Inc.?"

"That's Santa's company. He makes toys there. Well, the elves make the toys. Santa runs the place. They do a lot of business. And Gopal is studying for a Master's in Business Administration. He's the one with the books."

Sister didn't know who Gopal was.

"Where is this Santa Inc. company?" she asked.

"Next door," said Eric. "And that check that you are holding is my paycheck."

Sister Christine suddenly had a strange feeling about Eric. She couldn't quite discern it, but it was there. Then something strange happened. She began to laugh. And Eric laughed too. It felt good to laugh and it happened so rarely for her. It was like a release of energy that had been building up inside her.

"I brought you another book," said Eric eventually.

Eric placed a book on the table entitled *Getting Ahead in Real Estate*.

"Just in case you finished the others."

A little smile came to Sister Christine's face. She realized that she liked Eric. He had a good heart, despite his fanciful stories.

"On your way," she said.

As Eric approached the kitchen, he noticed that an unfamiliar aroma was emanating from between the doors. When he pushed the doors open, the smell became even more intense. A range of fresh ingredients were laid out on the large kitchen table. Mister Miller was chopping furiously fast, the blade missing his fingers by millimeters.

"What is all this stuff?" asked Eric, looking at the assorted produce.

"Garlic. Lemongrass. Coriander."

Mister Miller took the vegetable that he had just chopped and dropped it into a small pot that was bubbling away on the stove. Eric peered inside. Its contents didn't look too different to the usual lunchtime fare. It was the same consistency, maybe a little yellower in color than usual with an oily red film on top.

"Is this lunch?" asked Eric.

"No," said Mister Miller. "It's Laksa!"

Mister Miller handed him a small piece of chopped green vegetable.

"Try it," he said.

Eric looked at it, smelled it, and then placed it into his mouth.

"What is it?" he asked as he crunched down.

In seconds, an intense heat built in his mouth. It started on his tongue and worked its way down through his gums then up to his nose.

"I think something's wrong," spluttered Eric. "It hurts."

"That's a chili," said Mister Miller, letting out one of his guttural laughs.

Eric ran to the sink, jammed his face under the faucet, and let the cool water run into his mouth. The pain seared the soft flesh as he let the cool water run over it. Mister Miller roared with laughter. It took about ten minutes for the pain to finally dissipate. Now Eric understood what the other boys had experienced when he had added the chili.

"Sorry, young fella," said the old cook. "Couldn't resist."

He walked over to the stove and gave it a stir.

"Laksa is the food of Indonesia," he said. "Of jungles. And pirates. And storms so fierce that you never thought you would see land again. And beaches so beautiful you would never want to leave."

He took some noodles and dropped them into the pot.

"This was all you," said Mister Miller.

"What do you mean?" asked Eric.

"Those spices that you started throwing into my pot. The ones you dropped in without my knowing. I haven't so much as gotten a whiff of those in years. But when I smelled them, and when I tasted them, even in that disgusting swamp water that you boys eat, that started something, something within me that I thought was long gone."

Mister Miller took a large bound book on the shelf. He opened it, revealing page after page of hand-written notes, recipes, and stories.

"This is the journal of my life on the sea. You see, I wasn't just your average ship's cook. I was on an exploration of food from all over the world. That work has laid dormant on that shelf for many years. I almost forgot about it. I wanted to forget about it, but I could never bring myself to throw it away. Last night I took it down and read it from cover to cover."

"You did?"

"Yes. And I remembered."

"Remembered what?"

"I remembered why I love to cook," he said in a quiet but excited voice.

Mister Miller paused. Eric sensed that this was an important moment for him, so he decided to wait and see what he had to say.

"Ever since I was just a boy, no bigger than you, I wanted to see the world through its food. I wanted to live within the different cultures and learn their ways of cooking. I wanted to know their ingredients, the flavors, their methods. So I set off to sea at fifteen years old to learn. My apprenticeship lasted twenty years and took me from Singapore to Marseille, from Buenos Aires to Cape Town. And I wrote it all down, very carefully. My dream was to one day return to New York City and open the greatest restaurant the city had ever known, a place where you could circumnavigate the earth in an evening, where I could share my experiences of traveling the globe sampling the most incredible foods the world had to offer."

"And what happened?"

"I did it. I opened my restaurant to great fanfare. There were celebrities and socialites, Wall Street bankers and politicians. The great and the good. And the not so good. We got great reviews. I was the toast of this town."

"Wow," said Eric. "That sounds fantastic."

"Six months later we closed."

"Closed?"

Eric couldn't believe it.

"Closed," repeated Mister Miller. "You see, I knew everything there was to know about food, about cuisine, about cooking for people, about the artistry of taste. But I didn't know a thing about business."

Suddenly it all made sense.

"Business is tough," said Eric knowingly.

Mister Miller nodded his head in resigned agreement.

"Business is tough."

There was a moment's pause as Eric and Mister Miller reflected on that statement. They had both come to know it in their own ways and could very much attest to its truth.

"After that," said Mister Miller, "it was as though a light had been turned out. Overnight I lost all interest in the things that had been my passion. I didn't care if I never saw another clove of garlic or stem of lemongrass again. I lost everything in that restaurant. Everything except for a few jars of spices and my journals. I didn't have a penny to my name. So I looked for a job. But no one wanted to hire me. Until I saw a small advertisement for a cook at Our Lady of Mercy Orphanage. I didn't want to be a cook anymore. But I had no choice. It was the only thing I knew. So I gave nothing to it. My heart was broken."

Mister Miller paused again.

"That was until you arrived. I don't know how you did it, but you changed everything once more."

Eric took a small spoon and dipped it into the pot. He brought the fiery liquid to his mouth. The taste was even more intense than the smell. There were flavors that he had never even conceived of, nothing like garlic powder in an otherwise tasteless stew. It was as though a completely new universe of flavor had opened up in front of him. There was an energy coursing through Mister Miller that could not be contained. He was grinning from ear to ear.

"I'm ready to cook again."

The Perfect Toy

J ust as Santa Inc. was in turmoil, a wave of calm descended upon Our Lady of Mercy Orphanage. It was quite palpable. There were no pointless fights. No stomping on people's feet. No switching bowls of food at dinner. Just a sense of tranquility. The boys seemed to enjoy it, like sailors on a becalmed sea after a long and rough voyage.

Classes, chores, and recess all proceeded without a fuss. Maybe it was because their bellies were full of good food, or because Kevin O'Malley had put the fear into them, but things were immeasurably better inside that old building.

Lucius and Clive had become better friends too. Clive didn't have any stories to tell or adventures to recount, so Lucius found himself in the odd position of doing most of the talking. This gave Lucius a growing confidence that he had not possessed before. It was during this time, while the new friends were going about their chores, that Lucius decided to tell Clive a story.

"You know that building," he said pointing to Santa Inc. "Eric works in there."

"Really?" said Clive.

"Yes," said Lucius. "He gets there through a grate in the basement."

Lucius had never told a story before, but it was in that moment that he got his first glimpse at the secret power that they could hold.

Sister Prudence noticed the change at the orphanage too. She could not quite describe it, but she knew that all was not as it should be. She didn't like it. She was suspicious, and the otherwise calm atmosphere gave her an uneasy feeling. She set about trying to get to the root of the problem. She watched the boys carefully in class. She observed them during recess and dinner. She spied on them in the Rec. They were too well behaved.

Like a bloodhound, she picked up the scent of something that was not quite right. Something subtle and not easily defined. But the trail went cold. The Sister returned to the office, closed the door, and sat down in her chair. She did not like it at all. There was something deep in her old bones that told her so.

She stared at the wooden carving of Jesus Christ, then her eyes scanned across the room, and she noticed for the first time that Sister Christine's desk was remarkably tidy. Her eyes were drawn to a stack of letters. The outbox. She stood up, reached across and picked up a handful of envelopes, reading the addresses one by one: the Gas Company, the Water Company, and the Electric company. She placed them back down, her eyes scanning about for clues.

She was drawn to the drawers at the side of the desk. She had no compunction about opening them up, searching through them, moving papers and stationery. Then she laid her hand on something different. She pulled it out. A book. Tucked away. Almost designed to be concealed.

"Getting Ahead in Real Estate," she read aloud.

The lines on her face creased a little deeper.

In his lab, Huxley sat at his drafting table. But he couldn't work. He couldn't concentrate. He was gripped by a terrible dilemma. He knew very well the gravity of the situation that Santa Inc. was facing. He desperately wanted to help, but at the same time he felt completely stuck. He stood and walked to his kitchenette, but even the thought of tea was unappealing. He knew that this was his moment, that now and only now was his time, but he also felt unprepared and not ready for the world. That created within him a great anxiety. When Eric came shooting out of the air duct, it was a welcome relief to sitting with his own thoughts.

"Professor?" asked Eric, getting up off the bed.

"Hello," he said forlornly.

"I came to see if I could help."

"I don't think anyone can help," said Huxley.

"I could try," suggested Eric.

Huxley eased himself down to the table.

"My boy," he said. "I have been deluding myself for a long time. I have been preoccupied in my workshop while the world above has passed by. I've grown so used to it. No deadlines. No opinions. Just the endless potential to create something great."

Huxley sighed.

"The truth is I am scared," he said.

"Scared of what?"

"Scared that the world will not think that I am great. That people will not like my toys. That they will think that I am out of touch. That I am an old man with nothing but harebrained ideas."

"I like your ideas," said Eric.

Eric made Huxley a nice cup of tea, and the old professor summoned just enough energy to drink it. Eric walked around the toy laboratory thinking that maybe he would never see it again. As he dragged his finger along a dusty shelf, he focused for a moment on the old wooden toys that were set upon it. There was a motor car made of metal, a wooden train, and a horse made from wood that could articulate every joint and limb of its body. He looked up at the paints stacked up to the ceiling upon rows and rows of shelves, every color neatly ordered across the spectrum from light to dark.

He decided to hang around in the toy laboratory to offer Huxley some kind of moral support but soon found that he was bored. As Eric returned to the kitchenette, he noticed Huxley's jacket hanging on a rack with a couple of old coat-hangers to keep it company. Eric smiled as he took one of the coat-hangers in his hands. He held it forward and allowed it to become a bow. Then he searched the room for an appropriate target and spotted one of the paint cans on the top shelf. He pulled an arrow from its quiver and loaded it into the bowstring. Then closing one eye, he focused on the target. Whoosh! He let the arrow fly.

"Bullseye!" he called out.

Direct hit.

Huxley looked up from the table, peering over his glasses. Eric did not see him. Instead, he focused on his next shot. He pulled another imaginary arrow out and drew the string back. This time he swiveled his body a little and directed his aim toward the wooden figure. He carefully centered the arrow as Huxley watched. Once again, he let it fly.

"Ah!" he called out, noting that the shot had been unsuccessful.

"What are you doing?" asked Huxley.

"Target practice."

Huxley observed more closely as Eric continued to find new targets and repeated the process. His game became more elaborate as he crouched behind tables and took more and more difficult shots. Eventually, Huxley abandoned his tea altogether to more keenly observe. Eric took the coat-hanger and zip lined from one side of the room to the other with it.

"Remarkable," whispered Huxley.

Something was happening inside the old professor's mind. A thought was brewing like a pot of tea as Eric continued to use the coat-hanger in all manner of ways.

"By George! That's it!" called Huxley.

Eric stopped as Huxley jumped up from his chair, an ecstatic smile across his face.

"That's it," he repeated.

He danced over to Eric and took the coat-hanger from his hand. He held it aloft.

"This is it!" he called again. "It's all clear to me now."

"That's mine," said Eric. "Get your own."

"Don't you see?" he asked. "This is just an ordinary coat-hanger. Nothing special at all. But in the hands of a young, bright mind, it's a bow for an arrow. It's a zip line. It's a motorbike. It's the hook on a pirate's hand. Do you not see? It's everything and anything that you want it to be."

Huxley chuckled joyfully.

"The greatest toy in the world is not one single thing. Not an object at all. It is... imagination."

Now Eric started to understand.

"All this time, I have been trying to invent something new, the greatest toy known to man, and it has vexed me to the moon and back, provided me with more sleepiness nights than I care to recall," said Huxley. "And all this time I was looking in the wrong place."

Huxley tapped lightly on Eric's head.

"It was up here the whole time. All we need to do is stimulate the imagination and we can be anyone we want to be——travel to faraway lands, ride motorbikes across deserts, and whoosh through forest canopies."

Big Ideas

It was very unusual for the Sisters to spend any time in the kitchen at all, but when Mister Miller appeared from the pantry where he had spent much of the afternoon cataloguing his spices, he found Sister Christine sitting at the small table.

"Hello, Sister Christine," he said. "What brings you here?"

"There's been a remarkable change in the boys of late," she said. "I do wonder what has been the cause of this abrupt shift in behavior."

"Hard to say," said Mister Miller. "Maybe there's something in the air."

"I believe that you have found some way to improve the food here" she added.

"Not me," said Mister Miller. "Not at first anyway. It was the boy."

"How do you mean?" asked Sister Christine.

"He just dropped a few spices in the stew."

"How did he do it?"

Mister Miller thought for a moment.

"He just has a way of getting things done. You know, he got us free food from the delivery company."

"There is something about him, but I can't quite figure out what it is. All he does is ask questions," said Sister Christine.

"But what good questions they are," noted Mister Miller.

Sister Christine thought carefully about Mister Miller's words and concluded that he was right.

"I hope you don't think me rude, Sister, but as you're here, I may as well speak my mind."

"Go ahead."

"It's the boys," he started. "They have it real bad, cooped up like chickens day and night. That ain't right for growing boys. And they need to know that someone cares about them. Take Christmas Day. Not even a stick o' gum for a present. That's no way to live."

He shook his head regretfully.

"Mister Miller, I happen to agree with you," said Sister Christine.

"You do?"

"Boys are not built to sit at desks for hours. That's not how they learn. They learn by getting their hands on things, by building and smashing things and seeing how things fit together. And they need fresh air. And dirt."

"Well Amen to that," said Mister Miller.

But Sister Christine was not done. The conversation had stirred in her a feeling that she had suppressed for many long years.

"If I had my way," she continued, "we would do away with these old classrooms altogether. We would surround ourselves with interesting and stimulating things and take advantage of the wonderful learning opportunities that this city has to offer, like the museums, the music, the art galleries, architecture, and history. Instead of having our education scratched onto an ancient chalkboard, we would experience it in all its glorious color."

Sister Christine suddenly caught herself.

"I'm sorry, Mister Miller. I did not mean to speak out of turn either. I just came to tell you that I found a few extra dollars to put toward food next month. Some generous soul made a large donation."

"Thank you, Sister," said Mister Miller. "I'm sure it will help."

Sister Christine stood up to leave.

"Sister," added Mister Miller. "I believe that you could do all those things if you put your mind to it."

When Sister Christine left the kitchen, she felt that a charge of energy was pulsing through her. It was undeniable and stronger than it had been for a long time, as though her conversation had crystalized an idea in her mind. She wanted to do something, to act in some way. As she reached her office, she saw Eric coming down the stairs.

"Come here please," she said in her officious tone.

Eric made his way across the hall to the office.

"I would like you to help me think of ways to make some money," she said. "Seeing as you appear to know about these things."

"Why?" said Eric.

"I want to give this place a coat of paint. Maybe new windows," said Sister Christine. "Saving money will only get us so far."

"Did you know that New York City has some of the most expensive buildings in the world?" said Eric. "Maybe this building is worth something?"

"I can't see that," said Sister Christine.

Eric shrugged.

"We could do chores for other people?" he suggested. "We're good at chores."

"Now that's a good idea," said Sister Christine.

"We could launder, and press shirts, and polish shoes."

"Perfect."

"It would be nice to get a whiteboard and new chairs. Or new desks," said Eric.

"And the water pipes. The boiler. And the electrics."

"What about some new games for the Rec?"

Sister Christine sat back in her chair. Her smile disappeared.

"There's so much that we need," she said.

For a few moments, Eric and Sister Christine sat in silence, thinking to themselves about all the things they might buy if money were no concern.

"Sister Christine, where are you from?"

That question took Sister Christine by surprise. A thousand memories flooded back to her, memories that had laid dormant for so long, too many to sift through in the time she had to answer.

"I'm from Greenport," she said finally.

"Where's that?" asked Eric.

"It's way out on Long Island," she said. "Out of the city, due east, down the country roads until the dunes and the sands converge on each side and you cannot go any further. Then you're there."

"What's it like?" asked Eric.

"It's beautiful," she said. "There are green fields and long white beaches. There's a port where the fishing boats bring in their catch and a breeze that blows in off the Atlantic that invigorates the senses."

Sister Christine was quite taken with that thought, and her words stirred even more memories, times spent as a child that were carefree and full of adventure.

"Why did you leave?" asked Eric.

"I had a calling."

"From who?"

"From God," said Sister Christine.

"Isn't there an orphanage there?" asked Eric.

"No," said Sister Christine with a smile.

She observed that Eric seemed to be a little puzzled, as though the idea of her not being in an orphanage was too difficult to comprehend.

"Greenport is where I grew up," she said.

"With a family?" asked Eric.

"Yes."

"That sounds nice," said Eric. "Do they still live there?"

Sister Christine shook her head.

After Eric left, Sister Christine sat in her chair for a while longer. She wasn't prone to long periods of contemplation, but the conversation had affected her quite deeply. It had transported her back to a time and a place that she had almost forgotten, or certainly long put out of her mind. For some time, she allowed the memories to come to her, watching each one of them carefully before it moved on, allowing them to linger and then dance away into nothingness. It was only after some unknown time had passed that she felt a cold, dark fog descend upon the room, not in keeping with those memories at all, something malevolent and twisted.

Sister Prudence stood in the doorway. "What are you doing?" she asked.

Sister Christine gathered herself. "Just finishing up," she said, trying to smile.

Sister Prudence waited in silence for a moment, observing carefully for any signs of weakness. "What's this?" she asked, holding *Getting Ahead in Real Estate* aloft. Sister Christine looked at it silently as a pang of fear ran through her.

"I... I was... It's a book," she stuttered.

"I can see that. Isn't there another more important book that you should be reading?" inquired Sister Prudence.

"It was just for interest. I have our accounts in order. Everything is paid and up to date."

Sister Christine smiled, but Sister Prudence was not pleased at all.

"I just thought..." continued Sister Christine, but then she hesitated. Sister Prudence was driving that stare into her that could melt rock.

"Thought what?" she asked dismissively.

"I just thought maybe if we did things a little differently here that we could make life better for the boys, maybe try to make the food better and even make some repairs."

"Must you be so foolish, Sister? This orphanage has stood here for more than one hundred years and it will stand for another hundred without your naïve dreaming. Now, where did this book come from?"

Sister Christine once again stuttered. She couldn't tell the truth. She couldn't implicate Eric or even let it be known that he was the one who had given her the book.

"I found it," she said eventually.

"Found it?" said Sister Prudence doubtfully. "Where?"

"In the basement."

Sister Christine felt terrible about lying. Sister Prudence stared at her once more through a long-drawn silence. Then she looked at the book one last time, reading each word in the title.

"This is not for you," said Sister Prudence with a particularly harsh tone.

She threw it in the garbage can by her desk and left.

Coat-Hanger

Huxley put his best jacket on and carefully tied his bow tie so that it was perfectly symmetrical on both sides. He combed his hair, making sure that there was not a single stray out of place. Then he looked at himself in the mirror. He seemed older than he remembered.

"Here goes nothing, old chap," he said to himself.

He and Eric rode the main elevator to the 77th floor, coat-hanger in hand.

Soon the doors pinged open to the executive suite.

"You'll be fine," said Eric with a smile.

Huxley took a deep breath and then stepped out onto the thick carpet.

"Good morning, Martha," said Eric without breaking stride.

"Good morning, Eric."

When they reached Santa's office, Eric tapped on the door. Huxley fiddled with his bow tie again, even though there was nothing wrong with it.

"Come in," called Santa.

Eric pushed the door open and they walked in.

"Hello, Santa," said Huxley.

"Hello, Owen," said Santa with a smile.

Both of them recognized that it was a big moment but neither wanted to let their guard down.

"It's been a long time," said Huxley.

"You've come to save us. Just in the nick of time."

For a few moments the three of them stood somewhat awkwardly together. There was so much that Huxley and Santa could talk about, and yet there was something that prevented them from saying anything. Eric thought that a little odd, but they had a job to do and there was no time for dallying.

"Did you want to hang up your jacket?" asked Santa.

"Pardon me?" said Huxley at the odd question.

Santa motioned toward the coat-hanger in Huxley's hand.

"No, no," Huxley replied.

They sat down at Santa's desk.

"So," said Santa expectantly.

"Professor Huxley has come up with a great idea," said Eric.

"Let's hear it then."

"For a very long time, I've been toiling away in my laboratory," said Huxley. "You may think that I was living out my senior years in relaxation, but the reality could not be further from the truth. I have been trying to develop a toy so magnificent, so universally lauded that it would send Santa Inc. back to the top. But unfortunately, I must say that I failed in this endeavor. That was until young Eric here showed me a completely different way of observing the challenge. Then it became quite simple. You see, the most perfect toy conceivable is not a physical object at all. It is within the imagination of a child."

At that point Huxley handed the coat-hanger to Santa. He took it, rather confused, and looked at it for a moment.

"To you and me," Huxley continued, "this may appear to be nothing more than a mundane household item. But in the hands of a young boy with an active imagination, it is a bow, the handlebars of a motor bike, a zip line, and even the hooked hand of a pirate captain."

Huxley paused and waited for a reaction from Santa. Santa inspected the coat-hanger from a number of angles.

"It's a coat-hanger, though, right?" he asked eventually.

"Yes, it is."

Eric nodded in agreement.

"But it's so much more. It's anything that we want it to be, a conduit for a child's fertile mind."

Santa let out a long sigh. He put his head in his hands. There was a knock at the door. It was Martha.

"Mr. Rupee has arrived. He's waiting in the boardroom."

"Alright," said Santa rising to his feet. "We're going with a coat-hanger."

The boardroom filled quickly. There was an odd mix of Max's people, who were all young and casually dressed, and the Santa Inc. executives dressed in their heavy suits and suffocating ties. Santa was quiet and apprehensive. Eric was confident. He knew that Huxley's idea was very good. There was an undeniable and singular truth about it. There were greetings. Santa and Max shook hands. Huxley said hello to some of the executives that he knew. They were all surprised to see him.

"I thought you had passed away," said the man with the bald head.

Santa took his seat at the head of the large boardroom table and tapped his fingers against the polished wood, anxiously waiting for the meeting to start. Eric and Huxley sat off to the side, slightly behind Santa. Max took his seat at the opposite end of the table. Eventually, there were no seats left and the remaining stragglers had to stand up against the wall.

Santa looked around at the assembled faces. Their expressions gave little away, and it was impossible to tell if they were with him or not. He decided to continue, regardless.

"Colleagues, as you know, this company has had a bumpy ride over the last few years. But we have a plan to turn things around. Professor Owen Huxley has been working for many years to design the greatest toy that the world has ever seen, a toy that can reach every child across every continent. We believe that we have done that. Professor." Santa motioned for Huxley to take over, and Eric gave the professor a supportive nod.

Huxley took a step forward. Those seated at the table sat up a little taller to get a first look at the exciting new product. Huxley's palms were clammy, and a bead of sweat rolled down his forehead. It had been so long since he had faced a boardroom full of people.

"Ladies and gentlemen," he announced. "This toy is a coat-hanger. I mean, this is the greatest coat-hanger the world has ever seen. I've been working on this for the last twenty years."

There was silence, and then confused glances shot about the room. Huxley felt his mouth quickly drying up.

Santa took the coat-hanger from Huxley as the old professor sat down.

"Let me try to explain. To you, this may appear to be nothing more than a simple household object. Indeed, that is what appeared to me when I first saw it myself. But that's because as adults we have learned to see the world through blinkers, only perceiving what is, rather than what can be. You see, we have been making products for children to play with: a car, a plane, a dollhouse. Smaller versions of real life. Now we can replicate any product imaginable. But this is in fact unnecessary. You see, a child's imagination is rich enough to create something from nothing. This coat-hanger that you can only imagine hanging your shirt on and placing in a closet, can actually be a motorbike, or a zip line, or the hook of a pirate's severed arm."

Santa held the coat-hanger like a hook and swiped it at the man with the bald head who lurched back in shock. Santa looked at each one of them in turn, his eyes scanning the room. Max looked on, curious but expressionless.

"This is cheap and easy to manufacture. Every child will want one."

After a few moments, the silence and lack of reaction became more uncomfortable, and even Santa's enthusiastic expression started to fade. Nobody wanted to say anything. They were so used to Santa being the leader of the company, but they also recognized that Max was their new boss, and they did not want to appear stupid in front of him.

"Could I take a closer look?" asked Max.

Santa passed the coat-hanger along. It went from person to person, making its way down the table toward him. When it finally arrived, Max took a hold of it and inspected it carefully. He looked at the metal handle and the wooden frame. He spun it around to observe it from different angles. Everyone waited. Huxley looked on nervously. Eric remained confident.

"It really is a coat-hanger," said Max.

Santa nodded. "Yes, it is. The beauty of this design is its simplicity."

Max handed the coat-hanger to the man next to him. It made its way back, person by person, along the opposite side of the table.

"Santa," said Max. "You have built this company from nothing to what we see today. You have brought some of the best-loved toys to the world for many years."

Max paused.

"But the world is changing," he continued. "Kids don't want the same things that they did twenty-five years ago. They want action. They want adventure. They want it to feel like it's real life. They don't want a coat-hanger."

Max looked around the table.

"Santa Inc. is going to dominate the games industry of the twenty-first century. Who's with me?"

A big cheer went up. Eric noted that Max had a way of pumping his people up and Grubbs was loudest of all.

When the meeting finished, Max found Santa.

"Perhaps we can talk somewhere privately," he suggested.

They walked back down the corridor. Max closed the door to Santa's office. There was a quietness to the room.

"I'm not the kind of guy to beat around the bush," said Max. "I have big plans for this place. You are Santa. You'll be the face of the company. That's one heck of a brand. But we're not making toys anymore. Those days are over."

Santa did not reply. But he knew he didn't want to be just a face. For the first time in his life, he sensed a creeping inevitability to his future. More importantly, he decided not to resist it.

"I can assure you," Max continued with a bright smile, "I am going to make you a lot of money."

But the appeal of making millions was completely lost to Santa. The whole idea in that moment held no value and no sway over him. The drive that had pushed him forward for so long ebbed away to nothing.

"No one can deny that you have built an incredible legacy here," Max continued. "But it's time to move on. The company needs a new direction. A new leader. That leader is me."

Spaghetti Bolognese

Eric pushed the doors to the kitchen open to start the dinner preparation. He was unusually tired from his day at Santa Inc. The large metal table that was always empty was stacked full of raw ingredients. There was a box of sweet-smelling fresh tomatoes, bulging cloves of garlic, basil leaves, bottles of olive oil, and more. Somewhere behind it all was Mister Miller, busily sorting through the bounty. He shot Eric an excitedly nervous grin.

"I went to the Italian market this morning. I talked with the owner about the olive oil, and we sampled each bottle. I held the tomatoes in my hands and felt their firmness. I smelled each clove of garlic for its aroma. I tasted the basil for its freshness."

By this time, Mister Miller's voice had almost turned to a laugh. He looked so happy.

"My boy," he continued. "I haven't felt so alive in many years."

There was a sprightliness about him that Eric had not seen before.

"Look at this," he said, reaching for a large round object that was wrapped in white paper.

He pulled the paper off revealing a wedge of yellowish-white cheese. He pushed a knife into it and sliced off a wafer-thin piece, then handed it to Eric.

"It's not spicy, is it?" asked Eric warily.

Mister Miller laughed heartily.

"Parmigiano-Reggiano," he declared in his best Italian accent.

Eric placed the cheese onto his tongue. Immediately he felt the flavors cascading through his taste buds.

"A little sweet, a little salty, a little fatty," said the old cook with a smile. "It cost more than a month's worth of that slop that we usually make, but you can't put a price on quality, can you?"

Next he revealed a large slab of meat, deep read in color.

"Look at this beautiful cut. We'll grind our own mince today," he continued. "That way we can ensure the exact texture that we desire."

Eric prodded it with his finger. It was quite different from the *Meat* that came in the can. Finally, Mister Miller held out his hands, as if to welcome an old friend that he had not seen in a long time: a large box of flour.

"Today we will make our own pasta. Every strand of spaghetti that is consumed will be borne from our own hands."

Eric could not help but be enthused by Mister Miller's passion for his work.

"There's a lot to do," he said. "No time for naps, no time to slink away to wherever you go when you think that I'm asleep." Mister Miller grinned knowingly.

They got to work. Eric chopped the tomatoes while Mister Miller ground down the beef with a meat grinder. All of the machines and tools that had laid dormant for so long were now placed into service. Mister Miller turned his old radio on, and the sound of opera piped out through the tiny speaker into the room. Mister Miller sang a few words as he worked. He looked happier and more content than Eric had ever seen him. His heavy gait and limp seemed to have magically disappeared.

When it came to the pasta, they worked together——first mixing the flour with the eggs and water to create the dough, then slowly kneading it in a giant bowl so that it gradually became more elastic. They ran the dough through the pasta maker over and over until it became ever longer and thinner. Mister Miller inspected every length of pasta. His attention to detail never wavered, and he would not pass a single strand until he had satisfied himself that it was exactly right. They then carefully folded it and placed it into the fridge. He stirred the pot of Bolognese sauce, gave it a quick taste, and then sat down at his table.

"I tell you, Eric," he said. "I feel more alive today than I have felt in many years."

Eric sat down opposite him. He looked at his flour-covered hands. He was tired from the hard work, but the kitchen was filled with such a wonderful aroma that it was hard not to feel good. He was very excited about the prospect of finally getting to eat this delicious meal again.

"It's been so long since I foraged about the city to find the right ingredients and talked all morning to the merchants over coffee. Today I really used my chopping board and knife, and tasted the food to make sure that the flavor was exactly as I wanted it. I tell you, boy, it has filled me with a wonderful sense that anything in life is possible."

Mister Miller filled a giant pot with water and brought it to the boil. Eric looked at the clock for the first time. They had been working hard all afternoon, but it had flown by as though no time had passed at all, and now there were just a few minutes before five.

"These boys will not know what's hit them," said Mister Miller with a chuckle.

The opera was still playing on the tiny radio.

"If you have never seen *La Traviata* performed *al fresco* in Firenze, you must put it on your list."

Eric nodded.

The doors to the cafeteria opened and the boys came bustling through.

"Let us get to work," Mister Miller announced, one purposeful finger in the air.

He dropped the first batch of pasta into the pot. Eric watched the boy's faces. There was a moment of surprise and then excitement among each one of them as the delicious smell permeated their senses for the first time. So unaccustomed were they to the endless possibilities of food that at first they did not know how to process it. But then, as the garlic and basil and tomato went dancing up their noses, they became quite excited and hurried along to the serving hatch.

The pasta bubbled and churned in the water, and soon Mister Miller pulled it out, letting the water drain off and then glugging an ample serving of olive oil on top. He distributed the first batch among the bowls and handed them to Eric in a miniature production line. Eric carefully ladled on the sauce, added the cheese, and passed the bowls through the hatch to a pair of expectant hands.

Eric had never seen an expression on a boy's face quite like those that he saw when each bowl of pasta was received. Each boy took his meal back to his table with a silent glee. When Kevin O'Malley appeared, Eric scooped an extra large serving of sauce into his bowl.

It took a few moments for Sister Prudence to notice that something was different. When she first entered the cafeteria, her grim expression did not change at all. Eric wondered if maybe she had no sense of smell. After all, how could she fail to recognize that this food was the stuff of magic? But as she walked down the aisles and saw more carefully just what the boys were eating, she finally noticed that the food was altogether changed.

Eric and Mister Miller got their process going at full speed. Eric had never seen those boys devour their dinners with such gusto. They had never experienced such fantastical and unctuous delights. Eric grinned at Mister Miller, and Mister Miller grinned back. Sister Prudence marched back to the serving hatch and stared into the nearly empty pot.

"What is that?" she demanded.

"It's Bolognese sauce," said Mister Miller.

Sister Prudence eyed the concoction with great suspicion. One of the boys put his hand in the air.

"What is it, Martin?" she asked.

"Please, Sister," he said, holding out his bowl. "Can I have some more?"

"Don't be greedy," she spat.

Martin sat back down. Dinner was over at record speed that night. Even if the older boys had wanted to switch bowls, there was no time to do so as their contents disappeared inside joyful bellies almost immediately. As the boys filed out of the cafeteria, they stared wistfully at that pot, wishing that they could all have just a little more.

When the last boy left, Mister Miller pulled out two plates and served out two very handsome portions.

"Come, my boy," he said. "Now, we shall dine."

He turned the little radio back on as they sat at the small table, ready to eat. Mister Miller grated a good portion of Parmesan cheese onto each plate, and it slowly melted in the sauce.

"Now," he said.

Eric thought that he might burst with anticipation, but Mister Miller was intent on speaking first.

"My young friend, I want to thank you from the bottom of my heart."

"For what?" asked Eric.

"You have given me back my passion. You have given me back my love. I wake up in the morning and all I think about is cooking. I go to bed at night thinking about it. I feel so full of life that I could burst. I thought it was lost forever."

Mister Miller held out his hand. Eric placed his hand in it.

"Thank you," he repeated with a warm smile.

The door to the kitchen swung open, and there stood Sister Prudence with her tiresome, mean face staring at them.

"Good evening, Sister," said Mister Miller. "Would you care to join us?"

"Turn that music off."

Mister Miller clicked the radio off as silence befell the room.

"This boy was sent to you as a punishment," said Sister Prudence, her voice rising. "Because he could not be trusted to be with the other boys. Now he dines on these indulgent foods. Just like the rest of them."

"Sister, the boys deserve a good meal once in a while," replied Mister Miller.

"They deserve nothing!" Sister Prudence shouted.

Her eyes noticed the pile of papers that had been placed on the counter. She walked over and picked them up.

"What is all this?" she asked.

"Receipts. For the food," replied Mister Miller.

She flicked through them.

"Is this how much money you spent on this meal?" she asked.

"You can't compromise on quality. The olive oil is first pressing. From Calabria," protested Mister Miller.

Eric noticed the vein in Sister Prudence's forehead that so often appeared in his presence was now pumping like a fire hose.

"Eric. Leave us," she ordered.

Eric looked at the delicious bowl of Spaghetti Bolognese that was so tantalizingly close. His stomach groaned with desire for it. He placed his hands on it to take with him.

"Leave it," ordered Sister Prudence.

Back to School

It was early morning. Eric rose before the others and made his way to the kitchen to begin his morning duties. As he reached the door to the kitchen, he was stopped dead in his tracks by the unmistakable voice of Sister Prudence.

"Eric."

She stood in the corridor where he had passed only moments before.

"What are you doing?" she asked.

"Going to the kitchen."

She moved forward without taking her eyes off him for a second. She could not help but find everything about Eric suspicious, and she scanned him up and down, probing for the truth.

"Your punishment has come to an end," she announced. "You will return to class immediately."

Return to class! The news was calamitous. Eric did not want to go back to class. Class meant being stuck under the watchful eyes of the Sisters all day and not going to Santa Inc. at all. It was a disaster.

"Mister Miller needs me. He needs my help," Eric pleaded.

"Mister Miller is no longer in the employ of Our Lady of Mercy Orphanage," said Sister Prudence.

"But, Sister Prudence..."

Eric looked at the old Sister's face and knew that she would not yield.

"Back to the dorm," ordered Sister Prudence. "Get ready for the day."

She watched as Eric trudged back up the stairs. Eric felt defeated. He didn't know what to do. How could he go back to boring classes after all that he had done? And what about his job? What about Santa Inc.? Santa needed him now more than ever.

Sister Christine made the oatmeal that day. There were plenty of glances exchanged during breakfast, as the boys tried to figure out what had happened. There was only one conclusion: The delicious Spaghetti Bolognese had somehow gotten Mister Miller fired.

"Maybe he's just taken a day off," whispered Paul hopefully.

"Or not feeling well," added Carl.

The boys desperately hoped that Mister Miller would return. Over the course of the morning, they managed to convince themselves that his departure was only temporary and that the good food would return very soon. Eric sat in class. It felt very strange to him, the old desk, the rickety chairs, and the hours of mind-numbing subject matter dispensed with all the verve of a hard-bristled brush. He pretended to pay attention, but his mind was elsewhere, consumed with thoughts of the future of the large building that stood not fifty feet away, of his colleagues, of Huxley, and of course, of Santa.

After class, as the weather was clement, the boys were allowed outside. Eric sat on the steps in the courtyard still wrapped in those same thoughts. Lucius and Clive were throwing the ball to each other nearby. Lucius looked over to Eric.

"Do you want to play with us?" he asked.

"No thanks," said Eric. "Terrible things are happening."

Lucius knew he didn't want to engage in the conversation. He just wanted to play ball, but he made the mistake of asking, "Why?"

Eric looked around furtively. Lucius threw the ball to Clive for the last time and walked over to Eric. He wanted to give his friend a chance. But Eric was too preoccupied.

"Because..." he said.

Eric's eyes shifted upward. Lucius followed, craning his neck upwards.

"What is it?" asked Lucius with curiosity.

"Up there," pointed Eric. "On the 77th floor. There's a man called Max Rupee. He's taken over Santa Inc. He's going to change it forever."

There was nothing to see, just the giant building standing tall against the cloudy sky.

"Now that you are back at school, why don't you just forget about that stuff?" asked Lucius.

Eric didn't answer. He just continued to look up at the neighboring building. After a few moments, Sister Christine appeared at the door.

"End of recess," she called out.

Lucius walked back to the door with a glum look on his face.

"What were you guys talking about?" asked Clive.

"Nothing," said Lucius.

"You looked like you were talking about something important," said Clive.

As they stepped inside, Lucius hesitated, but then he decided that he should tell his friend. Lucius felt a confusing mixture of hurt and exasperation with Eric, and he needed to share it with somebody.

"The thing is," he said, "Eric has a lot of crazy ideas."

"Tell me," said Clive.

Lucius sighed.

"Alright," he said. "But you can't tell anybody about this."

Just a little later, Eric and Lucius made their way around the dorms collecting the laundry. They hauled the baskets down the main stairs, bumping it all the way down to the bottom then through the large hallway and to the laundry room opposite the kitchen. Eric strained to look through the kitchen doors when he got close, but he couldn't see anything. He wondered where Mister Miller might be, where he had gone to. The two friends began to sort through the clothes and sheets, depositing them in different washers according to color. Eric was too consumed in his own thoughts to make any conversation, and it left Lucius feeling more hurt than ever.

Eventually Lucius felt compelled to speak up. "Eric. I'm not sure that we can be friends anymore," he said.

"Why?" asked Eric.

"Because you are never here. And even when you are here, you're not really here. Clive, he's here and he talks about normal things. And he needs a friend."

Eric looked at Lucius.

"I'm sorry," he said. "I know I haven't been around too much. And I know that you have been on your own."

Lucius shrugged. He didn't really know how to respond. All he knew was that he was tired of the way things were. He had lost his friends. That was real.

Dark Night in New York

Changes came to Santa Inc. quicker than anyone could have imagined. Hordes of young people dressed in hoodies and sneakers arrived with laptops and coffee. They sat on beanbags on the 77th floor staring blankly at their screens. When one of them brought a ping-pong table in, Martha got up and left. Max met with an architect and instructed her to knock all the walls out so that he could see every corner of the city.

There was a constant parade of real estate developers all eager to discuss the conversion of the building into offices and apartments. Huxley was given forty-eight hours to vacate the basement, and the elves were all served with termination of employment letters. The machines would be sold for scrap. Only Grubbs seemed happy to accommodate the new regime, sensing that there was indeed money to be made.

Santa sat in his office staring forlornly out of the window. Many hours passed and the sun slowly went down behind the buildings. He was in a reflective mood. He thought about how he had built the great company that sat beneath him, his time at the North Pole all those years ago, and the uprooting of everyone to come to the great city of New York in pursuit of a dream. He thought about the friends that had come and gone while chasing that dream: Huxley, the elves, and the reindeer. He thought about the people that he had replaced them with. People who were only interested in the pursuit of money. He didn't know those people and they didn't know him.

He realized that there was a hole within him, something that had been missing for a long time but that he had been too busy to pay any attention to. Now, in the solace of his office and suddenly with little to do but think, it became quite obvious. As the sun made its way through the winter sky and finally dipped below the buildings, he could not help but feel that it was also setting on his time in the city.

Eventually, he stood up and left his office. The entire building was quiet. He walked past the bean bags and the ping pong table to the elevator. Then he made his way to the 27th floor. He stepped out into the quiet office space and looked around. This was the company that he had built. He walked through the rows of desks and offices, then down another level to an almost identical office, then down again. He felt some pride about what he had achieved. It's no easy task to build a company, he thought to himself.

Santa took the elevator down to the factory floor. As the doors pinged open onto the expanse of concrete, one thing was most clear to him. Silence. Never before had he experienced silence in that place. There was always movement, always the sound of industry. Now there was nothing.

He looked at the elf lodge. Inside, all the elves were sleeping. They would soon be in need of new accommodations. Max would never let them stay. He thought back to their long history together. How he had gathered them at the North Pole, in that cold and wintry place, and taught each one of them his ways of building toys. They were all great friends back then, and he had sat side by side with them as they made the toys together. Now, in the silence of that cavernous factory, he wondered how it had come to the point where he could barely speak to them at all.

He wandered over to the stables. There in the semi-darkness, the reindeer huffed and puffed and clopped about. Santa placed his hands upon the wooden gate. One of them wandered over and pushed its wet nose against his face.

"Hello, boy," said Santa with a smile.

He had missed the smell of those animals and the way that they butted their heads lovingly against his when they saw him. They bore him no ill will. In fact, they were pleased to see him. He stroked their fur as their tails twitched. Where would the reindeer go? He turned and walked back toward the elevator.

His heart was heavy, and he felt a strange feeling in his body that he couldn't quite understand. It was a pulling sensation, almost magnetic, unlike anything that he had ever experienced before. He couldn't tell where it was leading him, although it was certainly present and growing stronger.

There was another door in the corner of the factory floor that was only just visible. Santa could just about make it out in the distance, but once seen, he recognized it immediately. Without thinking, he changed direction and began to walk straight toward it. His footsteps echoed out against the gloom of the midnight hour. When he reached the door, he placed his hand on it for a moment. He knew it well from a time long passed. As he opened it, it all came back to him. The luge.

A smile came to his face as he stepped inside and pressed the button, and the rattling of wheels began from somewhere above. Soon, the contraption rolled out of the tunnel and came to a stop in front of him. Santa, without hesitation, climbed aboard. He adjusted his seat a little, shifted into a comfortable position and released the brake. The luge began to roll forward, slowly at first but then gaining in speed.

Soon he was whooshing around the corners and whizzing down the straights. He couldn't help but let out a call of glee as his grey hair was pushed backwards. He let the luge go as fast as it could possibly take him, and for a few moments Santa felt nothing but the unadulterated thrill of pure fun.

Eventually, Santa rolled into the basement and came to a stop. He stood up and stepped out into Huxley's toy laboratory. The lights were on. Everything was intact, but there were notes on many of the machines and tools that designated where they were to be taken. Some had already been sold, some were being scrapped. Santa walked around. He looked at the drawings and designs on the walls, and the prototypes that were scattered about the place. He looked at Huxley's drafting board, still with its paper and its pencils.

It had been years since he had ventured down to this place. The prototype toys had been hastily deposited in boxes. Santa pulled out a wooden doll that could articulate every limb. The craftsmanship was extraordinary. He pulled out a toy train and a wooden castle and looked at them carefully.

Santa realized that he had almost forgotten about his dear old friend, assuming that he had been doing nothing all these years and that he had lost his creative powers. But now he realized that he was wrong. Huxley had been working harder than ever in the service of Santa Inc., perfecting his craft and constructing fantastical toys, although none of his endeavors had ever been acknowledged.

Santa picked up the coat-hanger. He held the finished wood in his hands, observing carefully its grain and the texture of the finish. Maybe Huxley had been right all along. Maybe children could get by on their fertile imaginations alone.

As he spent more time wandering around the basement, a thought became clearer and clearer to him. He had spent years building a company, focusing on making as much money as he could, elevating his status and wealth, but in doing so he had somehow lost the very thing that had driven him in the first place——the simple desire to make children happy on Christmas Day.

He thought of the times that he had shared with Huxley, designing and testing new products, and the times with the elves figuring out how to build all of those toys in time for the big day, and finally with his beloved reindeer, feeling their warm breath against the cold of the winter air as they took off for their annual flight around the world on Christmas Eve. He realized that those were the best times that he'd ever had, a time when he was truly happy, when work was a day of fun and laughter. He'd long forgotten that in his endless drive to make more and more money. As those memories came flooding back, Santa became aware of exactly what that pull was.

"Santa," came a voice across the floor.

It was Huxley.

"I never knew about this place," said Santa.

"I couldn't sleep," said Huxley. "Wanted to take one final look at this place before it gets turned into a gym or a yoga studio or whatever they have planned for it."

Santa smiled. Huxley walked towards him, taking time to look about the room himself as Santa held Huxley's perfectly carved wooden train.

"These toys are superb," he said.

"I suppose it doesn't matter much now anyway," said Huxley with a shrug.

There was a moment of silence.

"I'm sorry that it's been so long," said Santa.

"No sense in fretting about that," said Huxley, never one to stand on sentiment.

At that moment, there was a whooshing of air and Eric came crashing down through the air duct and landed on Huxley's bed, which had fortunately not yet been moved.

"I couldn't sleep," he said.

Huxley rummaged around in the cupboards of his little kitchenette.

"I had packed up all my things," he said, head buried inside, "but then I remembered that I had this."

Huxley pulled out a small box that said *Break in Case of Emergency* on the top. It contained tea bags and Custard Creams. He put the kettle on, and he, Santa, and Eric pulled up three chairs around the small kitchenette table.

"So," said Huxley, "how do we get this upstart out of this building and return you to your rightful position?"

"We don't," said Santa, shaking his head.

"Why not?" asked Huxley.

Santa placed the wooden toy train back on the table.

"I have a different plan."

Bad Things

At six o'clock in the morning, Sister Prudence walked through the dorms vigorously banging her pot with the metal spoon. She had a suspicious look on her face and kept a keen eye for clues. A strange rumor had rippled through the orphanage. It had begun when Clive was cleaning the third floor toilets with Martin and had told him a fantastical story. Something about Eric and the building next door and Santa and a grate in the basement that he used to get there. Martin told Arvin and Arvin told others and it quickly spread up and down the building.

Sister Prudence had heard it in the whispers of the walls as she went about her business of patrolling the place. She caught words here and there but could not quite place it all together. She had been disturbed by the strange behavior of Mister Miller and the curious book in Sister Christine's desk. She sensed forces moving against her, and she knew that somehow she would get to the bottom of it.

The boys roused and opened their weary eyes. They rose to their feet and trudged down the stairs in the usual procession. When inspection and prayer was finished, they lined up in front of the serving hatch of the kitchen, stomachs rumbling and ready for breakfast. The shutters of the hatch rolled upwards but they were not greeted by Mister Miller, nor his bubbling milky sweet oatmeal, as they had hoped. They were not even met by Sister Christine. Instead, a severe-looking woman dressed in chef's whites stood in his place, arms folded, as though expecting trouble.

"This is Ms. Wickham," announced Sister Prudence.

Ms. Wickham began to ladle the oatmeal. Eric stood in line. He hated being there and longed to be back in the kitchen. When he reached the hatch, he held his bowl out, and the ration was deposited. There was a peculiar consistency to it. It clung to the ladle and refused to drop in the bowl. Ms. Wickham gave the spoon a strong shake and it eventually came free. One by one the boys took their breakfast and sat down at the long tables. One by one their faces told the same story. Eric sat down on the old bench among his friends. He was tired from the night before. Paul leaned over.

"I heard Sister Prudence last night when I went to the bathroom," he whispered. "She was shouting at the top of her lungs."

"At who?" asked Ryan.

"Don't know," said Paul.

"Maybe it was Mister Miller. Or even Sister Christine," added Santiago.

Eric pushed his spoon into the thick mush in his bowl and shoveled a mouthful in. The taste was of watery cardboard mixed together with hard little pieces that he thought might be glue. The unpleasant texture stuck to the top of his mouth and refused to move. Soon, all the boys had the same pained expressions upon their faces. Some of them even left food in their bowls. Things had taken another unexpected turn for the worse.

Within the blink of an eye, or the rumble of a stomach, the boys became antsy. There was an aggravation about them that was palpable. They were eager to argue and even more eager to fight. As they sat in the classroom and waited for the lesson to begin, Eric sensed that bad things were on the horizon.

John shoved Oscar, then Oscar punched Paul. Paul tried to trip Lucius as he walked by. Clive was pinched by Arvin. Punches were thrown. Shins were kicked. Ears were pulled. The boys managed to cool off moments before Sister Prudence arrived.

They silently rubbed their wounded parts as she sat down at her desk and looked over the group. Eric noticed that she carried the same expression in the cafeteria. It was a kind of satisfied glibness, as though she was pleased that life had just become that little bit harder for her wards.

"Mathematics," she announced. "Open your books."

Sister Prudence ordered each boy to repeat their multiplication tables. Eric played along, careful not to step out of line. The deep scratches in the old table punctured the paper as he wrote, and the old chairs wobbled precariously as they had always done.

At lunch, things got worse. There was talk that the oatmeal was a one-off, an anomaly as Ms. Wickham tried to get the consistency right for the first time. But with the second meal of the day, all hope dissipated as the boys realized that the same old nasty stew that they had endured for many a long year was back to stay.

"The stew is back!" they whispered in disbelief.

Their frustrations spilled out into more fighting, name calling, and general bad behavior. Outside, the weather had turned cold, as though an icy chill had fallen upon the city. The cold air blew a little colder through the cracks. The lights flickered on and off, and the water ran frigid as the boiler gave up for the day.

Eric retreated into the Rec and absorbed himself in a copy of National Geographic. But it was no good, and he could not concentrate. There were too many elements out of balance, too much disruption to the peace that had been so carefully cultivated. He had to try something. Eric placed the magazine back and walked across the hall to the office where Sister Christine was sitting at her desk. She was busy with the checkbook, carefully documenting each entry in her log.

"Hello, Eric," she said as he appeared at the door.

"Sister Christine," he said. "Bad things are happening."

She stopped what she was doing and focused her attention on the boy in front of her.

"I know," she said.

"We don't want to go back to the way things were," said Eric. "You saw what a difference the food made. Life was better for everybody. What can we do?"

"I don't know," said Sister Christine.

She was as deflated as the boys. Her enthusiasm had soured into despair.

"But you do know," said Eric. "Maybe just talk to Sister Prudence?"

At that moment the sound of Sister Prudence admonishing some poor boy echoed somewhere down the hallway. A sad expression came over Sister Christine.

"I'm sorry," she said to Eric, shaking her head. "I can't help you."

"But why?" asked Eric.

"Sister Prudence is my superior. I can't go against her orders. I just can't. There has to be order."

She reached down into her desk drawer, picked up Gopal's books, which she had rescued from the trash, and handed them to Eric.

"Please return these to wherever you got them, and do not bring me any more."

Eric figured that there was perhaps only one person who could help him, someone with the power to temper the hearts, minds, and stomachs of the group. Kevin O'Malley was in the fourth-floor dorm. He was alone, sitting on his bed and staring out of the window. Eric wondered if it was window gazing season because everybody seemed to be doing it. He deliberately cleared his throat so as not to alarm the angry beast.

"What do you want?" he growled.

"I need your help," said Eric, gingerly stepping forward.

Kevin didn't answer and turned back to the window.

"The fighting has started back up. The pranks. All of it. Worse than before."

"What did you expect?" said Kevin dismissively. "This place will never change."

Eric could not accept that answer.

"Maybe we can get Ms. Wickham to make better food?" suggested Eric, although he had no idea how they might go about doing it.

Eric stepped forward so that he could see Kevin O'Malley's face. He sensed that something was not right and carefully sat down on the bed opposite him.

"What's wrong?" Eric asked.

Eric waited for a moment and wondered how Kevin O'Malley could help. Maybe this was beyond even his power. Eric stood up to leave.

"None of this matters to me," said Kevin.

"Why?"

"I'm going to turn eighteen," said Kevin.

"When?" asked Eric, sitting back down.

"Soon."

They sat there for a few more moments.

"You must be so excited," said Eric. "You'll be a man. You can do whatever you want. Eat what you want. Go to bed when you want."

"Where am I going to go?" asked Kevin.

In that moment, sitting on the bed, the Head Boy, the strongest and oldest of all of them, the fiercest of the lot who had handed out punishments and fought his way to the top of the pile with his bare fists, was back to being the scared little boy who had walked through those big wooden orphanage doors at seven years old. That place was all he knew. He would not be the king out in the wide world. He would be that little boy again.

"Something will appear at the right time," said Eric. "Like Magic Dust."

"What's Magic Dust?"

Eric left Kevin O'Malley to his own thoughts.

"You'll know when you see it," he said.

Later that evening, as soon as everybody was in bed, Eric snuck back to Santa Inc. The laboratory was quiet, and Eric made his way directly to the factory. As the elevator doors opened, he was greeted with a flurry of activity. The elves looked very excited. Although the machines were silent, there was plenty to be done.

"Good evening," Stephen called out, a giant smile planted on his face.

"We're leaving," said Lofty as Eric approached.

"We're packing our things right now," added Stephen.

"We're going home!"

As Eric looked over the elves, he could see that they all possessed the same joyousness. They sang and danced as they went about their work. On the other side of the factory, Santa was working with Robbo and Huxley. They were loading timber into a large container. Eric made his way toward them, greeting the other elves as he went.

"Hello, Stanley!"

"Evening, Oswaldo!"

"Bonjour, Jean-Pierre."

When Santa saw Eric, he stopped and waited.

"Aha!" he called out when Eric was close enough. "We were expecting your return."

"You really are leaving," said Eric.

"Yes, we are," said Santa. "And there's something that we wanted to talk about with you."

"What is it?" asked Eric.

Huxley stopped what he was doing and walked over.

"I knew the moment that I saw you just what you were," said Santa.

"You did?" asked Eric.

"Don't forget, my friend, that I too was born from the stars. I thought you had been sent to help me rescue the company. Now I realize that was not the intention."

Huxley sat with them as Santa continued.

"We're going to make toys for children again. Nothing more. Nothing less."

A large smile spread across his face. He looked so happy.

"Owen and I have been doing this for a very long time," said Santa. "In our minds, we feel as though we are twenty-one years old, but our bodies disagree. Every year there are more and more children to deliver to, more and more toys to make. It's a lot of work. We think maybe we need some new blood in the organization. And we think you possess some magical qualities. What we're saying is..."

"We'd like you to come with us," interrupted Huxley.

"To the North Pole," added Santa.

Eric didn't know what to say. For once he was quite stunned. He had not considered that option before.

"Will you come with us?" asked Santa.

The Inquisition

T he clanging of Sister Prudence's pot rattled through the dorm, but as Lucius awoke, stretched and yawned, he saw that Eric's bed was empty. He looked at all the other boys getting ready and realized that no one else had noticed. Maybe Eric was in the kitchen? He looked at the empty bed for a moment and then quickly drew up the sheets to give the impression that Eric was present. He didn't want to be involved in whatever Eric was doing, but he felt compelled to do something to protect him.

As he lined up at the hatch, he stared into the kitchen. Eric was not there. Lucius began to worry. Where had his friend gone? He didn't want to, but he couldn't help it. Over breakfast, Lucius stared nervously at the clock. For some reason Eric's absence had not been noticed by anyone else, but Lucius knew that it would only be a matter of time until that situation changed.

"Come on, Eric," he said to himself quietly.

After breakfast, the boys readied themselves for classes. Lucius felt a terrible, anxious feeling in his body. There was nothing he could do to shake it.

"What's wrong?" asked Clive.

"It's Eric," replied Lucius. "He's disappeared."

"He's probably at that place he goes to," said Clive.

But Lucius had a feeling that something bad was happening, and as much as he wanted no part in it, he could not abandon his friend. Clive ran up the stairs to prepare for class and Lucius lingered in the Rec, looking at the basement door, waiting. He paced up and down from the old TV to the board games and back. Over and over. Peering down the hall every time, willing the door to open. But the clock would not stop ticking, and the minute hand slowly marched to the top of the hour.

Eventually, the inevitable happened. The bell rang for class. Lucius didn't know what to do. He wanted to stay and wait for his friend, but as the rest of the boys shouted and barged their way upstairs, he knew that he was out of time.

"Settle down," shouted Sister Prudence from above.

As they quietly jostled for room on the stairs, Lucius had no choice but to follow. He was wracked with fear, barely able to make the climb. Eric would most certainly be late for class, but that, Lucius feared, would be the least of his troubles. His knees shook as he walked up the final stairs, and they almost buckled when he saw Sister Prudence waiting by the chalkboard, perched like a vulture, her boney claws gripping the old leather seat.

He did not look at her. Instead he put his head down and walked silently to his desk hoping that by some miracle, Eric would arrive just in time. Lucius listened to the boys' footsteps as they entered the classroom, each one like a nail into a coffin. Then came the scraping of chair legs against the wood, the flipping open of books, and finally, the inevitable click of the shutting door. He looked up, hoping that his friend had miraculously made it, but it was not to be. Eric's desk was empty. Plain as day for all to see.

"Now then," said Sister Prudence, writing on the board, "long division."

Sister Prudence wrote a series of numbers out, scratching away with the chalk. Lucius thought that if she conducted the whole lesson facing the board, there could be some slim chance that Eric would be safe. But just as that thought had occurred, Sister Prudence turned around and her eyes were drawn to the conspicuous absence in the middle of the room.

"Where's Eric?"

Silence. The deafeningly loud kind.

"Where is Eric?" Sister Prudence repeated.

The boys stared silently ahead. Sister Prudence's eyes scanned the room, looking at each face in turn for a clue, a hint of who might possess some information. Lucius was the only boy who was staring at his desk. His eyes anchored to the old inkwell. He could not have lifted his head if he had wanted to. Sister Prudence slowly walked towards him, then stopped.

"Where is Eric?"

Lucius did not reply. BAM! The yardstick came crashing down on his desk. Slowly, he looked up. His body shook as fear coursed through his veins.

"I... I," he stuttered, "I don't know."

Sister Prudence stared directly at Lucius as though she was melting him like ice in the sun. But much to Lucius's surprise, Sister Prudence did not pursue the interrogation any further, instead she turned and pointed back to the board.

"You will divide the numbers on the left, by the numbers on the right."

The rest of the lesson progressed as normal. Lucius almost forgot about his friend as he struggled to keep up with the steady stream of arithmetic. Finally, the session drew to a close and Sister Prudence instructed the boys to pack up their books. Now two hours of laundry awaited. The boys filed quietly out of class, not yet far enough away to begin their rambunctiousness.

"Lucius, go to the office," Sister Prudence ordered.

Lucius had never been summoned to the office before, had never known what it was like to stand before Sister Prudence and be called to account. He stood on that same well-worn patch of carpet and observed the neatly ordered desks. There were a small number of letters organized in the 'Out' box and a small number in the 'In' box. He looked up at the wooden carving of the Lord Jesus Christ that was attached to the wall, still and silent. Sister Prudence arrived. She sat down and waited a few moments.

"Where is Eric?" she asked once more.

Lucius did not know what to do or say. He desperately didn't want to get his friend into any more trouble, but he knew that he would be compelled to give some answer. Sister Prudence's fingers wrapped around the yardstick, and she drew it upwards and rested it upon her desk.

"I don't know," said Lucius.

"Don't lie to me, boy!" she cried, rising to her feet. "You know exactly where he is. I've seen him talking to you. I've seen him telling you things. Where is he?"

She pointed the yardstick at him so that it was no more than an inch from his nose. Then her voice lowered again.

"I know what a corrupting influence he is. I know that the things he says can appear true. I don't want to punish you, Lucius. I don't want to make you scrub the steps all night. I don't want to make you spend the night outside in the yard. I don't want to send you to the basement..."

Sister Prudence stared into Lucius's eyes.

"But I will."

Lucius imagined the punishments that Sister Prudence had listed. He foresaw himself cowering in the dark of the basement with its strange sounds and menagerie of odd objects. He was terrified just thinking about it. He couldn't survive down there. He wasn't strong like his friend.

"You must tell me the truth, Lucius. Where is Eric?"

Lucius closed his eyes.

"Santa Inc.," he said meekly.

Sister Prudence's face crinkled only a little as she forced a neutral expression.

"Santa Inc.?"

"Right now, Max Rupee has taken over the company. He wants to get rid of the elves. He doesn't even want to make toys anymore."

"Whatever are you talking about, boy?" demanded Sister Prudence.

"That's where Eric is. At least I think that's where he is. He works there."

"Works?"

Lucius nodded.

"In the office."

"And how does he get to this job?" she asked, indulging the boy for a moment.

"Through the grate in the basement. To the building next door."

Sister Prudence sat back in her seat. Now it all made sense. Those little flurries of conversation that she had picked up all slotted into place. The grate. Of course that was it.

"If you do not tell me everything you know of this, Lucius, I will punish you like you have never been punished before."

Lucius stood silently for a moment. What choice did he have? He didn't want any part of Eric's story, and now he found himself in the middle of it.

"He found it when he got locked in the basement. He would go while he was working in the kitchen with Mister Miller. After breakfast and lunch."

Sister Prudence, although thoroughly unconvinced, caught the scent of a more interesting and plausible story, and decided to pursue the line of inquiry.

"So while Eric was working in the kitchen, he had another job?"

"Yes," said Lucius, growing in confidence a little. "At Santa Inc. Where Santa works, and the elves make things, and there's a man called Huxley who designs toys. But..."

"But what?"

"I don't know if it's true at all. Sometimes I believe it, and sometimes I'm just not sure."

But Sister Prudence was not giving up.

"And what does Eric do at this job?"

"Business," said Lucius, as though it was obvious. "He learned all about it. That's how he helped Sister Christine pay all of the bills."

"Carry on, Lucius," she said.

"The money that Sister Christine saved allowed her to give more to Mister Miller to make our food better."

"I see," she said.

"And that's what got Kevin O'Malley to stop all the fighting and the name calling and the pranks, just like you wanted, because that's why you gave Eric the special job in the first place, right?"

Suddenly Sister Prudence saw the situation in a whole different light. Far from being the punishment that she had designed, Eric had turned the entire orphanage against her and spun a web of lies to his own advantage. Even Sister Christine had been lured by his deceit. Everyone was in on it. Sister Prudence felt betrayed. She felt humiliated. Most of all she felt a burning anger rising up within her. But she did not let it show.

"That will be all, Lucius," she said calmly.

The Grate

When Lucius left Sister Prudence's office, he felt better. He had explained everything, and to his surprise Sister Prudence had not appeared to be too annoyed at all. Maybe it would all work out just fine, like Eric said. Sister Prudence followed Lucius out of the office.

"Sister Christine," she called out.

Sister Christine was walking down the stairs.

"In the office."

Sister Christine made her way to the office. Lucius heard the door close behind her. At that moment, the basement door opened, and Eric stepped out.

"Eric, quick," called Lucius.

Eric saw Lucius, who was desperately beckoning him in his direction, and ran toward him. They scurried into the Rec.

"I had to tell Sister Prudence," said Lucius.

"Tell her what?"

"Everything. About Santa Inc. About the food and Mister Miller and Sister Christine and Kevin O'Malley."

Eric thought about what Lucius was telling him. Lucius had expected Eric to be angry, but he wasn't. Eric had always figured that eventually Sister Prudence would find out. It was only a matter of time. Now that time had come.

"Santa is leaving," said Eric, concerned with more pressing matters.

"Leaving?" inquired Lucius.

"He's going back to the North Pole. He's taking the elves and the reindeer, and Huxley. He's leaving New York City."

"Why?" asked Lucius.

"Because he's done with business. He wants to make toys again. He asked me to go with him."

"He did?" said Lucius.

"He wants me to become his apprentice," said Eric.

"Are you going to go?"

Eric paused for a moment.

"I don't think he needs me," he said eventually. "You see, he's got all of his family back now. I think he's going to be alright."

Eric smiled at Lucius, and Lucius smiled back, hoping that maybe life would return to normal again.

"Come on," said Lucius, "let's start our chores. I can tell you all about Clive. He's a nice guy, just a little quiet."

At that moment, the door to the office swung open and Sister Prudence appeared. She looked about the place, then saw the boys standing in the Rec.

"You!" called Sister Prudence, pointing her boney finger directly at Eric all the way from the office.

She marched forward, grabbed Eric by the arm, and yanked him into the main hallway.

"This boy has taken over your minds," she called out. "He has corrupted you all in the very worst way."

Sister Prudence stood looking upwards, in front of the spiral staircase, still gripping Eric's arm. The boys ran out of the dorms to peer over the balcony and see what was going on.

"Has everyone been influenced with his malevolent schemes?"

Boys appeared from the laundry, from the Rec, and from outside. Eric stood in silence as the gallery grew around them.

"He has even taken over the minds of Sister Christine and Mister Miller," Sister Prudence declared.

Ms. Wickham appeared at the door to the kitchen. Sister Christine stood silently in observance.

"Am I the only one that he does not control?"

Sister Prudence looked about the room, now turning her attention to the rest of the boys. They backed away, even Kevin O'Malley. They had never seen the Sister in such a rage, and each was terrified.

"Well?" she called.

There was silence.

"Sister Prudence," suggested Sister Christine. "Perhaps we should..."

"Quiet," she shouted, cutting her off. "I don't need to hear any more from you."

Sister Prudence walked back toward the basement door, dragging Eric along beside her. She threw it open and stared into the darkness.

"All of you, down here," she ordered.

There was a minute of the quiet rumbling of feet as fifty boys anxiously made their way to the basement. When they were all gathered, Sister Prudence produced a light bulb from some place about her person and screwed it into the light fitting. The room was illuminated.

"Take a look around," she ordered, inviting each one to inspect the room.

Most of the boys had never seen the contents of that basement. They had heard the fables of it and were reluctant to even step inside, fearing for the horrors of what might befall them if they did.

"Go on," ordered Sister Prudence insistently.

Kevin O'Malley pushed his way to the front. He looked around. Then Ping and Terrence. Then the rest of them, all buoyed by the safety of numbers.

"There is no grate," called Sister Prudence so that everyone could hear it. "There is no grate! Come and see for yourselves."

Each boy stepped down onto the first stair, scanned quickly, and then moved on. Sister Christine looked on in horror, unable to do anything about the increasingly irrational actions of her superior. The boys were reluctant, but Sister Prudence pressed them into it. They walked further down the stairs into the damp mustiness and cool air of the basement. Umberto, who was not known for his smart decisions, stepped all the way down to the bottom. He was more curious than scared and wanted to take a good look around. There was no grate. No grate at all. Just boxes of old toys, books, tools, paint, offcuts of wood, and other knick-knacks. There was even a box of old Christmas decorations with a plastic Santa in it.

"He's a liar!" called Sister Prudence. "He fooled you all because you're too stupid to see."

Through it all, Eric remained silent and calm. Each boy walked down, scanned the room, and then quickly retreated. Santiago went down. Then Clive. Then it was Lucius's turn. He timidly stepped down into the basement and looked around. There was nothing of any consequence there. Nothing to see. Just old junk. Lucius felt a sense of disappointment. He didn't want to acknowledge that Eric's stories were not true, but the truth was plain to see.

Next, Arvin stepped down. He wasn't a shy or timid boy. In fact, he was quite daring. He took his time and looked across the room, trying to see into each box. He found their contents intriguing. Unlike the others, he calculated that there was some value in what lay before him.

"Move on, boy!" called Sister Prudence.

But Arvin would not be rushed. His eyes moved slowly to the back of the room, scanning over the boxes and junk in the far reaches. He thought about what he might pilfer if he could sneak back one night when everybody was sleeping. Maybe there was something that he could trade or that would allow him to elevate his status or gain some sway over his peers. Then at the very back, somewhat obscured by boxes, he saw something. It was blackish, square, metal.

"There's the grate," he called out.

The boys heard his words clearly in the silence of that moment. They gathered closer at the top of the stairs for a glimpse.

"Where?" demanded Sister Prudence.

"Right there," said Arvin, pointing directly at it.

Sister Prudence tromped down the stairs, and the boys followed, jostling for a view. Indeed there was a grate, metal with a crisscross pattern, and Arvin held out his hand and pointed directly at it so they could all see. A current of whispers ran back up and spread among those who did not have a direct view.

"There is a grate! There is a grate!"

"Everybody out!" shouted Sister Prudence, her eyes popping with rage. "Out!"

The boys quickly made their way back up the stairs until everyone was back in the main hall. The last to appear was Sister Prudence. She looked madder and redder than anyone had ever seen her before.

"You are a demon in the guise of boy!" she proclaimed. "We will purge this wicked creature from our presence."

"Now just wait," called Sister Christine finally.

Sister Prudence turned to her deputy.

"You can't say those things to him," said Sister Christine. "He's just a boy. He's good and honest."

"Do not tell me what I can and cannot do!" screamed Sister Prudence.

"You've lost your mind," said Sister Christine. "Leave him alone."

Sister Christine stepped forward to take a hold of Eric, but Sister Prudence pushed him behind her like some old lion guarding its kill. There was a rumbling among some of the boys, and Sister Prudence could tell that discontent was growing toward her. She did not like that at all.

"Let him go," ordered Sister Christine.

For a few moments, there was a tense standoff between the two as they stared each other down.

"Sister Christine," growled Sister Prudence. "You are relieved of your position. I will see that you are transferred from here with immediate effect. Now leave me to instill some discipline into these worthless creatures."

"I won't," responded Sister Christine.

"You will!" came the reply. "You will!"

In that moment, Sister Christine knew that Sister Prudence was nothing but a cruel bully herself. Unremorseful. The worst kind. She would never change. Nothing would ever change. She also knew that nothing would be gained by fighting with her superior in front of the boys. She stood down but resolved to find a way to alert the outside world to Sister Prudence. But Sister Prudence was not done.

"Go to your dorms. All of you," she ordered. "No dinner tonight as punishment."

As the boys walked glumly away, she turned to Eric.

"You," she sneered.

Without another word, she pushed him into the basement. He barely caught his footing before he stumbled and fell down the wooden steps to the floor. Sister Prudence removed the light bulb, slammed the door behind him and bolted it shut. Eric lay in the dark. His knee hurt a little where he had landed.

In the hallway, Sister Prudence scanned over the fifty pairs of eyes that had stopped and were silently watching her every move. Each one of them terrified in their own way. But she did not say or do anything. Instead, she stepped into the office and slammed the door closed behind her.

Fire

Astrange, uneasy feeling settled over Our Lady of Mercy Orphanage. Sister Prudence did not emerge from the office, and everyone else conducted the day in hushed tones, too afraid to make any noise at all. Sister Christine remained in her room where she prayed quietly as she packed the few belongings that she possessed. She had written a letter of complaint to the head of the church, but it felt worthless. She knew it would fall on deaf ears. She did not know where she would go, but that did not concern her. Her main worry was for the boys.

Kevin O'Malley took charge. Chores were conducted in silence. It was very odd, but there was no fighting and no arguing. The boys went to bed early that night and hungry, but they were glad to go, preferring to enter the realm of dreams and leave the taut atmosphere that lingered over the orphanage behind them.

In the middle of the night, when the building was dark and silent, the door of the office opened. Sister Prudence stepped out. Her anger had not abated in those hours. In fact, during that time, her thoughts had stewed like one of Mister Miller's dinners, so that they had become even more concentrated in her mind. She couldn't help but relive the events over and over again.

She couldn't stand that Eric had influenced so many people around her. She felt betrayed and humiliated. After all of her years of service, to be treated like a fool was insufferable. She had given her life to the orphanage and those stinking, ungrateful boys in it. Yet they had all been somehow turned by that wicked boy.

Eric was truly the devil in disguise. He had polluted the minds of all that he had come into contact with. His lies and stories had destroyed the very fabric of the place that she had carefully held together for so long. It wasn't good enough that he was just in the basement. That had not worked the first time. She wanted to punish him more. Maybe she would send him away to another orphanage. Maybe she would turn him loose onto the streets. Her rage would not abate, and a thousand voices screamed in her mind.

She marched to the Rec, flung open the door to the cupboard, and began pulling out all the National Geographic magazines, a handful at a time, babbling to herself about treachery and revenge. She threw them into the fireplace until there was a giant stack of them in there. She struck a match and held it under the pile until the small flame took and began to grow and spread.

Sister Prudence gazed into the dancing light as it reflected in her eyes. She would stamp out this madness once and for all. She would put an end to it even if it meant putting every single boy on lockdown for the rest of his life.

The fire grew higher and more powerful as the glossy photographs of the Inuit Tribes of Alaska, of the Australian Wombat, of the Elephants of the Ivory Coast shriveled and blackened in the heat. Soon the flames became so high and so intense that they rushed up and out of the fireplace scorching the mantelpiece above. Smoke billowed out silently, wrapping the room in a dark and malevolent fog. She did not notice that the chimney flue had been pushed closed to prevent cold air coming in. The smoke could not escape. Without hesitating, she threw more magazines on.

"Lord, give me strength," she cried.

The flames jumped back out of the fireplace. Sister Prudence did not care. She coughed and spluttered, but she willed them on. Her heart was filled with so much rage and so much hate that she barely had control over her senses. The fire hypnotized her as the flames danced higher and higher. Crackling embers spat out of the fireplace and landed on the carpet. As they burned their way into the fabric, flames sprung up all around her. Soon the entire room was ablaze, and the smoke became so thick that it obscured the light.

"This is what you have brought me to," she called out.

Within minutes the fire grew wildly out of control, voraciously consuming everything in its path. As it did so, the blackness filled Sister Prudence's lungs and she collapsed on the floor.

The fire alarm rang. It was shrill, startling, and deafeningly loud. The boys awoke quickly. They could smell the smoke in the darkness. Confused, they got out of bed to see what was happening. By the time they got to the main staircase, they could see that the fire had enveloped the entire bottom floor of Our Lady of Mercy Orphanage. Then there was panic.

Sister Christine awoke to the sound of shouting and noise. She leapt out of bed and opened the door to discover the fire all about her. She ran out into the corridor. Everything was burning. Smoke and heat. The grand wooden doors of the entrance were close by, but she couldn't leave the boys. She had to make sure they were safe.

"Use the fire exits!" she called out desperately.

She battled through the flames, holding her nightdress to her mouth to prevent her from inhaling the smoke. Boys were running in all directions, coughing and spluttering as they tried to figure out what to do.

"Use the fire exits!" she called out again.

The main staircase was already ablaze, but Sister Christine did not care. She made her way upwards, dodging the rapidly growing flames, continuously crying out all the time for the boys to get out. Her bare feet burned against the floor. Kevin O'Malley looked down on her from the top floor.

"This way," he called to the boys.

He opened up the sash windows and led them out toward the old metal fire exit. One by one they hopped through the window, escaping to the second floor, where they stopped. Kevin O'Malley ran down to the third floor where he repeated the action. The younger boys quickly made their way outside and onto the rusted metal staircase. Kevin pushed his way down, past the others. He unlocked the old ladder, forcing it to go scraping and banging downward. That allowed the boys passage to the street, where they made their way to safety.

"Find someone and call the fire department," shouted Kevin.

"Where's Eric?" asked Lucius.

In the chaos, nobody heard him.

Inside, Sister Christine checked every bed to make sure that no one was still in the building. Her nightdress no longer worked as a filter for the smoke. It was so thick that she too began to choke and splutter as the blackness enveloped her lungs.

As the boys assembled on the opposite side of the street, Santiago looked up. Every window of the building was alight with glowing orange. The flames were relentless, climbing higher and higher, snaking inside and out as those four stories turned into a furnace. The gargoyles' faces appeared to contort even more under the intense heat. Kevin desperately searched the line of boys, trying to take note in his mind of anyone who was missing.

"Eric and Sister Christine," shouted Lucius.

"I'm going back," Kevin shouted as he ran across the street.

He jumped up the ladder two rungs at a time, ran up the fire stairs, and re-entered the building through the third-floor window. The inside of the building was twice as hot as when he had left moments before. The sound of the flames was deafening, and he struggled to see through the intense heat. Immediately, he felt the smoke attack his lungs.

"Sister Christine," he called out, shielding his eyes with his forearm.

As he moved further inside, a giant burning beam crashed to the ground in front of him. He jumped backwards, narrowly avoiding being crushed by its weight.

"Sister Christine," he called again.

No answer. Refusing to retreat, he forced his way forward onto the main stairs as the fire funneled upwards like a great chimney. He darted up the stairs as they crumbled and fell below him. He barely made it to the fourth floor before the entire staircase disintegrated and crashed to the ground far below. Undeterred, he searched the fourth floor and the bathrooms. She was not there. On the street, the boys anxiously waited. A distant sound pricked their ears. Sirens.

"Sister Christine," called Kevin.

He staggered back into the hallway and looked all the way down to the ground floor. The ceiling and roof had begun to burn. The whole place began to creak and groan under the pressure. But there was something in him that refused to give up.

Outside, the boys waited, huddled together and unable to do anything but watch the sight unfolding in front of them. Then, from a few blocks away, came a wave of flashing red light and the wailing of sirens. Five engines in all, led by a giant gleaming hook and ladder, raced down the street. They skidded to a halt in front of the burning building, and firefighters in their bright yellow protective suits, helmets on, poured from the vehicles.

"They're still inside!" called Terrence.

In moments, two of the firefighters placed more protective gear over their heads with breathing apparatus. The giant ladder ascended into the air, spraying a jet of water into the building.

"Look!" called Santiago, pointing upwards.

Kevin O'Malley appeared on the third-floor escape. He was dragging another body out with him. It was Sister Christine. As soon as he got outside, he collapsed onto the metal walkway. The firemen rushed to them, bringing the ladder down and loading both Kevin and Sister Christine onto it. When they reached the ground, the medics took over, pushing oxygen masks against their faces, checking pulses, transferring to gurneys, and into the ambulance. Lucius ran forward to where some of the firefighters were standing.

"Eric is still in there," he called. "He's still inside."

One of the firefighters heard him and turned around.

"There's another kid in there?" he asked.

"Yes," cried Lucius, "in the basement."

Without a moment of hesitation, the firefighter pulled on his breathing apparatus and ran towards the building. He ran up the old steps and pushed his way through the door. Then he was gone. The boys waited anxiously, their eyes trained on the door. Time seemed to stand still during those moments, and looking at the cavernous inferno, it appeared impossible that anyone could survive inside. Water sprayed from all directions into the building but did little to abate the flames. Lucius could barely stand it, he was so consumed with worry.

Then after some time, the firefighter appeared in the entrance. He was holding Eric in his arms. His crew rushed forward to assist as he too collapsed in the doorway from the intense heat that he had endured. Another picked up Eric. Lucius looked on in despair. Eric was not moving at all, his arms dangled down, and his head rolled back. They took him to an ambulance where a team of emergency medical technicians was waiting. Lucius strained to see as they worked quickly to check his vital signs. The look of concern on their faces was not comforting at all. Then the doors were closed and Lucius could see nothing. Lights flashing and sirens wailing, they disappeared into the night.

The police cordoned off the street. The fire crews handed out blankets to the boys, most of whom were shivering in their pajamas. But the fire raged on, determined to incinerate every last inch of that place.

Ruins

Three days later, Sister Christine opened her eyes. She looked around and found that she was in an unfamiliar place. There were beeps and machines, and the scent of bleach. She was lying in a hospital bed. Slowly her eyes fluttered open, not quite sure of what had happened or why she was there. Eventually, after some time had passed, a nurse appeared and saw that she was awake.

"Where am I?" she asked weakly.

"Hospital," replied the nurse. "You were lucky to survive the fire."

"Fire?" repeated Sister Christine to herself, unable to re-assemble those fateful moments before she lost consciousness. "What happened?"

"You were in the building. The boy pulled you out."

Sister Christine thought hard. A ripple of memory moved toward her. Darkness. Flames. Smoke.

"What boy?" asked Sister Christine.

"Kevin."

"How is he?" asked Sister Christine.

"He's fine," said the nurse. "He saved your life."

Sister Christine could not yet put a face to the name Kevin, but with each moment, her thoughts became clearer. The nurse handed her a cup of water. Sister Christine sipped and allowed it to revive her senses some more. Suddenly images began rushing toward her——the fire escape, the burning staircase, the crashing of the timbers.

"Kevin O'Malley," she called, as though something had become clear.

"You need to rest," said the nurse.

But Sister Christine strengthened, and a rush of images became more fully formed in her mind.

"Sister Prudence?" she called out, grabbing the nurse's arm.

"Sister!" called the nurse.

"What happened to her? Is she alright? Where is she?"

She had no recollection of Sister Prudence from that night. There was a blank spot where her image would be. The nurse paused, not quite sure how to say what she wanted to say.

"I'll get the doctor," she said finally.

"Tell me," demanded Sister Christine.

"I'm sorry. She did not make it," replied the nurse.

Sister Christine was quiet. In those brief moments her entire life at Our Lady of Mercy passed in front of her. All those years. They had been obliterated. It was hard for her to understand, hard for her to make any kind of sense of it all. Everything had turned to soot and ash.

The twisted world of Sister Prudence was all that she had known in so many years. But she felt no sadness. In fact, the news that Sister Prudence was no more left her with a strange sense of lightness, as though she had been released from invisible shackles, shackles that had been with her for so long that they were only detectable once removed.

"What about the boys?" she asked.

"The boys are being looked after at a Salvation Army Hall across town," said the nurse.

"How are they?" she asked.

"They are fine," said the nurse. "Except..."

Then the nurse paused again, and her expression changed.

"One of them is here. In the intensive care unit," she continued. "We're not sure if he's is going to pull through."

Sister Christine's heart sank. She did not need to be told the name of the boy. She began to cry. As her body moved, she felt pain coursing through it. The nurse walked over and placed her hand on Sister Christine's shoulder. But Sister Christine forced herself up, pulling the tubes out of her as she did.

"Sister, you can't get up. You must stay in your bed," warned the nurse.

But Sister Christine would not be stopped. She limped as fast as she could down the halls of the hospital toward the intensive care unit. Her body was wracked with pain and refused to work as normal, but she paid no attention to it. As she pushed through the door, she saw someone in front of her that she recognized. It was Mister Miller. He was in the waiting area. He looked up and saw her.

"I came as soon as I heard the news," he said, standing up. "What a tragedy."

"How is he?" asked Sister Christine.

"He's not yet woken up. But they've let me in to see him a couple of times."

Soon after, the nurse arrived with the doctor, and Sister Christine and Mister Miller were permitted to visit Eric by his bedside. Although the doctor insisted that Sister Christine use a wheelchair. Eric lay in the hospital bed with his eyes closed and tubes and breathing equipment attached to him. There were lots of machines that beeped and whirred.

"Will he be alright?" asked Sister Christine.

"We don't know yet," said the doctor. "We'll have to wait and see. He inhaled a lot of smoke."

Sister Christine stared intently at his face. She felt a terrible guilt that she didn't do more, that she didn't fight her way past Sister Prudence.

"Sister, please," said the doctor, "you must return to your bed."

There was an equal sense of collective shock among the boys in those first few days. Their usual rowdiness was gone, there was no fighting or arguing, none of the boisterous noise that accompanied their waking hours. Instead they spoke quietly to one another as they sat about waiting for something. What they were waiting for, no one was quite sure.

In the beginning, the Salvation Army Hall was a hive of activity. Television cameras were positioned outside as the local news reported on the fate of the homeless orphans, and police and city officials swarmed the building busily writing reports and talking amongst themselves.

The boys watched, quietly intimidated by all of those important-looking adults. They sat and waited, and nobody told them anything. Temporary beds were assembled to accommodate them, spread out in a long room that was usually used to house the city's homeless.

Lucius sat on his metal-framed bed. It had a thin mattress that squeaked any time he moved. He was still in the pajamas that he awoke to in the smoky chaos of that night. He looked about the place and could see the shock and disbelief written across the other boys' faces. He knew nothing of the fate of his friend since Eric had disappeared into the night. He too hated the feeling of being powerless to do anything.

"Clive," he asked. "You alright?"

Clive was sitting on the opposite bed.

"I don't know," said Clive. "I don't know what is happening."

Lucius stood up and got Clive a glass of water and an apple from the bowl that had been laid out for the boys. Clive took a sip then a bite.

"You'll feel better soon," said Lucius.

Then he moved on to Santiago. His old friend was lying on another bed and staring at the floor. For some reason, all of

Lucius' hurt from being abandoned by Santiago was gone and was instead replaced by a need to make sure that he was taken care of. Santiago smiled when Lucius handed him the water.

"Hi, Santiago," said Lucius. "How are you?"

Santiago looked up and smiled timidly. Lucius went around to every boy one at a time. He tended to Umberto, Carl, Arvin, and all the others he used to be scared of. And they were very grateful for the help and his comforting smile. Just when the world appeared to have turned on them again, there was someone who cared for their wellbeing. Someone who didn't treat them like another name on a form but a real person. And in those moments, something strange happened to Lucius. It was so noticeable that he felt it deep into his bones, and it made him stand up a little taller. He felt strong.

Sister Christine, now fully awake but confined to her bed under strict doctor's orders, also spent her time deep in thought. She was troubled by the events that had taken place that fateful night. So much so that she considered leaving her life in the church altogether. She did not know anything but that life. It had been everything to her since she was little more than a girl herself, but she saw so clearly just how much damage it had done.

What would she do? Where would she go? She remembered her own childhood. It was so different to that of the boys. It was full of laughter, love, and joy. She was surrounded by the ocean, fresh air, and green hills. Maybe she would go back there for a while and think some more. She felt certain that she did not want to remain in New York City. She felt lost. She felt unsure of the world in which she was now living, as though its very foundations had been forever corroded by those recent events. She wondered if the destruction of the orphanage was a sign from God. She pushed her head back onto the pillow and stared into the space of the room, unable to think any more.

In that moment, something odd happened. A glint of sunlight shone directly through a small crack in the closed curtains of the hospital room. As it did so, it illuminated a shaft of light within the room itself. Sister Christine could see quite clearly something magical sparkling all around her. She felt enveloped by a warmth that was both familiar and foreign, resonating within her like the pipe organ of a great cathedral. She sensed a path opening up before her, and then to her own surprise, she could see the way forward more clearly than she had ever seen before.

Sister Christine felt a strength return to her body, as though she had suddenly been charged with a great purpose. It was almost immediate. With it came a full realization. She was no longer the person that she had been, a meek subordinate beholden to the whims of a cruel superior. By default, she had now become the head of Our Lady of Mercy Orphanage, such as it was. She could not give up on the boys. She was all they had.

The old Sister Christine would have been daunted by this thought, maybe even cowered from it, but now she perceived her circumstance as a great opportunity. She could give those boys the life that they deserved. She understood how to run the orphanage better than anyone, she understood how to educate those boys, she knew how to give them their best start in life. It was clear. A door had been opened. There was no one else in front of her, no one to tell her how to do it. This was her moment. She almost jumped out of bed and began to change into her clothes as the nurse came running back in.

"Sister," she called. "Get back into bed."

"There's no time to lose," said Sister Christine. "The time is now."

The Salvation Army Hall was quiet. The television cameras had gone, the police had moved on to the next emergency, and the officials had filed their reports and returned to City Hall. It was as though the boys, for whom the whole world had cared so much for a few days, had once again been forgotten. Sister Christine, assisted by a walking cane, limped purposefully into the building.

She saw clearly how the events had shaken the boisterousness out of them, but she felt sure that it could be brought back. She felt a deep desire to help every one of them, and despite her own recovery, she felt ready for what she knew she had to do. There were no doubts anymore, just a feeling of possibility that she knew to be true to the core of her being.

"Good morning," she called out, in a clear voice. "Gather round."

"We have all experienced something terrible," she said to them. "Our friend is fighting for his life. We've lost our home. We've lost our school. But we are not lost. I will not give up on you. I will not leave you. We will find a new home. And our lives will be better. In every respect. We will respect each other. No more bad food. No more cold showers and icy chills. That is my promise."

A huge roar of cheer exploded into the room.

Hospital

Sister Christine knew that although Our Lady of Mercy Orphanage had been condemned to nothing but rubble and ruins, the land on which it had stood was still very much intact. That land, in New York City, was some of the most valuable in the whole world. She immediately placed it on sale and worked tirelessly day after day with great purpose to find those boys a new home.

There was a flurry of activity as interested buyers came to see the site where Our Lady of Mercy Orphanage had once stood. Each had grand schemes of skyscrapers full of offices and apartments. Many were interested, for they could see a great amount of potential in it. They made generous offers, but Sister Christine drove a hard bargain, pitching one buyer against another to drive up the price.

Mister Miller stayed at the hospital day and night. When he was allowed to visit Eric, he sat at his bedside in an old armchair; otherwise he sat in the waiting room, sleeping across a row of four seats. He watched Eric, still and silent, eyes closed. During these times, he would talk to Eric, and even though Eric showed no response, Mister Miller felt that somehow his words were being heard.

"I remember when you walked into my kitchen," the old cook recounted. "I didn't know what to make of you. Asking me odd questions."

He smiled, remembering all the things they had done together.

267

"And that chili in the boys' food," he chuckled to himself.

When he looked back on it, he realized that despite all his previous adventures, his times with Eric were some of the happiest of his life.

"I never had much of a family," said Mister Miller becoming serious. "So I never knew what I was missing out on. But when I left the orphanage, I felt that there was a hole that I could not fill, and I realized that it was because you were no longer around."

The machines beeped and Eric remained still and silent. Mister Miller lay his head on the side of Eric's bed and fell asleep.

The weeks in the Salvation Army Hall were not easy, and Sister Christine knew that she had to work fast before the boys gave up all hope. Life did not stand still during this time, and the boys continued to grow and change every day. Kevin O'Malley turned eighteen years old. Sister Christine bought him a cake for the occasion. Everybody cheered. Sister Christine remembered when he had first come through the orphanage doors as a scared little boy taking his first steps alone in the world. Now he was a man.

"I made a decision," he announced as everyone was enjoying the cake. "I'm going to become a firefighter."

Everybody cheered again, and although none of them knew it at the time, they were cheering for the greatest Fire Chief that New York City would ever know.

"They'll train me and give me a place to stay," he said.

Kevin O'Malley was hopeful for his future. He had found a direction in which to go.

Mister Miller was exhausted. He had not slept in a bed for a long time. He had run out of good stories to tell Eric, and a long and indeterminable period had opened up in front of him.

Thoughts began creeping into his mind that Eric would never wake up and that maybe he should go home. But something else within him refused to leave, refused to believe in that ending.

"Come on, Eric," said Mister Miller. "Don't give up. There's too much life to experience and beauty to see."

Mister Miller placed his hand onto Eric's. Then an incredible thought came to him.

"When you wake up," he said, "I'm going to take you all over the world and show you all of those places. That's a promise."

Eric's eyelids fluttered a little. Just for a second. But Mister Miller saw it.

"We'll visit the Yangtze River and Alaska and Belo Horizonte," he continued.

Eric's eyes moved under his eyelids, and Mister Miller felt a wave of hope flooding through him.

"We'll travel by freighter. And by bus. And train. And see everything that the entire glorious world has to offer."

Then another thought suddenly came to him, something so fantastic that he shuddered at the thought of it. He paused for a moment before speaking, wondering whether he could even release the words from his mouth.

"I guess the only way they'd let us go is if I became your father."

Mister Miller waited, heart pounding, full of hope and expectancy. He couldn't believe that he had uttered those words, but now they felt so right, so obvious, as though his entire life was somehow leading to that moment. Suddenly Eric's eyes opened. He blinked a couple of times and stared at Mister Miller.

"Do you really mean that?" he asked quietly.

"Yes!" cried Mister Miller as tears of joy welled uncontrollably in his eyes. "Yes, I do."

Eric slowly sat up in the bed and looked around. He coughed.

"Do you think that you would want to do that?" asked Mister Miller. "I mean, if I was to become your father?"

"Oh yes," said Eric. "I really would."

Mister Miller threw his arms around Eric and hugged him. In that moment, his life took on a completely new meaning and he couldn't help but weep with tears of happiness. For the first time, Eric experienced the loving embrace of a parent.

"What's your first name?" asked Eric.

"Gaston," replied Mister Miller.

"Gaston," repeated Eric to himself. "I like that. This is going to be great."

Goodbye, New York City

By the time she was done with the sale of Our Lady of Mercy Orphanage, Sister Christine had carried off one of the most lucrative deals that the city had ever seen. She had pitted buyers against each other, whipping them into a bidding frenzy, and elevating the price to stratospheric heights.

When the money was finally deposited in the orphanage's bank account, she was overjoyed, for she had jurisdiction over more wealth than she could ever fathom. But she was not driven by greed or the desire to acquire money for money's sake. She carried with her a deep desire to reach her goal, and a vision for the new life that she saw a single opportunity to reach.

But no amount of money could equal the joy that Sister Christine felt when Eric appeared in the Salvation Army hall one afternoon. The boys whooped and hollered and gathered around him, peppering him with all types of questions. He was a little fragile and prone to fits of tremendous coughing, but with the help of Mister Miller, he was able to walk. Lucius pushed his way to the front and greeted his friend.

"Eric!" he said, staring at him as if he could barely believe it. "Do you remember what happened to you on that night?"

"I went to see Santa to tell him that I wasn't coming with him," Eric replied. "Plus I had to hand in my ID card. Then I came back through the tunnel. That's when I smelled smoke. So I ran to the basement door, but it was locked."

"Why didn't you go back through the tunnel?" asked Lucius.

"I got a strange feeling that Sister Prudence needed me."

That sounded like a very odd answer to the boys, but it made complete sense to Eric.

"Then everything just went dark," he added.

"Why is Mister Miller here?" asked Santiago.

Eric looked up at him and smiled.

"I'm going to become Eric's dad," he said with a proud smile. "I'm going to adopt him."

This was the most incredible news that any of the boys had heard, and it invited another extensive round of questions. Eric looked at Lucius again.

"I never thought I would have a family," he said, "and you have been dreaming of one your whole life."

But Lucius felt different too, his newfound dedication to the service of others had changed him. He no longer felt scared or worried. He no longer had those dreams of finding a family because he realized that he already had one, it just looked a little different.

"You know what," started Lucius, "I just have this feeling that everything is going to be alright."

Eric smiled broadly.

So the arrangements were put in place for Mister Miller to formally adopt Eric. There was a lot of paperwork and several interviews, but it was such an exciting time that it didn't feel like work at all. Sister Christine helped the process along by vouching for Mister Miller as an upstanding citizen. Finally the process was complete, and upon receiving the official documents, Mister Miller presented Eric with a piece of paper.

"What's that?" asked Eric.

"We have a passage on a freighter. We set sail for the Ivory Coast of Africa in three days time," said Mister Miller.

Eric's eyes bulged in excitement.

There was a big celebration to send Eric and Mister Miller off on their adventure. Soon after that, Sister Christine appeared in the Salvation Army hall with an unusually large smile on her face, in fact she could barely contain her excitement.

"Pack up your things," she called. "We are leaving."

The boys began to gather their few possessions, whispering among themselves as Sister Christine ushered them out to the street where a large motor coach was parked. The boys assembled on the sidewalk.

"Where are we going?" they asked.

"What's happening?"

"All aboard," called Sister Christine. "We're going on our own adventure."

The boys stepped aboard tentatively. They were unsure. Nothing good had ever become of them in their entire lives. But Lucius sensed that something good was going to happen.

"Come on," he said, stepping aboard.

Clive, Santiago, and Lucius found seats and sat down. Soon they were moving. They made a slow route through the clogged streets of New York City. Despite the place being their home, they were not so familiar with its boulevards and avenues, and they watched in wide-eyed wonder as they travelled through the packed streets full of yellow cabs, buses, and rivers of people.

Soon they were crossing the Long Island Bridge, watching the ships passing beneath them and the trains ferrying the commuters to their offices. Then they were out into Long Island, and slowly but surely, the dense city yielded to suburbs of single-family homes which yielded to trees and grass and greenery with intermittent houses and farms.

Eventually, the highway joined the coast and the boys stared at the vast expanse of sea that lay before them. For the first time, Lucius laid his eyes on the Atlantic Ocean. The sheer size of it, the waves breaking on the shore, was magnificent. The coach slowed on the highway and turned off, down a small single-lane road, until it came to stop. The boys jumped up immediately to get their first views of their new home.

"Here we are," announced Sister Christine. "Gather your things."

As the boys filed off the coach, they stared at the building in front of them. The paint shone a brilliant white. Three young sisters stood at the entrance.

"This is Sister Eloise from France, Sister Damiola from the Ivory Coast of Africa, and Sister Madeline from the Philippines," said Sister Christine.

The sisters smiled at the boys, welcoming them to their new home. But the boys simply stood in front of the building looking at it. They could barely comprehend their surroundings.

"Go ahead," said Sister Christine, nudging them forward. "Explore."

Slowly and tentatively they stepped toward the large front door. The place smelled new, of cut wood and fresh paint.

"Don't be shy," said Sister Christine. "This is your home."

Terrence stepped inside as the rest followed. After some time, the boys became more confident, peering into rooms, running between the floors. There were no old sash windows that let the cold in, no gargoyles lurking with their grizzly stares on top of the building, no rows of hard benches in a dark canteen. It was bright and modern and capable of comfortably housing up to one hundred children.

There were now four dorms. There were computers in every classroom and indoor and outdoor play areas, including a full basketball court. The classrooms were built so that children, young and old, could learn and grow in different and stimulating ways. The kitchen was stocked with fresh fruits and vegetables, and there was a new cook who had studied nutrition.

There were tables and chairs, some large and some small to accommodate all sizes. And there was a new library that had been filled with books. In one corner was a bookcase that contained every issue of National Geographic magazine ever published. Sister Christine gave the library a special name, *Eric's Library.*

"Wow!" exclaimed Lucius.

Everyone was very happy that day. It felt, just for a moment, that the world was a good place.

A Realization

Aand so, life became very different for the boys of Our
Lady of Mercy Orphanage in Greenport. Sister Christine was determined that their new home would be a
place of safety and learning, where young boys' minds and bodies could grow and become strong, so they could enter the wide
world with confidence. She was determined that they should be
given the best possible start in life, in spite of their provenance.

The boys took to Sister Christine's new methods very well.
Gone was the discipline for discipline's sake. Questions were
encouraged, and the boys gladly accepted responsibilities and
proved to be quite trustworthy. The uniforms were modernized,
and Sister Christine allowed the boys to wear casual clothes in
their free time and on weekends. The food was varied and tasty,
and a new tradition was started of serving Spaghetti Bolognese
on Thursdays.

Of course, there was still the odd fight, a nasty prank here
and there, and calling of a bad name. Because after all, they were
still very much boys. But those things no longer ran through their
lives like a jagged edge.

Slowly, the boys became a part of the Greenport community.
They helped the local residents with chores like mowing lawns
and washing cars, all of which greatly endeared them to their
neighbors. When the weather permitted, they explored the area
in kayaks and on bikes, and they worked on the grounds. They
got plenty of fresh, healthy sea air. And so, just as Sister Christine
had promised, life became immeasurably better.

Slowly, the memories of their old life started to fade and were replaced with new memories of picking apples from the tree by the wood and taking lessons outside with Sister Eloise on warm days.

It was on one such day in the summer when Sister Christine was sitting on the porch watching the boys at their afternoon activities. Some were gardening, some were throwing a ball around, and some were simply doing nothing in the grass. In the distance, she watched a figure approach.

It soon became clear that it was Lucius, walking all the way from the end of the driveway where he had collected the mail. He had grown taller since the move. A benefit of the good food and clean air, she thought. He had transformed in that time from a timid little boy to one of the most respected, and well liked young men in the orphanage. It was not because he was tough or preyed on others either. It was because he was always there to help. That was his great strength. When Sister Christine saw Lucius, she always thought of Eric.

"Hello, Lucius," she said as he handed her an assortment of envelopes.

"Another postcard!" Lucius exclaimed.

Sister Christine looked at the brightly colored postcard among the dreary-looking bills. The back contained the familiar handwriting of Eric. On the front was a photograph of an exotic city with the caption *'Bem Vindo a Manaus'*. Sister Christine read aloud:

"Dear Sister Christine and the boys of Our Lady of Mercy Orphanage, we have recently arrived in Manaus, after a long journey up the Amazon River on a local trader's boat. We saw Piranha fish and caiman along the way. Perhaps the best food yet was Tapioquinha, a delicious local pancake. I'm doing a project on indigenous species, and

Dad spends his days cooking. At night, he does a little carousing, but not too much.

Your friends, Eric and Gaston Miller."

Sister Christine smiled. She enjoyed Eric's postcards. He wrote every time they arrived at a new destination. Sister Christine had taken to pinning them on a large map in the room that they used for geography lessons.

The clock chimed two o'clock, and Lucius walked into the library and sat down. He had taken to telling his own stories to the younger boys, some of whom were new to the orphanage and feeling alone and scared. His favorite was how they came to arrive in such a wonderful place.

Lucius told them about Eric, and how terrible the old orphanage was, and how he had found a grate that led to a magical place called Santa Inc. He did not miss any details, and his memory of those conversations was very well preserved. The young boys listened in awe.

Sister Christine finally walked inside and paused in the doorway to the library where the boys were gathered. She observed carefully. When Lucius was done, the boys had free time to choose their own books. Sister Christine approached Lucius.

"Do you think it was true?" she asked "Santa Inc."

Lucius thought for a moment.

"I'd like to think so," he replied. "But I guess I don't really know."

"Does it matter? It's still part of our story," said Sister Christine.

As Sister Christine watched the boys, she started to understand the sequence of events in a way that she had not understood them before. She thought about the books that Eric had given her, the skills that he had taught her, and the confidence with which she was finally imbued. How he had changed Mister Miller and given him back his enthusiasm for cooking. Then she thought of how the orphanage had eventually been saved from Sister Prudence and delivered to the wonderful place where they now resided. She started to see that those events were not isolated but perhaps part of a grander plan. It was a remarkable thought. Everything fit together so neatly, and Eric was at the center of them all.

She recalled the moment that Eric had appeared at her desk when she had prayed for help. Maybe that wasn't a coincidence at all. Maybe the good Lord himself had provided Our Lady of Mercy Orphanage with precisely what it needed at exactly the right time. They had encountered a miracle without even knowing it.

Christmas in Greenport

Nearly a whole year passed since Our Lady of Mercy Orphanage moved to Greenport. The days drew in and became shorter, the winds blew hard, and the icy Atlantic air howled along the cape.

As Christmas approached, they cut down a large pine tree from the grounds that stood over twelve feet high and placed it in the center of the hallway. The entire day was spent adorning it with baubles and lights. They made decorations and hung them up in every room.

Their days were filled with the delights of the festive season. Sister Damiola assembled the choir to sing, and Ryan, who had become a proficient pianist as a result of his weekly lessons, accompanied them, this time putting his footing stomping to good use. The boys practiced for an entire month and performed for the people of the town. For the boys, singing in the choir was no longer a chore but something they enjoyed. The people of Greenport cheered them, and the boys were rewarded with cups of hot chocolate and Yuletide cookies. By the time that the actual day arrived, the entire building had been whipped up into a frenzy of Christmas cheer.

On Christmas morning, the excitement had reached fever pitch. The boys woke extra early, as did the Sisters. Some had barely slept that night. They barreled out of their beds and ran downstairs to a stack of presents so high that they could barely believe their own eyes. There was shouting and jostling as each scrambled to find a box with his own name on it. Soon the melee grew so raucous that Sister Christine had to take charge. She ordered the boys to sit around the edge of the room while the other Sisters distributed the gifts in a more orderly fashion.

The boys sat down with as much patience as they could muster, wriggling and squirming with anticipation until their gifts were handed to them. Many had never unwrapped a present before, but they tore at the paper as though they had done it a thousand times. Lucius received an atlas, and he delightedly opened its pages and scanned through the pictures of countries and continents. Clive got a basketball. Santiago got a baseball mitt.

Lucius looked back inside his gift box because all children have to check their gift boxes at least twice. There was something else in there. He reached in and pulled it out. It was a small laminated card with a photograph on it——Eric's photograph. Above his picture, *Santa Inc.* was printed in black letters. It was Eric's Santa Inc. identification card. Lucius studied it quietly. He peered back inside the box. There were no other markings on it at all.

Lucius looked at Eric's picture. A warm sense enveloped him, and he felt a certainty become present in his mind and body. Lucius pushed the card into his pocket, jumped up, and joined the riotous party. Sister Christine smiled to herself. She also felt a deep sense of contentment for she knew that her prayers had been heard.

Made in the USA
San Bernardino, CA
23 July 2020